Praise for the Books of Devon Delaney

"The Cook-Off Mystery series by Devon Delaney is a very tasty treat of a series. Readers will be glued to their seats wrestling with continuing reading the story or getting up to get a tasty treat to eat . . . I highly recommend getting something to eat before you sit down to indulge yourself in the story . . ."

—*Cozy Mystery book Reviews*

"This is a very fun and rollicking mystery that stays light-hearted even as the case gets more complicated, building toward a get-all-of-the-suspects-together-in-a-room conclusion. Cooking, holiday celebrations, and moving family drama all make for the perfect end-of-the-year escape."

—*Kings River Life*

"I've read several in the series and enjoyed them all. It was interesting to see Sherry acting as a judge rather than a competitor. The book kept my interest from the beginning but any book that combines cookies and murder has to be interesting. The characters are varied and seem like a lot of fun. I look forward to more in this series."

—Alicia F.

Books by Devon Delaney

Cook-Off Mysteries

Expiration Date
Final Roasting Place
Guilty as Charred
Eat, Drink and Be Wary
Double Chocolate Cookie Murder
A Half-Baked Alibi
Murder for Good Measure
Serving Up Spite
A Holiday for Homicide
Farm-Fresh and Fatal

Farm-Fresh and Fatal

A Cook-Off Mystery

Devon Delaney

Chapter 1

"If there's one thing that ruffles my feathers, it's a practice recipe failure," Sherry said to her sister-in-law. The dismay was evident in her tone. "The potatoes are undercooked, and the chicken is overdone. That's a bad sign. Something's not right with the universe. How is my recipe for the potato cook-off going to be chosen for the finals if I can't even prepare it successfully?"

"Don't take it so hard." Charlotte offered Sherry a conciliatory hug. "You got two out of three versions correct. We rushed the last batch. Haste makes waste, as everyone knows." Charlotte rearranged the mound of small yellow potatoes on the kitchen counter. "We've run out of sweet potatoes. We'll have to call it a day. I give this cooking lesson high marks except for the last batch. We killed two birds with one stone, or potato. You got to practice your recipe, and I can now add a talent to my résumé. I'm a student chef."

"You're right. I need to focus on the big picture. The takeaway is using dark meat cut into strips, not white meat. That's where the flavor is. Cut the potato cubes about an inch square, not an inch and a half. That's how the first two attempts succeeded. Smaller cuts equal less cooking time, and that's always a plus in cooking competitions." Sherry pushed the small casserole dish to the side, banishing it from the acceptable batches. "I hope this isn't a bad omen for the cook-off. If I make it past the initial entry phase, that is."

"There's no bad omen here. Your Speedy African Groundnut Stew is fantastic. Sweet potato, chicken, mango chutney. And peanut butter. Wow! Who knew all those ingredients could result in such a luscious stew? And everything comes together so quickly. You're a genius." Charlotte licked the wooden spoon with serenity on her face, sealing her praise of Sherry's recipe. "After it comes out of the oven, when is the best time to eat it?"

"Let it cool a bit. The flavors will marry completely when the bubbling settles down."

"Perfect. Let's clean up while the marriage is happening."

Sherry wiped the counters and stove while Charlotte washed the dishes. She reflected on her sister-in-law's contributions to the Oliveri family since marrying her brother, Pep. Besides making Pep wildly happy, Sherry was proud of Charlotte's ability to take off her marine biologist hat to don a chef's hat for a few hours a week. Sherry didn't have the DNA that kept Charlotte organized in every aspect of her work life, or the analytical abilities required to achieve a master's degree in ocean research. Sherry's innate strengths lay in the ability to win multiple cooking competitions, garden productively, and keep her family's hooked rug shop prospering.

The kitchen was Sherry's territory. She was more than happy to fulfill Charlotte's desire to learn to cook while she was on temporary leave from her research position. Sherry considered Charlotte's recent decision to take a right turn in her life while suffering a crisis of guilt about not spending enough quality time with her toddler daughter, Mimi. Unfortunately, time spent with the family was a different variety of satisfaction than cleaning up the ocean for the next generation. Charlotte was struggling to make the adjustment. Sherry was more than willing to ease the transition by sharing some of her cooking knowledge.

"To be honest with you, I didn't think I'd like the sweet potatoes in the recipe," Charlotte said. She set her wooden spoon down in the sink. "I'm a white potato girl, or so I thought. You've opened my eyes to other options. Us scientists thrive on uncovering convincing evidence, and cooking that sweet potato convinced me there's nothing to fear from the orange spud. How about you? What's your favorite type of potato?"

"I love buttery yellow potatoes, like Yukon Golds. As a matter of fact, I considered swapping out the sweet potato for Yukons when I submitted this recipe to the Local and Vocal Farmers' Day potato recipe contest last month. My thought was a Yukon Gold is more appealing to the masses. But that took away the nod to African cuisine I was striving for. I reconsidered. Second-guessing a recipe hardly ever works in my favor. I went with my gut and put the sweet potato back in. I hope that was the right choice."

"You taught me one of your winning cook-off recipes." Charlotte pumped her fist over her head. "Pep's going to be the best-fed husband in Augustin."

"Hold on, not so fast," Sherry said. "I've only submitted the recipe to the potato cook-off. I won't hear if I'm selected to be in the cook-off until day after tomorrow. The recipe goes through an evaluation process before the finalists are chosen. The reviewers read through the recipe, assess whether it makes sense in every way, most importantly whether the potato is used to its maximum potential in the recipe, and whether the title of the recipe is catchy. If the typed-up submission passes those evaluations, the judges may or may not cook the recipe to taste test it. Some contests take that step, others don't. If it's an on-site cook-off, the judges want to see how the recipe creator cooks the recipe up in real time to its full potential. That's the part I have the passion for. I like to persuade the judges I've submitted my best effort for their judging discretion. All these steps are why the finalist announcement date can be anywhere from a month to a couple of months from when they receive my submission. This contest has a fast turnaround. The cook-off is next Wednesday." She raised a hand with two fingers crossed.

"I know November is past harvest season for most produce around here. Are you able to use local potatoes at this time of year?" Charlotte asked.

"The cook-off entry form gave some information about the storage of potatoes. If stored correctly, potatoes can be fresh for months," Sherry said.

"Why is the local farmers' festival being held in November? Why not the middle of summer?"

"My guess is the organizers didn't want to crowd the farmers' market season. Slightly after most crops are harvested is a great time to promote the produce for next year. Building anticipation is an advertising trick that even farmers can benefit from. Think of the event as more of a winter farmers' market. A pre-holiday chance to showcase local farmers and keep them on everyone's minds."

"Okay. You've convinced me your hobby is as much of a challenge as my job, just in a different way." Charlotte's laugh was subdued and reminded Sherry, once again, how lucky the Oliveris were to have welcomed Charlotte into their family. For a tall athletic woman who was the picture of self-confidence, her sister-in-law was reserved and thoughtful in all she said and did. Sherry admired her greatly for how her gentle demeanor convinced her brother, Pep, to give up his wandering ways for a more settled life that included starting his now-thriving food truck business.

"On another note, I've brought you a present."

"No, I'm the one who should be giving you a present," Charlotte said. She waved her hands in front of her chest. "No presents."

"Too late," Sherry said. Sherry reached for a large canvas bag she had lugged in from her car when she arrived and removed a cast-iron skillet. "This hefty workhorse was popular in the United States as early as the sixteen hundreds. Not only has it not gone out of style after all that time, it's enjoying a current resurgence in popularity. Helps build biceps, too. Every kitchen needs one. I'm gifting this one to you."

"I couldn't. You're too generous," Charlotte said. She snatched the skillet from Sherry's hands despite her half-hearted refusal. "I've always wanted one. My Nanna had one that my sister inherited because no one thought I would ever demonstrate cooking talent."

"They were so wrong about you," Sherry said. "You needed some free time to hone your skills, that's all."

"I've changed my mind. I'll gladly accept your gift," Charlotte said. "How do I care for it?"

Sherry ran through a quick tutorial on keeping the skillet rust-free and well-seasoned. Charlotte absorbed all the information and proclaimed the skillet would henceforth be named Bernie, not in reference to any mishaps she's had in the kitchen prior to receiving the pan, but rather a nod to her Nanna Bernice.

"What time is Pep coming home with Mimi?" Sherry asked.

Charlotte glanced at the oven clock. "He wants to do his shopping for tomorrow's food truck menu before dinner, so I'd say soon. He'll be tempted to stay for an early dinner once he smells our masterpiece." Charlotte opened the window behind the sink. "It gets warm in this tiny kitchen when the oven's being used. Even in November."

A series of bangs outside paused the ladies' cleanup.

"Our neighbors can be noisy," Charlotte said. "Comes with the territory, living on a farm."

Sherry cozied up next to Charlotte and peered over the sink. Not far from Charlotte's house three men and a woman were hatching a plan to unhook a trailer from the back of a pickup truck. The process didn't appear to be going smoothly. Fingers wagged, faces wore scowls, and pebbles were being kicked across the dirt driveway.

Charlotte pinched her forehead tight. "The Colton family can be as cold to each other as the winter winds. I feel sorry for Perry Colton. He's trying to preserve a way of life for his two sons. I'm not convinced they have an appreciation for his efforts." She pointed to the men facing the older man. "Especially Jarrod."

"I haven't been introduced to the Coltons. I'm guessing that's Perry?" Sherry asked as she kept her sights on the older man.

"That's Perry," Charlotte said.

Sherry estimated one of the men was in his thirties he was the spitting image of the older man, apart from the absence of gray flecks in his hair. He wore a scruffy beard and canvas-colored overalls. The other man shared similar features, minus the facial hair.

"Jarrod is the taller one wearing the leather bomber jacket and corduroys. He's got his foot out the door when it comes to his contribution to the farm. He's got his real estate license, and he doesn't show up here too often," Charlotte said. "His wife, Liz, does pitch in for certain tasks."

"The majority of their crop are potatoes?"

Charlotte nodded. "Yes."

"I put two and two together by the farm's name, Coastal Greater Tator Farms." Sherry held her gaze on the eldest man until he must have sensed he was being watched. He raised his sights and gave Sherry and Charlotte a wave. Sherry waved back.

"We haven't lived here long enough to see the full harvest from start to completion, but they're winding down this season. They've been storing the harvest as it comes in. The potatoes are released to vendors on demand."

"Perry's the farm's CEO?"

"Absolutely. Perry is a potato aficionado. I've had some interesting talks with him about the life cycle of a potato plant. I may not know much about cooking them, but I bet you I could grow them based on the knowledge he's shared."

"That could come in handy for the next hobby I'll be teaching you, gardening," Sherry said with a broad grin.

"Maybe this spring. Right outside the kitchen window is a perfect location."

"How could you not be inspired by your surroundings," Sherry said.

"We were lucky to get this rental cottage on the farm property."

"It's a gem," Sherry said. "Especially for a potato lover."

"It's a lovely location. The bonus is, from the second floor you can see the Long Island Sound." Charlotte shifted her sights from the window and began drying bowls.

"How did you and Pep find the house? Through an agent?"

"Luck of the not-so-Irish," Charlotte said. "A perk of Toasts of the Town food truck is when Pep strikes up a conversation with a customer. Great things can happen. One of the Coltons, Jarrod, was served breakfast along with a side of Pep chat. One thing led to another, and Pep had a lead on the cottage vacancy. We skipped to the top of the rental wait list when Jarrod bartered with Pep to create a potato-topped toast for Toasts of the Town's menu in exchange for a spot on the cottage vacancy interest list."

Sherry laughed. "Pep is a born negotiator. Anyone who can pitch a 'how to start a food truck for beginners' and get the deal done is a master of persuasion."

"I agree. And he convinced me to marry him when others have tried and failed."

"He's a lucky guy," Sherry said.

"I like to remind him of that often," Charlotte said with a laugh. "Problem is, I'm not sure how much longer I'll be able to enjoy the view of the Long Island Sound from my bedroom window."

"Why's that?"

"Unfortunately, my sense is we'll be the last renters the Coltons accept before they sell out," Charlotte said. "That only means one thing. Bulldozers, development, and McMansions. This coastal real estate is worth its weight in gold developed. Not so much as farmland."

Chapter 2

Sherry returned home with her portion of the Speedy African Groundnut Stew. She knew Don loved the sweet-heat ginger sauce that bathed the chicken and tender sweet potato chunks. He was also a big fan of peanut butter. That was the hint of background flavor that wed all the ingredients together and tied the recipe to its African origins. When they sat down to eat dinner, Sherry shared the story of her time in the kitchen teaching Charlotte.

"Maybe it's time for you to switch professions. Teaching cooking might be your calling," Don said.

Sherry reflected on the events since meeting the man who stole her heart, years after her traumatic divorce from her ex-husband, Charlie. Don followed his heart and left his investment firm in Long Island to move to Augustin months after he met Sherry at a cook-off. He also traded in his financial career to pursue his passion for boating which he morphed into a commuter transport business. Was he serious about Sherry leaving her part-time managerial position at the Ruggery, her family's artisan hooked rug business? Or her job editing the Augustin town newsletter, and her volunteer position at the Augustin Community Garden? What about her beloved hobby of participating in cooking competitions? Was he suddenly questioning the time she spent experimenting in the kitchen? Sherry was close to forty years old, with the milestone year looming in the not-too-distant future. She still considered herself young enough to give the weighty matter of a major career change the consideration it deserved. She opened her mouth to reply but the words wouldn't come. She didn't know what the right answer was.

"You've gone completely pale. You've got to know I was kidding. You wouldn't be you if you didn't have your finger dipped in many pies." Don reached across the table and clutched Sherry's hand.

"You had me worried."

"I obviously struck a nerve. What's going on?" Don asked.

"The topic of switching careers has been on the table lately. Not for me, but for Charlotte. She's considering not returning to work after her leave is up. She feels as if she's missing out on quality time with baby Mimi. Maybe subconsciously you brought the subject up because *you* need more quality time with *me*," Sherry said, her sentiment punctuated with a sigh.

"If you saw the frown on your face even contemplating giving up all you do in a day to wait idly by for me to get home every day, you'd know how ridiculous the notion is. This isn't the eighteenth century. I don't need anyone giving up their passions for me. I want you to include me in them. Stay out there, you're making the world a better place one recipe at a time." Don squeezed her hand before taking another bite of stew. He swallowed with a guttural moan of satisfaction. "When did you say you'd hear back from the potato recipe contest you entered?"

"If I make the cook-off round, I'll be notified by email day after tomorrow."

"I'm glad the cooking lesson went well today," Don said. He scooped a bite of the stew into his mouth.

"Pretty good, right? Does the recipe shout 'potatoes are the star'?"

Don could only manage a head bob with his mouth full.

"Coincidentally, the property Charlotte and Pep are renting their cottage on is primarily a potato farm. Maybe the farm will be exhibiting at Farmers' Day. They're as local as local can be. The family's name is Colton."

"Colton? Is one of the family members named Jarrod? A spiffy dresser and meticulously well-groomed?"

"Exactly." Sherry was amazed at Don's precise description.

"He doesn't give off farmer vibes," Don said. "More Wall Street than Green Acres."

"Where do you know Jarrod from?"

"It would be hard to forget the guy. He booked a ticket on the *Current Sea* about two weeks ago. He was with another man who I could only assume was a lawyer because, well, he had a lawyerly air about him. Together they were quite a dapper couple of gents."

"What did Jarrod do to make himself unforgettable? He can't be the first passenger with keen fashion sense," Sherry said.

"You're right. We have a very tastefully dressed group of repeat customers. What happened was, after all the passengers were aboard, I backed the *Current Sea* away from the dock as usual. Suddenly, Jarrod called out to me at the top of his lungs to move the boat along. I turned to see who was playing backseat driver to my captainship and I saw him pointing to a man running down the dock to board. The approaching man's clothing was disheveled, and his beard was spraying in all directions. I took the order to continue pulling away seriously, as I deemed the running man a threat. The desperation on his face spooked me. I nodded toward Jarrod to thank him for the heads-up."

"How did you know his name?" Sherry asked.

"I have a list of names I check off. I also heard his traveling companion announce 'Jarrod Colton gets what he wants. Good job.'"

"I wish I could always get what I wanted," Sherry said.

"Would your wish be me?" Don asked. He cocked his head and shined a sly smile.

"Of course," Sherry said with confidence. She poked at a chicken chunk and swirled it in the luscious sauce. "I wonder where Jarrod Colton was traveling to in Long Island," Sherry said.

"I can only assume he was on business. He was buddy-buddy with the man seated next to him."

"Charlotte said he had a real estate license. But Long Island isn't in Connecticut, so he'd need a New York license to do business there."

"The man he sat next to introduced himself with a handshake. Harry something."

"Didn't you have his full name on your list?" Sherry asked.

"His secretary made the reservation under her name for some reason. I didn't change it on the printout because he gave me his business card and I figured I could do it after the trip. He even offered his services. I didn't even read the card to see what his specialty was. I don't need a lawyer right now if that's what he is. I have the card in my rain jacket at my house. I haven't gotten around to updating my passenger information. I'll check it out by tomorrow if you're really interested."

"Just curious," Sherry said.

"That's what makes you a successful amateur sleuth. Your curiosity. Just ask Detective Ray Bease, he'll double down on that after all the murder investigations you've helped him solve."

"If I can be of help, I pitch in where I can," Sherry said. "In this case, all I'm being is nosy."

"That's an honest admission."

"I was thinking about the man you said ran down the dock after the *Current Sea*," Sherry said. "Should I be nervous that you're in danger from a lunatic?"

"I don't think so. I hope not. My sense was the man would have jumped aboard if given half a chance. I have no way to know what his intentions were beyond a free ride across the Long Island Sound."

"Strange," Sherry said. "Did he say anything?"

"He did. He called out, 'Don't do this.'"

"To you?"

"I couldn't tell who he was yelling at. If it was to me, I ignored him."

"Please, be careful."

"I'm not worried and you shouldn't be either."

"Do you have room for dessert?" Sherry asked.

Don patted his stomach. "No, thanks. That stew really hit the spot. Put your feet up while I do the dishes."

No sooner had Sherry risen from the table than her phone buzzed. She gathered it off the front hall table and made herself comfortable on the couch in the television room. She was surprised to see the name of the food journalist for the local media corporation on her phone's display.

"Hi, Patti. Always great to hear from you." As happy as Sherry was to hear from Patti Mellit, she was curious about the nature of the call. Sherry was in a waiting period between cooking competitions, and she usually heard from Patti during or after a cook-off for an interview. "What can I do for you?"

"I'm writing a series of articles introducing local farmers and their products in anticipation of Local Farmers' Day. I was wondering if you'd provide some moral support. I know you're vying for a spot in the potato cook-off, so I won't use your name in an article. I need a partner to come with me to visit a farm for a tour of the facility. Help me absorb the valuable information. Your take is priceless. Tomorrow. Sorry for the short notice but that's the nature of news. It waits for no one."

"I'm on at the Ruggery until two o'clock and then I can do it. Where can I meet you?" Sherry asked.

"Coastal Greater Tator Farm on Beachside Avenue. Doesn't Pep rent a home down that way?" Patti asked.

"Yes, he does. I was just at their house today. I haven't been down there much since they've moved in this summer. Most of our outings were to the beach. I'd be happy to get a closer look at the farm. What time?"

"Let's say three o'clock. I'll send the owner of the farm, Perry Colton, a text. Oh, maybe not him. His son said his father never knows where his flip phone is. I'll send his son Wellington a text saying I'll be there at three. We'll keep you a secret until we get there. I get the impression they don't take too kindly to many strangers on their property, judging by the interrogation I was put through trying to set up this meeting. Geesh, you'd think they were keeping secrets by the number of questions I had to answer to substantiate the reason for my visit."

"Sounds good. See you there," Sherry said before clicking off the call.

She returned to the kitchen and found Don elbow deep in dishes. "I've got a date tomorrow afternoon. With Patti Mellit. At the Coltons' farm."

"Maybe you could get some inside info on the best ways to serve up the spuds for the cook-off," Don said with a wink.

"Too late for that. My recipe entry is long emailed and it's up to the contest gods to decide if my recipe makes the final round," Sherry said.

"You know, it's said the potato fueled the rise of western civilization after the plant arrived from South America. It's a cinch to grow, produces an abundance of potato babies and is said to have saved much of what is now Europe from famine when their other crops failed. The potato traveled better than many crops when the settlers shipped it over on their long-voyage vessels. It's easily propagated and grows well in many different agricultural zones, and it's the staple food of millions across the globe." Don crossed his arms on his chest. His damp hand left a mark on his navy blue T-shirt.

"How do you know all this, O wise one?" Sherry asked.

"Remember, my middle name is Cormac. Can't get more Irish than that. That was my mother's maiden name. Along with the name, plenty of potato knowledge was handed down to me as a wee one. The Irish and potatoes go hand in hand over the course of history."

Sherry sighed a note of contentment. "My man is brilliant. If you dry your hands we can go anywhere you want, hand in hand," Sherry said with a returning wink. "You are the Irish and I'll be your potato." She reached her hand toward Don's.

Chapter 3

Sherry and her Jack Russell terrier, Chutney, spent Thursday morning at the Ruggery sharing management duties with her good friend Amber. The morning tasks centered on addressing a variety of customer needs. A new bride romanticized over the purchase of an authentic Erno Oliveri hand-designed hooked rug commemorating her new union. A set of first-time grandparents wished to gift their precious family addition an area rug to ratchet up the ambiance of her nursery. A tour group from Ohio was directed to the Ruggery to get a feel for the way things are done in a decades-old New England family-run business. Sherry wasn't sure her father would love the giant tour bus that blocked access to the store frontage for over an hour. She was mistaken. When Erno returned early from lunch he expressed delight.

Sherry sold the new bride a rug featuring two birds enjoying their perch on a branch. Erno pulled a canvas featuring a fawn in the woods to be hooked into the perfect nursery rug. Amber was instrumental in selling the tour group the rugs they didn't know they needed.

"Amber, you remind me every day, you've found your calling," Sherry said as the last of the tour group exited the store. "When we first met at a cook-off you were out of your element."

"That's an understatement," Amber said as she replaced an empty bin with the contents of a newly opened box of yarn. "Competition cooking isn't for the faint of heart."

"Thank goodness I was smart enough to put you to work here because you're a master of sales. I've overheard people saying, 'How did that woman know my favorite color was lavender?' and 'If everyone in Augustin is as nice as her let's just spend the week here.'"

"Just doing my job the best way I know how," Amber said with her trademark humility.

By the time the tour group pulled away in their bus both Sherry and Amber were yearning for a revitalizing cup of tea. The chance never materialized. Instead, customer after browsing customer walked through the door with no letup. Sherry worked the floor alone for an hour before her shift was up, giving Amber a chance to feed her rumbling belly.

Sherry clocked out of the Ruggery when two o'clock rolled around. Her first destination was home to drop off Chutney. She changed her shoes from comfy sneakers to waterproof ankle boots. As she drove in the farm's entrance she immediately realized her choice of footwear was a good one. The farm's driveway was surfaced with loose pebbles and mud, allowing the formation of deep ruts that guided the wheels of Sherry's car without much assistance. She took the drive cautiously, as there were potholes every few feet.

The handful of times Sherry visited Charlotte at the farm she'd been instructed to follow a single-lane paved street that delivered her to the south side of the farm. She had never ventured beyond the three cottages that the lane provided access to. Seeing the farmhouse for the first time was an eye-opener. The property was vast, with no obvious parking area for visitors. Twice she steered her car to an open space, only to be rebuffed by a massive piece of farm equipment taking up half the spot. As she steered her car back toward the house, she was relieved to see what she hoped was Patti's sedan beside an oddly low triangular building. Her relief was confirmed when the car door opened and out stepped Patti.

Sherry parked her car next to Patti's. She waited for the dust and muck her car's tires had stirred up to settle before she could open her door. Sherry lowered her window a sliver and called out, "Wait for me." Sherry stepped out of her car and met Patti halfway between the cars.

"Good afternoon. How are you?" Patti greeted her friend with a hug. "It's been too long. I thought this was a great excuse to get together."

"Any excuse is a great one," Sherry said. "This is quite a place. I can picture the hustle and bustle of farmers' wagons and horses tending the land in the warm weather. More modern equipment is probably used, but I prefer the historic sepia images my mind is conjuring up. Kind of romantic."

"I'm not sure how romantic real farming is," Patti said. "Harvesting potatoes is dirty work."

Sherry pointed to the distant triangular building. "That building is like none I've ever seen. Can you explain?"

A voice that brought sandpaper to mind called out from the porch of the red farmhouse. "Ladies. No wandering the grounds unescorted." A glance toward the farmhouse revealed a man seated under the overhang. "Head over here."

"I'd say that's our welcome wagon," Patti said in a muted tone. "That's Perry Colton, the patriarch of the family." She waved Sherry forward. "His son Wellington, behind him, is his mini-me. Jarrod may be somewhere around, but he's not as hands-on as these two. He may not show up."

Perry made no effort to offer a standing greeting. He continued a slow rock in his chair. His oversized fleece coat needed a wash or, at the least, spot stain removal in many areas. He waited for Sherry and Patti to come within an arm's length before he struggled to rise. His groans were painful to hear.

"Please, don't get up," Patti said.

"Don't patronize an old man," Perry grumbled. "I'm perfectly able to get up." His hand jutted toward Patti. The callus across his palm told the tale of years of manual labor. "I'm Perry Colton. Pleasure to meet you. We don't get too many of your kind on the farm." He directed his penetrating scowl at Sherry. "I didn't get the notice you were bringing a friend. I don't take kindly to unannounced visitors. Too many lookie-loos trespass, hoping to get their fill of the land people would kill for around these parts. Especially no-good, self-serving developers who don't give a hoot about the farms that feed their greedy appetites."

"Dad, take it down a notch. We're all friends here." A young man in soiled overalls, no coat, and a short-sleeved shirt nodded a greeting. "I'm Perry's son, Wellie. That's short for Wellington. I'm much more of a Wellie than a Wellington." He emphasized the lengthy version of his name with a proper English accent. He lifted his palms. I'd shake hands but then you'd have potato dust all over you." His laugh was hearty and welcoming.

Patti leaned into Sherry's ear. "I'm going to withhold a full introduction because you've entered the recipe contest, and the farm is providing the potatoes. I don't want to compromise your chances."

"Okay, better safe than sorry," Sherry said.

"I'm Patti Mellit, journalist for the Media Pie Communications group, and I've brought my friend Sherry to help take notes. Nice to meet you all in person."

Perry stepped forward with a halting gait. "What is it you ladies would like to know about the farm? I forget what Jarrod told me you'd like to see." Perry's gaze softened and he squinted. "Something about a festival? You know, we give to charities but there's a limit to how much we can afford. This season was a boom, but next season is already knocking on the door. It only takes a family of potato beetles to spoil the entire crop."

Sherry's gaze drifted to Wellie, who was shaking his head. "Dad, we're already giving the potatoes for the potato cook-off. It's all for a good cause. Try to concentrate. The festival is only a few days away. These ladies are the good people. They're on our side if we present ourselves well."

"Your son is right," Patti said. "We're not here to ask for anything except a quick tour of how a potato farm works. I'm writing an article about the kinds of farms Augustin is lucky enough to call theirs. Farms like yours are few and far between these days. Local potatoes are a treasure." Patti managed to put a smile on the elder man's face.

"Buttering me up is the best way to see my softer side," Perry said. "Compliments are currency around someone like me." He pointed to the odd building Sherry spotted when she parked. "Come on, let me show you the potato storage building. It's where the magic happens."

Everyone waited for Perry to manage the uneven terrain leading away from the porch. Wellie held back and leaned into Patti and Sherry. "I've told him so many times Coastal Farm is supplying the potatoes for the festival's cook-off. It'll dawn on him soon why you're here."

Perry waved the group forward. "Move along, folks. I have lots of potato information for you. Wellie will jump in, too."

Sherry's eyes widened with a deepening interest to absorb all the information the Coltons would provide.

"For starters, if you like vitamins and minerals you need to eat more potatoes. If you've got some extra weight to lose, eat potatoes. They're low in calories and they fill you up. Skip the cream, butter and bacon crumbles, though."

Sherry laughed as she walked alongside Patti. She had the feeling she had stepped back in time as they ambled deeper into the farm property. To their left was a pickup truck that succumbed to the ravages of rust. The bumper was partially missing, and the tires were bald. It was the same truck being worked on when Sherry caught a glimpse out Charlotte's window.

"Does this truck still run?" Patti asked.

"As good as I do," Perry said.

"Grunts and groans like you, too," Wellie said.

Chapter 4

Perry led the group to the storage building. There were no windows, and most of the building appeared to be underground. A dirt and grass bank was pushed up against one of the sides. Sherry swore the building was lopsided. The only way inside appeared to be through a massive double door.

"Are we going in there?" Sherry asked. She had second thoughts entering such a claustrophobic-looking structure.

"Yup. Why? It doesn't suit your taste in architecture?" Perry asked.

"Dad," Wellie scolded. "Be nice."

"If you were a potato you'd feel right at home in there," Perry said. "The temperature and humidity are perfect for storage. The ground is sloped to insure proper drainage. It may look like something from a horror movie, the place where the villain hides, but I guarantee there are no bad guys in there." He paused. "That I'm aware of. Why don't we go—"

Perry stopped in mid-sentence and looked around. His mouth drooped.

"Where's Jarrod? Is he stopping by today? Be nice if he attended school occasionally," Perry said. "If I'm called into the principal's office one more time, I'll have to sit in on his classes for him. Maybe embarrassing him is the ticket to get him a perfect attendance record."

Wellie slowed his pace until Sherry and Patti were at his side. "Dad gets a bit confused about what decade we're in. When Jarrod's not here he thinks he's playing hooky from high school. Play along. He'll come back to the present soon."

Patti's reply was interrupted as a champagne-hued luxury sedan honked and came to a stop by the edge of the driveway.

"Speak of the devil," Perry said.

"Hey, guys. Sorry I'm late. Welcome." The man Sherry assumed was Jarrod was attired in a stylish camel-colored double-breasted overcoat. He stepped out of a car. His shiny black shoes were no match for the unpaved driveway. After a few steps they were covered in grit. He introduced himself as Jarrod and joined the tour.

"How's Dad today?" Jarrod asked his brother, as if his father weren't six feet from him.

"He could use your help more often around here," Wellie snapped. "The day you ran off to Long Island he was out of it. I had no choice but to bring someone in to fill in. You know how against that he is."

"If we hadn't brought in extra hands at the height of harvest how do you think the process would have been completed? What's the problem with paying someone else to pitch in? Dad's so paranoid we're losing the farm," Jarrod said. "Guess what. If the demise of the farm is meant to be, we need to let go. Heck, we could all use the money."

Sherry exchanged glances with Patti. The tension between the brothers eased as the conversation returned to the potato storage building in front of them. Perry's gait quickened as they came within feet of the structure.

"The building is built on a graded slope to provide better drainage." Perry's voice had perked up.

"You said that already, Dad," Wellie said.

"This marvel is nearly one hundred years old and she's still a beaut," Perry continued. "Let's move on."

"Dad, you skipped a few pieces of information," Wellie said. He lowered his voice and faced Patti and Sherry. "He's back with us."

"Why don't you take over, Jarrod," Perry said.

"I'm Wellie, Dad," he corrected. "Okay, sure. I'll add that if this appears to be a roof over a sunken building, that's exactly what it is. The potatoes are often loaded through an opening in the roof. Follow me."

Wellie reached for the metal door handle. The hinges groaned as he struggled to haul the heavy door open. Despite his efforts the door didn't budge.

"Another task to add to the list. The door is either warped or the frame is settling with the cold weather. Either way, this baby needs a good coaxing to open." Wellie raised his foot and kicked the doorframe in various places with the sole of his boot. "It's like opening a vacuum-sealed jar. Banging the lid on the edge of a counter breaks the seal. A swift kick loosens the sealed door." He tried the handle again and was successful.

The door opened to a room unlike any Sherry had ever seen. Thick, moist air hit her in the face as soon as the door was ajar. She had to bend low to provide herself a decent view of the interior of the building while not bumping her head on the low beams. The interior light was dim to nonexistent, but where there was filtered light, she was able to identify purple, gold, and white potatoes in shallow bins. The fresh scent of the abundant crop compounded within the controlled environment was a smell reminiscent of her own garden. The comforting earthiness quickly grew on her.

"I don't want the group to go inside the building because that would change the humidity level," Perry said.

"And the door handle isn't behaving. One of us has been locked in there at least once over the last month," Jarrod said. "That would not be a good way to go."

"It's not going to kill someone to be locked in the potato storage building. You can pound on the wall until someone hears you. That's what we've all done over the years. No one is worse for the wear," Wellie said.

"Why not get the door fixed?" Jarrod said. "Has anyone thought of that solution?"

"I'll get to that right after we adjust the tractor brakes or possibly replace them," Wellie said. "Oh, and the new hitch on the back of the pickup truck needs to be ordered and attached. Not to mention the need for instruments to measure soil moisture with all this climate change shenanigans wreaking havoc on the weather patterns. We need a Fort Knox gold reserve to cover all those purchases."

"Dang. Can we stay on topic?" Jarrod said.

"Take a gander inside," Perry said. "You can see we've had a very good year." He turned to his sons. "It's October, right?"

"November, Dad," Jarrod said. "Yes, this is one of the most productive years on record. The spring came early, and the autumn frost is late. All we need now is to maintain the impossibly demanding twenty-four-seven schedule and next year will yield the same results." The sarcasm dripped from his voice.

Perry exhaled with an intensity that made Sherry's skin prickle. She attempted to get Patti's attention for reassurance the situation wasn't flammable, but Patti was busy taking notes on her phone.

"You get the picture. Potatoes, potatoes, and more potatoes. That's the name of the game," Perry said.

"Let me show you gals how the magic happens. We have a few more plants that can be pulled up. That way you can see exactly how the potato grows. Right this way," Wellie said. "Jarrod, can you hold the door?"

Jarrod stepped forward. When the heavy door was entrusted to his grip, he faltered. The glare he shot at his brother did nothing to quell Sherry's growing concern for the unsettled circumstances of the Colton family.

Chapter 5

The group parked themselves in front of a tired brown plant collapsed in the field beyond the storage building.

"Is a sweet potato considered a true potato?" Sherry asked.

"Good question," Patti said.

"The difference confuses a lot of people," Wellie said. "*Considered* is the operative word. In my opinion, the label *potato* was applied to sweet potatoes way back when to make the starchy vegetable more relatable to consumers. Now, it's too ingrained in people's heads to be more specific. Sweets look like an orange potato, they cook like a potato, so darn it, it's a potato."

"I agree," Patti said. "Why fix a problem that doesn't exist."

"There are differences, though. The taste, the texture, and the fact the sweet potato is a root and the potato, as we know it, is a tuber, part of the stem and not the root," Jarrod said. "But they grow in common conditions, although sweets require a longer growth period. Sweets need the same amount of care and attention while in the ground, and after harvest. We grow heirloom sweets and most every other type of potato."

"We'll be at the local farmers' event Wednesday showing up the other venders." Wellie puffed out his chest.

Perry's ample brows merged. "Where did you say we will be? You know I'm not a willing traveler."

"Don't worry, Dad," Jarrod said. "Hopefully this is the last time we'll have to do this."

Sherry glanced at Patti. If she had a follow-up question the timing was right. Patti stayed mute.

Wellie bent over and gently coaxed the wilted plant out of a sizable dirt hill. "The plant's roots are covered in soil mounds we have to rebuild every few days, so the growing potato never sees the light of day." He held up a root high in the air. The wiry stem was teaming with purple potatoes. "Beauties."

Sherry opened her mouth with a question but was denied when a man rushed forward.

"Mr. Colton? Perry?"

"Yes, Isaac, what can we do for you?" Jarrod asked. He stepped in front of his father to field the question.

The man in the winter hat, sunglasses, and a puffy coat threw up his hands. "Jarrod, your father said he would address the leak in the kitchen sink days ago and now the dishwasher is leaking. It's become an emergency."

"I've got this, honey." A woman trotted forward from the direction of the gold sedan. When she reached Jarrod she put her hand across his chest. "You finish up with our visitors. Isaac, let's have a look. Perry's been sidetracked recently. It'll be fixed by dinner."

"That's a big promise, Liz," Wellie said. "Plumbers aren't usually sitting by the phone twiddling their thumbs waiting for calls."

The chill in Liz's expression froze any rebuttal from the others. "I've got this covered."

"My wife is in charge," Jarrod said. "Better listen to her."

"Yoo-hoo." A shrill hail traveled from a porch across the driveway. The woman waved and yoo-hooed a second time. "Jarrod? Is that you?"

"Okay, Madeline. I hear you," Jarrod called back. He lowered his voice to a reasonable volume. "Do me a favor and stop by Madeline's cottage after Isaac's. She left a voicemail her garbage can lid is missing. We may need to buy her a whole new can. Thanks, hon."

"This way," Isaac said. He and Liz followed a driveway rut past the potato field.

"Your wife's a go-getter," Wellie said to Jarrod. "She gets things done."

"Give me some credit, too," Jarrod said.

"That cottage number three guy is never satisfied," Perry grumbled. "Rather than asking for nonessential maintenance all the time he should be more like the Oliveri family in cottage number one. Never a peep out of them and the sweet gal offers *me* a hand. Fancy that notion."

"Plugging a leak is essential, Dad," Wellie said.

"That's my brother, his wife, and my niece in cottage number one," Sherry said. "They're the sweetest."

"They're a great family. I'm a big fan of Pep's food truck," Jarrod said. "That's where we met."

"Well, don't that beat all," Perry said. He slapped his thigh. "In that case, you're welcome here any time, pretty lady. Any Oliveri is a friend of mine."

Patti lifted her eyebrows and donned a beaming smile. "Sherry's just as sweet. I can attest to that."

"Time will tell," Perry said. "You've seen the storage facility and the field, what else is on the agenda, boys?"

"Would you like to see the big machinery?" Wellie asked. "The lot is outdated, and the plough, rototiller, seed potato planter, harvester and tractor may be rusty, like me, but we have more good days than bad."

"Yes, please," Patti said. "We're here for the full experience."

Jarrod faced Sherry. "Patti's here to research for her article. What are you here for?"

"I love to cook, and potatoes are one of my favorite ingredients. Knowing as much as I can about what I cook helps me produce a better recipe."

"You should enter the local farmers' cook-off," Jarrod said. "May already be closed for entries. You'd have to check. Coastal Farm is the potato supplier."

Sherry nodded and turned her attention to Perry to avoid any follow-up.

"Is it time for supper did you say?" Perry asked.

"Not quite yet, Dad," Wellie said. "These ladies would like to see the heavy equipment before they leave."

"Is that why you're here?" Perry asked.

"I'll tell you why they're here again as we walk," Wellie said to his father. "Just stay with the group." Wellie led the way to the rusty tractor.

"You can see what we're up against," Jarrod said. "I don't have time to spend all day on-site here, Wellie's practically on his own when I'm at my second job. Dad is here one minute and far away the next, sometimes selectively, it seems. Now a cook-off's been added to the to-do list. Might be the straw that breaks the camel's back."

"I think the cook-off is a perfect way to showcase your produce," Patti said. She trotted after Wellie, who had created a separation from the others.

Jarrod shrugged his shoulders.

"Who oversees the cottage rentals?" Sherry asked. "Charlotte and Pep are so happy with theirs. I'm sorry if the other tenants are demanding."

"They're not demanding at all," Jarrod said. "It's our job to provide upkeep. The sink is stopped up and it's our responsibility to maintain it in working order. If the extra income generated by the cottages on the farm is too much work to maintain, the Coltons need another plan." His voice grew strained as he continued. "It won't be long before Dad needs more care than we're able to provide. I don't want everything to collide at once. Sorry to vent. No one else will listen."

Wellie turned back and called out, "You all coming?"

The tour concluded thirty minutes later. The time spent canvassing the property opened Sherry's eyes to how many steps are undertaken to provide potatoes to the grocery store. She left the farm with a new appreciation for local farmers and their dedication to making sure their customers eat the finest product. She also left the farm with a certainty the Colton family was on the verge of a fork in the road concerning the farm's future.

Chapter 6

The day the Local and Vocal Farmers' Cook-off organizers were to contact the cooks moving on to the final round couldn't have moved along at a slower pace. To pass the time, rather than obsessively checking her email, Sherry organized notes for an upcoming middle school visit. Those notes included the story behind her current pet project. She'd be talking to a fifth-grade science class about the Augustin Community Garden's newest addition, a children's garden, in two months. The garden was the brainchild of her tennis partner, Kat, and funded in part by a recipe contest win months ago. The cook-off sponsors generously matched the amount Sherry was awarded with a donation to the charity of her choice. Thanks to a suggestion by Kat, she chose to fund the creation of an outdoor space to teach children the importance of learning where their food comes from—namely, a local garden or farm. If the children became the stewards of their own plots, all the better. She hoped the story behind the project would serve as an inspiration to the youngsters to live a more local life. When she finished her assignment her stomach told her what was next.

Friday's lunch was an unimaginative tuna salad sandwich. No capers, no horseradish, only celery salt and mayonnaise to flavor the fish. She ate the sandwich while checking her email multiple times. She began to lose hope she'd made the cook-off. She was expected at the Ruggery at two o'clock, and at one fifteen she was so antsy she decided to go to work a few minutes early. She put on her down vest and scooped up Chutney.

Sherry sighed as she recalled the disastrous recipe attempt she cooked with Charlotte two days prior. The drive down Augustin's idyllic Main Street did nothing to lift her dipping mood. She was coming to grips with the idea that the bad outcome was an omen she hadn't been chosen to participate in the cook-off. A dejected Sherry parked her car in the alley adjacent to the store. She trudged across the mud-splattered driveway they shared with the neighboring store while cradling her canine bundle. Carrying Chutney was mandatory to prevent the small dog from painting the Ruggery's antique wooden floors with muddy paw prints courtesy of the fickle November freeze and thaw cycle.

"Good afternoon," she announced as she entered the store. The brass bell overhead chimed as the doorframe brushed the ancient mechanism. There was no one in sight. She set Chutney down, which signaled Amber's adopted Jack Russell terrier, Bean, to scamper from the store's mini kitchen to greet his best canine buddy.

"Here I come," Amber called out as she followed her dog into the artisan rug showroom. "Hi, how are you? You're early."

"Pretty good. I've worn out the keys on my computer checking my email for any word about Wednesday's cook-off, and that left me with nothing to do. But seriously, no news is bad news in this case. So, here I am in my happy place, hoping to brighten my mood." Sherry was surprised Amber found no amusement in her humor. Her solemn expression sent a chill up Sherry's arms.

"Is something wrong?"

"You must have heard the awful news," Amber said. "I can't believe you were just there yesterday. Did you see anything suspicious?"

"Whoa, whoa. What news? I wasn't anywhere yesterday except here, home and, oh yes, Coastal Greater Tator Farm. What do you mean suspicious?" Sherry unsnapped her vest as a sour wave overtook her stomach.

"Hi, sweetheart." Sherry's father, Erno Oliveri, carried a collection of rolled area rugs from the far end of the showroom. "Can you lend me a hand? I'm switching out the fall foliage rugs for harvest themes in respect to the upcoming Local Farmers' Day celebration. Farms are what put Augustin on the map and gave the original inhabitants their first taste of wealth. We must honor those that remain." He handed Sherry three rolled and bound rugs.

"Hi, Dad. Amber was about to tell me some news that I don't think will be good," Sherry said. She stood staring at her co-manager.

"I haven't shared the news with Erno yet. I have no idea if either one of you has heard. A body was found at the farm you visited with Patti. It was identified as Jarrod Colton. The Colton family runs the farm, right?" Amber sucked in a breath.

"That's right," Sherry said. "Perry Colton is the senior Colton. Jarrod and Wellington are his sons. Wellie lives on the farm, Jarrod doesn't. How awful."

"If that don't beat all. You know, I went to school with Perry Colton," Erno said. His face grew ashen.

"I didn't know that. Does Pep know that? Have you seen Perry since Pep moved to the farm?" Sherry asked.

"I didn't tell Pep outright. I assumed Pep knows I know everyone in Augustin, because I do. Some better than others."

"Perry is Pep's landlord," Sherry said.

"That's right. I suspect most people have a connection to me, one way or another. Pep living on my old schoolmate's farm would have come up eventually. No need to rush the revelation. Unfortunately, I have a bad habit of not making time for old friends," Erno said. "I knew I'd get over to the farm eventually, but Pep brings baby Mimi here so often I haven't needed to make a visit."

"Jarrod Colton. Dead. I'm speechless," Sherry said. She caught her breath as she pictured the man who had showed her the ways of potato farming a day ago.

"Troy was called to the scene early this morning. At first light," Amber said. "I just got off the phone with him for an update."

"Your boyfriend must have been in shock when he got to the farm," Erno said.

"What police have to deal with daily may hardly faze him anymore," Amber said.

"I hope it wasn't Perry who found the body. What a shock," Erno said.

"I didn't ask who found the body. Who else would be there at that time of the day? It was the crack of dawn."

"Did Troy mention anything else?" Sherry asked.

"He said the man was dressed in a spiffy suit. Not something one would wear to run a tractor. I say that because the body was found where the tractor was parked. The tractor was running when Troy arrived."

"When questioned about the tractor use, Perry Colton said he may have left the tractor running, but then he retracted his statement. He then told Troy he didn't remember leaving the tractor running," Amber continued. "He'd relocated it from the field back by the potato storage building around first light. Troy said Mr. Colton immediately corrected himself and said he may have done that the day before, in which case he didn't know why the tractor was running."

"Wasn't Wellington, his other son, there to corroborate the story?" Sherry asked.

"You're getting ahead of me, Sher," Amber said. "I apologize for the lack of details."

"I'm very sorry for the family," Erno said. "Their farm is one of the relics from generations gone by."

"So, you and Perry went to school together," Sherry said. "No wonder he said any Oliveri is a friend of his."

"He said that? That old goat can be a real charmer when he puts his mind to it," Erno said. "Yup. We went to school together, but only when we felt like it, which wasn't often."

"Erno. I'm surprised," Amber said.

"Ha! Funny thing is, Perry and I shared a common dislike for school. He wanted to be on the farm instead of at school and I wanted to be in my dad's rug shop instead of Mrs. Tuttle's English class. Neither one of us continued past high school and I'm not sure we even got credit for those years. Look at us both now. Pretty successful if you ask me. Take that, Mrs. Tuttle. She called Perry Perry Alfresco, because all he wanted was to be outside in the fresh air, not cooped up in front of a blackboard. I'll send my condolences to the Coltons."

"How awful for the family," Sherry said. She gripped the rugs tighter. "I can see how there could be an accident with all the heavy machinery around the farm. Is that what happened?"

"Oh, one more detail. Sorry if it's too graphic. His body was found tangled in the potato harvester attachment that's pulled by the tractor. It digs up the potatoes without mangling them, but Jarrod wasn't so lucky," Amber said.

"Must be convenient having a boyfriend on the Augustin police force," Erno said to Amber. "Unless one of your friends is arrested."

"Dad, why would you say that?" Sherry scolded.

"Officer Sedgeman has to do his job, and that includes no special favors for Amber's friends," Erno said. "She gets to learn all the sordid details before anyone else."

"Don't listen to him, Amber. But since you do know all the sordid details, you said the body was tangled in the machinery?" Sherry asked. "Makes sense from what I gathered in my short time there. I got the impression Jarrod was the least hands-on farmer on the farm. Maybe that would explain how he got tangled up. He might have been rusty using the equipment. Accidents happen when you're not prepared enough."

Amber shut her eyes. "Last detail. It wasn't an accident."

"Oh, no," Sherry said. "A murder?"

"Troy said it's being investigated as one, yes."

"What kind of shape was the farm in yesterday when you were there?" Erno asked Sherry.

"Why do you ask, Dad?"

"I haven't seen hide nor hair of Perry Colton in ages. Farming at any age is a back breaker. He and I are not spring chickens. I can't imagine the stamina needed to keep all the parts in working order."

"You hit the nail on the head. The farm was a throwback to decades ago," Sherry said. "The machinery was certainly worse for wear and hanging on for dear life. The tractor that took Jarrod's life was a rusty dinosaur, but it must have worked to some degree."

"Nothing wrong with preserving the past," Erno said. "As long as the broken-down machinery doesn't malfunction and eat you up."

"Dad, that's not what happened. Well, maybe not."

"The farm was still producing at this time of year?" Amber asked.

"The fields were mostly harvested out for the year so the work at hand seemed all about the potato storage. That building is dark and ominous."

"A good place for a crime?" Erno asked.

"Hard to say. If I let my imagination loose, then yes, it's a good place for a crime. The building serves the purpose the farm needs. The environment inside is exactly where I'd like my freshly harvested potatoes living. There were all sorts of potato varieties in shallow piles. It's a potato gold mine. The farm had a good year they said."

"For that I'm glad for Perry. He's a hard worker." Erno's words were solemn. "I don't mean I'm glad for what happened to Jarrod. You know what I mean."

"When we were there Jarrod wasn't waving a victory flag in celebration for a bountiful harvest," Sherry said. "More like a flag of surrender. I think he wanted out of the farm business."

"Be careful what you wish for," Erno said. "He's now out."

"Is there a Mrs. Colton?" Amber asked.

"Jarrod is married. I caught a quick glimpse of his wife yesterday. She was very helpful with a rental cottage problem. The farm has three cottages they rent out. Pep lives in cottage number one. As for Jarrod, he is, I mean was, being pulled in three directions, the farm, the rental maintenance, and who knows how his other job as real estate agent is going." Sherry turned her attention to Erno. "Dad, is there a Mrs. Perry Colton?"

"She passed on ten years ago, give or take a year," Erno said. "In a strange way her passing helped spur on the farm's dominance around these parts. Perry put all his resources into the farm, and it became a potato powerhouse. I know because Perry had me refurbish two of Alice's hooked rugs after she was gone. He said she had asked him many times to repair the rugs. He felt such remorse putting off her request. I was thrilled to honor her with my designs in their farmhouse. I picked up the rugs that were truly loved and in need of rehooking in spots. That was before planting season, and I returned them when the harvest came in. Holy Toledo, you should have seen the mountain of spuds that day waiting to be distributed to grocery stores. Trucks from all over were lined up to pick up the potatoes. I remarked on the harvest and Perry humbly said his wife, Alice, was his priority while she was alive, and afterward he found the time to concentrate on his business."

"Sounds like a caring man," Sherry said.

"I wonder if Pep and Charlotte are aware of the crime scene at the farm?" Sherry asked.

"I don't know how they couldn't be," Amber said. "I assume there was plenty of police activity apart from Troy's first response."

No sooner had Amber spoken than Sherry's phone buzzed. Charlotte was calling. The call was brief and to the point. She clicked off the call and sighed.

"Ray Bease is on his way to talk to Pep and Charlotte and the others in the rental cottages," Sherry said. "Charlotte didn't want us to worry if we heard the news of a murder on the farm."

"Of course I'm worried," Erno said. "There's a madman running around Augustin."

Chapter 7

"You didn't need to come all the way downtown to the store, Charlotte. Although Grandpa is beside himself baby Mimi came with you. You may not get her back." Sherry's gaze followed in the direction of her niece's squealing. Mimi was testing out unsteady toddler legs while roughhousing with the two pint-size dogs in the middle of the showroom floor. Erno refereed the battle of wills between the little girl and the Jack Russells.

"I have so much to tell you. I wanted to see your reaction for myself," Charlotte said.

"That's not good," Sherry said. "I'm aware of a lot of the details of Jarrod's passing. I was shocked it was murder."

"That's only the beginning. Something's going on at the farm and I may be caught in the middle of it."

"I don't like the sound of that. Tell me everything while I bundle Mrs. Taliaferro's yarn. She's coming to pick up some colors in a half hour for the rug she's making, and Amber didn't get a chance to pack up the purchase before she clocked out. Go ahead, I'll multitask. I'm all ears."

Charlotte sat down on a stool behind the cash register. Sherry set three skeins of the highest-quality lamb's wool yarn on the counter. She snipped the tie that held the wool in a compressed state. Unbound, the wool flowed into a large oval.

"Hand me one, I'll help." Charlotte reached forward to receive the sage green oval of yarn. "I talked to Detective Bease in person after I called you. I was sensitive to what you told me many times about the detective losing patience with speculation, hypotheses, or guesswork when it comes to recounting a crime scene. Thank goodness I knew that because he was in a bad mood. His mood really took a turn when I mentioned the Coltons were about to supply the farmers' day cook-off with their heirloom potatoes. He literally winced when I spoke the word *cook-off*."

Sherry couldn't contain the adverse effects of a gulp of air gone wrong. She coughed and dropped a loop of her yarn. "Don't take his mood personally. That's his hyper-focused first day of a new investigation. He can get a little dramatic. Not all cook-offs end in murder."

"I wanted to share with you what I didn't tell him," Charlotte said.

"Are you saying you saw something happen associated with Jarrod's murder at the farm?"

"I think so," Charlotte said with hesitation. "This morning, I was awakened by Mimi, who I think was awakened by a disturbance outside her bedroom window. The farm is an incredibly quiet place at night. No traffic noises, no people, not even a dog barking. This is the first time a noise might have woken her up. Her toddler self-talk woke me up. I found her perched at her bed rail staring out the window and narrating the action she was observing."

"When you got into her room what did you see out the window?" Sherry asked.

"The police arriving. I thought one officer was Amber's friend, Troy. They were assembling around the old tractor Pep and I have named Ruby because she's so red with rust. The sun was rising right behind Ruby and turning most of the background into silhouettes. Precise images were hard to make out at first. Then I realized what was tangled in the rake blades. I quickly snapped down the window shade to keep Mimi from seeing any more."

"Oh, that's awful," Sherry said.

"I'm glad I did because Detective Bease said Jarrod was clobbered over the head before ending up in the tractor prongs. I don't want Mimi seeing anything like that."

"He gave you some insight into the cause of death? That's unusual. I have to pry that information out of him before it's public knowledge."

"I may have tricked him by suggesting the harvester was a temperamental tool that Perry couldn't count on to run when needed."

"How did that trick him into spilling the beans?" Sherry asked.

"I suggested that Jarrod might have escaped the sharp prongs if they weren't rotating properly. I questioned whether that is what killed him. He said a preliminary exam of the body indicated there had been additional trauma. He emphasized preliminary. He said Jarrod was likely unconscious or worse when he became entangled."

"I'll have to remember that trick of questioning the early findings to trick Ray into adding more information," Sherry said.

"Worked for me," Charlotte said.

"What do you mean you're caught in the middle of something going on at the farm? You had nothing to do with Jarrod's murder except being on the same property at the time."

"I mean, I see people come and go. Jarrod meets with people. Wellie keeps mostly to himself. He hangs out with his father for the most part. My view from my kitchen window is limited, so I don't see all angles." Charlotte paused. After a moment she continued. "I don't know whether to share with the investigation that I was beginning to work with Perry Colton on a journal of sorts, documenting the farm from a management perspective."

"Is that a paid position?" Sherry asked. "With a contract?"

"I'm being paid some and I'm under intermittent deadlines. There's no written contract between us but a verbal contract is good enough for me. We shook hands."

"That's an interesting project," Sherry said. "So, you're spending time with the family collecting information?"

"Not the family. Only Perry. It's his baby."

"Only him? For what reason, I wonder?"

"Perry didn't give me the specific reason for cataloging the farm's processes. He did say he approached me first for the position when he learned that Pep's book about a year in the life of opening a food truck was due for publication soon. He said that type of publication was what was needed for the future of the farm property. I was surprised he thought I was a good candidate. I've been at it for weeks now and I'm having a ton of fun. Who knew my secret passion was writing?"

"You're good at everything and perfect for the job," Sherry said. "Scientists are obligated to present their work with clarity and that's what anyone who wants something documented would want."

Charlotte frowned. "During my sessions with Perry I've made observations around the farm I'm not so sure how to interpret. He's been open about the mechanics of the farm, but the fine details are vague."

"For example?" Sherry prompted.

"He can't decide whether to show me the accounting books. One day he said he would, then ten minutes later, when I asked about the books, he said he never intended to show me. He has some memory issues. He forgot he'd said anything about the books."

"I encountered that when I was there," Sherry said. "Jarrod hadn't arrived for our tour of the farm yet and Perry thought Jarrod wasn't there because he was playing hooky from school. Another moment he didn't know what month it was. I mentioned his memory hiccups to Wellie. He didn't seem overly concerned."

"I witnessed episodes like that, also," Charlotte said. "I tread lightly when he flip-flops. Perry also insists I don't include his sons in the documentation. That's the part that makes me feel like I'm caught in the middle of something bigger. He wants me to take notes as if his were the only position of importance. That's tricky because there will be gaps unless his sons truly don't add value. I'm sure that's not the case."

"Everything might change with Jarrod's passing. From what I've observed, Jarrod wasn't the strongest cog in the farm wheel, by his own choosing, but he was a cog."

"I've made the same observation," Charlotte said. "He had one foot out the door."

"I get it. Farming is a difficult, often unsuccessful venture. Not everyone is cut out to make a living in such a physically demanding way that can go sour at the whim of Mother Nature."

"It can't help to have pressure to take up your father's profession on your shoulders, either," Charlotte said. She scanned the store. "Oops. Don't take that the wrong way. You work here voluntarily. You could quit at any time without the store tanking." Charlotte huffed. "Don't take that the wrong way, either. You're very valuable here. Ugh. My foot is so far in my mouth I can hardly speak."

"I'm not taking anything you say the wrong way. I gather this year was a banner yield for the Coastal farm. The Coltons should be reveling in the farm's success. Instead, there seems to be an undercurrent of discontent."

"Definitely," Charlotte said. "That's why I feel like I might be caught in the middle of a crisis. I'm working with Perry to save the farm, and his sons may be hoping otherwise."

"Was Jarrod in charge of the rental cottages?" Sherry asked. "Managing the rental is up his alley if he's a real estate agent."

"We haven't covered that yet in any detail."

"When I was at the farm a man living in one of the farm cottages had a pipe leak issue. Just as Jarrod was going to act on it his wife took the reins, so Jarrod didn't have to leave our tour."

"I do know that Liz Colton has been very helpful with cottage issues. But we leave our monthly rent with Jarrod. Must be an equal split."

"That's some help to the farm income. The rentals, I mean," Sherry said.

Charlotte shrugged. "In the end, my job isn't to judge the family dynamics. I'm neutral noting all Perry's telling me. My job isn't to advise him. Beyond that, if I don't understand something I've had Wellington provide a dumbed-down version I can translate into relatable words."

"Who is the intended audience of your project?" Sherry asked. "For example, Pep told me when his book, *Opening a Food Truck, From Soup to Nuts*, is released next month the publisher will be targeting wannabe entrepreneurs, age range twenty to fifty and beyond."

"We have yet to discuss that aspect of the book. I'm not even sure the result will be in traditional book form. The result could be a farm manual or a published or personal journal. I'm still in the note-taking phase. Perry is a delicate individual to work with. If I bombard him with questions, he shuts down or retreats into someone with no memory whatsoever. At that point, the session is over."

Sherry considered all Charlotte was telling her. "Is this side job too complicated for you? I don't mean in a work sense, more in a messy family affair sense. Especially now that one of the family members has turned up dead?" Sherry studied the developing furrow in Charlotte's brow. "Your idea was to use your work leave to bond with baby Mimi. That was your stated intention, you said."

"I know, but this project has captured my attention," Charlotte said. "And I might be a tiny bit emotionally invested in seeing Perry succeed. Especially now."

"Listen to what you're saying. And I'm speaking from the heart. You've taken on a project that could be very time-consuming. Are you sure you know what you're getting into?"

Charlotte took her time responding. After a period of silence, she began, emotion creeping into her voice, "I'm not good at sitting idle. I'm going nuts spending all my time with a two-year-old. That's my honest confession. With Pep's work schedule I'm afforded time to explore something new and I love it. Am I the worst mother ever?"

Sherry raised her free hand to stop Charlotte from continuing. "You're definitely never idle. Mimi never sits still. Mothering is anything but idle time. From everything I see you could write a manual on excellent mothering."

"Thanks, Sher," Charlotte said.

"May I add, if I were faced with the decision to keep up my frenetic schedule or give it all up for a moment of peace, I would choose to keep my crazy schedule." Sherry laughed at her admission.

"That's the Sherry I know and love," Charlotte said.

"Now, let's get back to Perry Colton and what he's not sharing with you." Sherry put down her hand and returned to the task of balling yarn.

"Here's a list of current questions Perry's not interested in going into detail about; Why doesn't he include his sons' contributions in the manual? Do the farm's rental cottages add value to the operation or just more work?

Why not hire outside helping hands more often? And finally, if the farm had a banner year, why is cash flow so tight?"

"That's a lot," Sherry said.

"And that was before Jarrod's murder."

"I can see how you might think you're in the epicenter of the situation," Sherry said. "Do you have any idea who might have done this to Jarrod, and why?"

Charlotte shook her head. "I'm racking my brain to come up with anything that would be of help to the detective. Right now, I don't want to raise red flags where there shouldn't be any. I'm choosing my words carefully."

"Did Detective Bease have any intel on whether the cook-off would move forward?" Sherry asked. "Mind you, the point may be mute where I'm concerned as I haven't received any word whether I'm in the finals. I'm still planning on attending to see who beat me out."

"He didn't offer any. Remember, he prickled when I mentioned a cook-off. You and he have history with cooking competitions. He had a set of questions and stuck to them. I was glad because I got a little nervous about my answers. He has such a practiced poker face I never knew what he was thinking."

Sherry pictured her friend Ray Bease measuring Charlotte's words with a stern glare. He never lingered over witnesses' responses because he said that caused undo nerves. He never pressed beyond a reasonable reply. He had a gentle yet serious way about him that drew out information without any unnecessary discomfort. Sherry had tremendous appreciation of her friendship with Augustin's homicide detective. Their common love of cooking, along with the many times Sherry aided in murder investigations involving cooking competitions, built a strong foundation for a lasting friendship. Sherry was also keenly aware of the fact cook-offs seemed to be magnets for bad behavior. Detective Bease was always wary when she mentioned she was entering a new culinary competition.

"I wonder how Jarrod's passing will affect the cook-off? Since Coastal Greater Tator Farm was supplying the potatoes to the cook-off, another supplier might have to be found."

"The Coltons' farm is the number-one best-selling potato farm for fifty miles," Charlotte said. "It would be a shame for Perry not to have his shining moment. If the cook-off was dedicated to Jarrod, that would be a wonderful tribute."

"Let's hope the potato cook-off goes forward, for the sake of Augustin's local farmers and the Coltons," Sherry said. "And let's hope Jarrod's murder is solved before that."

"For Perry's sake," Charlotte added.

Chapter 8

Sherry and Erno said goodbye to Charlotte and Mimi after an animated lesson in sorting yarn colors and placing each skein in its appropriately labeled bin. Sherry preferred to sort colors overseen by the expert eye of Amber, in case there was a dispute over shade variations. In the absence of Amber, Mimi was up to the task. The little one knew most colors, thanks to her consistent exposure to the family business. That knowledge proved invaluable to start the process. From that point on, the task became a fun game of sort and re-sort depending on the toddler's whim.

As soon as Charlotte and Mimi left, Sherry and Erno made the necessary color sort corrections that in-charge Mimi wouldn't have tolerated. The adults were patient with Mimi's innate stubborn streak, a familial trait of the Oliveris. Pep's success at creating his food truck would not have been possible without his steadfast conviction. The trait shared among the family members served Sherry well in her cooking competitions. She never gave up easily.

As the afternoon wore on the Ruggery was quiet, and then the front doorbell chimed. In walked Patti Mellit, bundled in a long fleece coat and humming a merry tune.

"Good afternoon," Patti called out.

Sherry emerged from behind the sales desk.

"Hi, Patti," Sherry said. "You're a ray of sunshine and happiness."

"Thanks." Patti continued humming as she scanned the store. When she finished her tune she asked, "Is your dad here?"

"Yes, I can call him for you."

"I was just wondering if we were alone. It's you I want to talk to. I wouldn't mind if we could tuck into a corner for a private word," Patti said.

"Okay, sure," Sherry said. "Let me grab you a stool and we can sit behind the sales desk. I need to keep an eye out for customers while Dad is in the storeroom." Sherry lifted a wooden stool and set it down next to hers.

"Thanks. I think you'll have a lot to think about after we talk," Patti said.

"Is this about Jarrod Colton?" Sherry asked.

"No. What about Jarrod Colton? I was about to send the family a thank-you basket of goodies for showing us around the farm. I got so much great material from our visit."

"You should change that to a condolence basket."

"Oh no! What happened?"

"Jarrod was found entangled in the harvester rake that is attached to the ancient tractor we saw."

"What a terrible accident," Patti said with a groan.

"Murder is suspected because he was dressed in a jacket and tie. The tractor was running, and no one says they were using it. Not to mention, he suffered nasty trauma to the head."

Patti shook her head. "Murder. How horrible. That may change everything. Do you think the cook-off is off now since Coastal was the potato supplier? It's the eleventh hour and finding a substitute local heirloom supplier who's stocked away a harvest for such an event would be next to impossible."

"I'd say yes the cook-off is canceled, but I haven't checked my email in a few hours for any word from the organizers one way or another. The finalists' notification day is today." Sherry met Patti's glance. "No time like the present." She lifted the lid of her laptop, which sat to the side of the cash register. "I'll check again right now."

"Can you hold off for a minute?" Patti had softened her voice, as if she were about to deliver bad news.

Sherry hovered her fingers over the keys. "What's wrong? I'm not sure I can take any more bad news."

"As horrible as I feel about the news of Jarrod's passing after he was so kind to us yesterday, I have some good news."

"Phew," Sherry said. "I can't imagine what it is."

"I've been asked for any recommendation for a position opening in the prestigious North-Eats Test Kitchen. The wonderful program on public television that has caught on like wildfire. I never miss an episode, and I've had many of the cooks on my podcast."

"How exciting. Are you thinking of taking the position?" Sherry asked. She signaled her pleasure at her friend's good fortune with a broad smile.

"Oh no, not me. I'm a journalist who researches food, food trends, culinary history and the like. I'm not a practicing cook with much talent, except for following a recipe step by step," Patti said. "You. You are who I would recommend being among the elite recipe creators on that show."

Sherry's mouth dropped open. She produced a bizarre noise that originated deep in her chest and emerged as a squeak.

"That's not going to win you the position," Patti said. "You'll have to form words when you're interviewed."

"I don't know what to say," Sherry said. "Except I am not worthy."

"Don't be ridiculous. Of course you are. If you're interested, the producer who contacted me gave me a choice of audition dates for you. They're intrigued with your background as a home cook who turned into an amateur cooking competition champion slash recipe innovator."

"Is it a full-time position?" Sherry asked.

"It is. The job would bring a lot of change to your life. I'm sure you could continue your volunteer work and edit the mayor's newsletter after hours, but you and I both know the cook-offs you take part in are for amateurs. If you worked at the test kitchen you'd be deemed a food industry professional, and that would disqualify you from amateur cooking competitions."

Sherry winced as her thoughts collided. She'd met the most remarkable people through cook-offs. She had traveled to many wonderful venues and hoped for many more trips to competitions. She'd miss the experience beyond words. On the other hand, maybe she was ready for a change while she was still young enough to adapt.

"Can I think about it for a day or two?" Sherry asked. Her voice was uncertain, her nerves were heightened, her head was spinning. "I'll take more days if allowed."

"These things move quickly. The producers would like an answer by next Wednesday. You're getting a bit of an extension because they are wrapping up a current show and they're on location somewhere."

"That's fine. Wednesday was the cook-off, but it doesn't seem as if I made the finals anyway. For that matter, the whole event might be canceled," Sherry said. She swiped her sneaker sole across the floor. The screech elicited a bark from Bean on the other side of the room.

"Off the record, are you excited about the prospect of working for such a prestigious show?" Patti asked.

Sherry sighed. "I have to say my gut reaction is to say thanks for the offer, but no thanks. I'm not that adventurous. On the flip side, the job is something I've fantasized would be a perfect fit for me if I was ten years younger."

"You've seen the show? The average age of the cooks is mid-fifties. You'd be the baby on the set. Age aside, what you'd be learning is invaluable. I'm biased because I'd have you on my podcast as a regular to pick your brain."

"You're making an attractive case for applying," Sherry said. She knew her friend had her best interests in mind. "I'll call you Wednesday with my answer. I promise."

"You've got a deal, my friend," Patti said. "Any decision you make is the right decision. On another note, do you want to check to see if you've heard from the potato cook-off?"

Sherry had forgotten all about the open email app on her computer screen. "Let me check."

At the top of her unopened email list the subject line read *Congratulations*. The sender was the Local and Vocal Farmers of Hillsboro County. She clicked the message open and read the introductory paragraph, which touched on the loss of a member of the preeminent potato farm in the county. The message went on to explain how the Colton family would like the cook-off to continue with a special dedication to the lost family member and his contribution to the farm's enduring success. The second paragraph welcomed Sherry to the cook-off, featuring ten of the best cooks in the northeast. Her dish, Speedy African Groundnut Stew with Heirloom Sweet Potatoes, was the recipe she would be preparing at the fairground's convention center Wednesday. Sherry rehashed the email to Patti.

"The cook-off will have a somber mood but it's on and you're in it," Patti said. "The Colton family will be rallying to keep their farm and their crop in the forefront while keeping Jarrod's memory alive. Not an easy task. Is that a problem for you to cook then call me with your decision? I don't want to stress you out."

"No, I can do both. I think."

Chapter 9

"Congratulations, sweetie. I knew you could do it," Don said. "The African Groundnut Stew is a winner. I can attest to that. Not to minimize tonight's dinner, which also is a winner." He sat in front of his empty dinner plate waiting for Sherry to finish her last bite of grilled steak bruschetta. She finished the seasoned steak and sopped up the herby, garlicky juices with her toasted baguette slice, all the while aware of Don's longing stare. She wasn't about to fork over her last bites no matter how good he was at making sad puppy eyes.

"Don't forget the word *speedy* in the recipe title. The cook-off committee added 'With Heirloom Sweet Potatoes' to the title for a nod to the cook-off theme."

"I like that," Don said.

"That often happens. The title is adjusted slightly to reflect the sponsor's products in a brighter light."

"Smart."

"The word *speedy* is the game-changer twist. Traditionally, the stew is a long slow process. I've introduced a couple of time-saving secret ingredients that pack a flavor punch and serve double duty to lower the ingredient count. That makes the recipe more user-friendly."

"Genius. Let me guess, chutney is in the recipe? Not the dog. The gingery, sweet, fruity condiment you love to love."

"You know me so well, my dear," Sherry said with a chuckle. "Would you like seconds? You're practically drooling over what's left on my plate."

"Yes, please," Don said.

"Tomorrow is a cooking lesson with Charlotte at her house and we may make the stew again," Sherry said. "Or we might make a different potato dish for variety's sake. I stocked up in case I got into the cook-off final round and needed to learn the ins and outs of cooking a potato. Charlotte says she has free access to the potatoes stored on the farm, so she has a backup supply."

Sherry placed the toast on Don's plate. She angled thin slices of New York strip steak boldly seasoned with smoked paprika, cumin, and garlic atop the toast. She spooned the cherry tomato halves, basil, and red onion bruschetta topping across the meat. Then she sprinkled on flaky finishing salt and ground some black pepper for the final kiss of flavor. He was silent while he savored his seconds.

"On a different subject, I got an offer to interview for a job," Sherry said.

Don's expression lifted. "Really? I didn't know you were looking. What's the job?"

"I wasn't looking at all. I love my gig at the Ruggery, my editing job, and my volunteering. I'd have to give all that up."

"You'd never do that," Don said. He shook his head. "I'm sorry. I shouldn't say that. Of course your options are always open. What's the job?"

"Recipe creator and tester at North-Eats Test Kitchen television. The kitchen complex is about forty-five minutes from here. They asked Patti to recommend someone, and I'm honored to say she recommended me."

"That's a chance of a lifetime for someone with your talents." The sincerity in his voice was paired with Don grasping Sherry's hand.

"A job like that would bring a lot of change," Sherry said.

"I can't believe you'd call creating and testing recipes for pay a job. You already do all that by your own volition."

"True," Sherry said. "And I only get paid if I win."

"If you're asking my opinion, go through the interview process and see if you like the position. One step at a time or you might get overwhelmed. I know you. You're already projecting into the future about leaving the family business, working full-time again, putting some volunteering on the sidelines and telling the mayor to find a new editor. Or you may also be thinking you can still do all those things and still have an hour left in the day to be with me. Either way, you're amazing." Don laughed cautiously.

Sherry's heart skipped a beat as his support washed over her.

After dinner Sherry and Don relaxed on the couch with Chutney curled up between them. The relaxation ended with a phone ringing. Chutney jumped down and repositioned himself on the rug. Don reached for his phone resting on the side table.

"Hello?" Don's brow lowered. "Detective Bease? Do you want to speak to Sherry?" He continued after a pause, "Okay. Do you mind if I put you on speaker phone?" Don clicked on the phone's speaker without waiting for a reply.

"I assume Sherry is within the sound of my voice?" Detective Ray Bease's familiar tone filled the room. His neutral lilt, framing carefully chosen words, indicated he was on duty.

"Yes, she's right beside me."

"Hi, Ray. I didn't know you had Don's number," Sherry said.

"There's a lot of things you don't know about me," Ray said. "I have a recipe question I've been meaning to call you about, but that can wait. I have a few questions for Don. Don, you still there? Don't let Sherry hijack this call."

"Hey!" Sherry scoffed. "I take offense at your insinuation that I, well, whatever it is you're insinuating."

"Don, you had a man named Jarrod Colton on your boat, the *Current Sea*, sixteen days ago. Is that correct?" Ray asked.

"I'll take your word for the number of days ago that was. Yes, that sounds about right. Sherry told me he passed away."

"Do you have a minute to answer a few questions about your time with Jarrod Colton?" Ray asked.

"As best I can. I've had a lot of different passengers since he was on board. My memory might be cloudy."

"Remember as best you can," Ray said. "Please let me know if any answer is beyond your recollection. I can't work with guesswork and speculation."

Don smiled at Sherry. She'd described Ray's fact-gathering methods to Don in the past and here they were on full display.

"May I ask how you knew he had ridden the *Current Sea*?" Don asked. "Did Sherry tell you?"

Sherry straightened up in anticipation of Ray having to answer a question even though he was the interrogator. Experience dictated Ray's intention was to always maintain control of witness interviews rather than having a question posed to him. Throwing a wrench in the works could ignite prickliness at any moment.

"I questioned Wellington Colton. He mentioned there were periods in the last two to three weeks when his brother was unreachable by phone even after multiple attempts. Jarrod had been visiting the farm less and less. As the property's cottage manager, Jarrod was obligated to be on call for all manner of problems. Wellington said one day he'd had enough of Jarrod's disappearing act. Wellington's new approach was to pester Jarrod's wife, Liz, until she revealed where he was. On the aforementioned day, Wellington dashed down to the marina to confront Jarrod when Liz mentioned he was on his way, by boat, to Long Island and may be out of telephone contact."

"So, that was Wellington Colton who threatened you?" Sherry asked. "Was he wearing overalls that day?"

"Yes. No coat, only overalls and a T-shirt. How did you know?" Don asked.

"Lucky guess," Sherry said. "If you had mentioned that detail I might have guessed who the man trying to stop the boat was."

"Whoa, whoa. He threatened you? He tried to stop the boat? And why should I be interested in the fact he was wearing overalls?" Ray asked.

"Before I knew the man booking it down the dock wasn't trying to hijack us, yes, I thought he was a threat. Until now I've been thanking my stars the man wasn't an Olympic swimmer, diving in to catch us."

"Why was he trying to stop the boat?" Ray asked.

"We're putting these pieces of the puzzle together in real time just like you, Ray," Sherry said.

"I'm not sure except that now I'm learning his brother was on the boat," Don said. "I can tell you, though, the man wasn't running down the dock to wish his brother a bon voyage. He was madder than the buggers in a poked hornets' nest."

"Madder than the buggers of a poked hornets' nest," Ray repeated.

"That's what I saw," Don said. "A man in overalls hauling it down the dock. Remember, I had no idea who the man was at the time. I wasn't taking any chances with the look of exasperation on his face. Safety of the passengers is my top priority. I kept the boat in reverse and stayed on schedule. Anyway, yes, Jarrod Colton rode the *Current Sea* to Long Island. Round trip."

"You mention a look of exasperation on Wellington's face."

"Definitely. He was huffing and puffing, yes, but he was gritting his teeth and his fists were clenched. He wasn't just winded, he was raging. Not knowing who the man was, I couldn't get away fast enough. I was grateful to Jarrod for pointing the potential intruder out."

"Jarrod knew who the man was," Sherry said. "He called out his own brother to avoid some sort of confrontation without naming him. Was that to pardon Wellington's behavior or to diminish him, I wonder?"

Ray let a moment pass, during which time Sherry heard what she thought was paper being shuffled. She grinned because she recalled the training Ray went through to become a requisite e-detective, armed with a laptop. Despite his unit chief's best efforts, Ray continually reverted to his trusty pen and notebook for ongoing investigations.

When the paper shuffling ceased, Ray continued, "Was Jarrod Colton traveling alone?"

"When you interviewed Wellington, didn't he tell you whether or not his brother was traveling alone?" Don asked.

Sherry winced at the question. Another question for Ray wouldn't make him happy.

"I'm asking you for your recollections," Ray said. "Different people have different recollections. All are important."

"Jarrod arrived with another man. They sat together. Both were in business suits," Don said.

"Wellington didn't mention a travel mate," Ray said. "And I didn't ask. I should have."

"You can't be expected to know something like that," Don said. "Most passengers are commuting to work at that time of the day. It's much more common that he or she travels solo."

Sherry was bursting with a question. The words flew out of her mouth before she could stop them. "Did Jarrod mention what type of business he was doing or where he was going in Long Island? I would think his real estate license is for Connecticut transactions, not New York."

Ray chimed in before Don could answer. "Did you hear any of their conversation?"

"I'm not an eavesdropper. My job is to get the boat to Long Island and back safely." Don put his hand on Sherry's knee. "I had already had one scare. I became particularly vigilant about my boat's instrumentation. My focus is on the boat, the dials on the console, and my communication with the outgoing and incoming marina radio commander. So no, I didn't hear more than small doses of their conversation, which is especially difficult when the engine is in full throttle."

"In the little conversation you heard between the two men, were there any outstanding emotions exhibited? Maybe a raised voice, a curse word, that sort of thing?" Ray asked.

"Hmmm." Don's sight drifted back to Sherry's face. If he was seeking guidance she gave none. Sherry pinched her mouth shut. She was enjoying the banter between the two men.

"Even though they were seated only a few feet from me the boat is too noisy to hear beyond a foot or two, especially when my attention is forward. I did see them shake hands when I announced it was time to disembark. Not a see-you-later handshake. More of a the-deal's-done handshake."

"Interesting," Ray said. "Anything else, Don?"

"Nope, that's all," Don said.

"Got it. Many thanks. Oh, and Sherry, I need a word with you, but someone's trying to call through so I'm out. I'll contact you tomorrow. Good night, both of you." Ray clicked off before Sherry or Don could bid him a pleasant evening.

Chapter 10

After Ray's phone call Sherry nestled into Don's arms. They were joined by Chutney, who curled up by Sherry's side. Don sunk his hand into his pants pocket and pulled out a small card.

"What's that?"

"I brought over the business card given to me by the man who rode with Jarrod Colton," Don said. He handed the card to Sherry.

"I'm surprised Ray didn't ask any other questions about that man," Sherry said. "Ray has a method to his questioning though, and I've learned not to second-guess any of it. I'd expect a follow-up call if I were you."

Sherry held the blue and yellow business card up to eye level. "*Harry Chan, Residential Development Sales and Acquisitions.* The card doesn't specify where he's based out of. Just says *Specializing in the Northeast region.* The area code is one of many out of New York City."

"I have a New York area code. Doesn't indicate where you live these days. Most people who move keep their old numbers."

"He's not a lawyer after all. Developmental sales and acquisitions specialist? That's not good for the future of the farm," Sherry said. "You're sure he was traveling with Jarrod? Maybe they were friends who happened to be on the same commuter boat. A boat captained by the handsomest sea captain there is."

"I'll take that compliment and raise you one. You're the most delectable cook on land or sea, who happens to be a decorated cooking competitor. I'm lucky enough to have a job where I can see you every night and taste test your latest recipe creations."

"I'm blushing," Sherry said. "Stay on track. Was Jarrod with Mr. Harry Chan for business or social purposes? That's what Ray should pin down."

"Thinking back, I saw them exit the Long Island marina in the same car. They had a driver. The car pulled extraordinarily close to the dock entrance. I suppose that was to save the men extra steps. On the return trip, the same thing. I would call that a business meeting."

"I wonder if the meeting had anything to do with Jarrod's murder?" Sherry asked. "And I wonder if Jarrod being together with Harry Chan had anything to do with Wellington being so angry and aggressive."

"You're the amateur sleuth extraordinaire," Don said. "I'd be surprised if you didn't already know the answer."

"I don't. Do you think Charlotte, Pep, and Mimi are safe on the farm? I mean, they were yards from the murder scene. What if they know something that they don't know they know? What if the murderer thinks they know something?"

"I think I see what you're getting at," Don said. He squeezed his eyes into slits, as if measuring Sherry's words.

"Why else would Jarrod be meeting with a developer if he weren't interested in turning one of the last precious waterfront farms in the area into a mass of overpriced condos," Sherry said. She wasn't posing a question so much as mourning the loss of another plot of underappreciated food-producing land. "Maybe the idea of cashing in on the family property without everyone's knowledge caught up to him. Look how he's ended up." The words left a bitter taste in her mouth.

"You said the word *maybe*. You're not sure that's the case, are you?" Don asked.

"No, I'm not."

"How could Jarrod sell the land out from under his father? Whose name is on the title?"

"I don't know any of that. For all I know, Jarrod may have been having a job interview and that's all. I might be jumping to conclusions, and if there's one thing I've learned from Detective Ray Bease, it's don't jump."

"Sage advice," Don said.

"What I do know is, Perry Colton is getting older. Wellington was angry at Jarrod. The family wasn't having a bonding moment when Patti and I arrived on the farm. Something's gone wrong and murder is the result. Dad is Perry's friend, and Pep and his family are living on the Coltons' farm. This is all a little too close to home."

"I see the wheels turning," Don said. "What are you up to?"

"Don't worry. Just a little information gathering. I'm going to the farm tomorrow to work with Charlotte in the kitchen. Let's see what I can dig up other than a fresh potato."

Chapter 11

Saturday morning Sherry headed to the Coastal Greater Tator Farm to give Charlotte another cooking lesson. She found Charlotte in her kitchen, donning an apron and eager to get started.

"Do you ever get tired of potatoes?" Charlotte asked as she ran the water over a handful of heirloom fingerling potatoes.

"Never. There are so many ways to incorporate potatoes into recipes. These beauties are from the Coltons' farm right outside your window. How amazing is that?" Sherry said. Her enthusiasm brought a smile to Charlotte's face.

The first task was forming a potato rinsing assembly line. At the end of the line was Mimi, who oversaw putting the clean spuds in a bowl positioned on the tray of her high chair.

"Pep and I are very lucky to live here," Charlotte said. "The frosting on the cake is Perry gives me a share of his harvest. I wish you'd let me pay you for your time spent giving me cooking lessons."

"Absolutely not. I enjoy our time together so much." Sherry reached down and rescued an escaped potato off the floor. "This needs a rewash." She put the escapee aside and handed a clean pinkie-sized potato to Charlotte. "How long is the lease on your cottage for?"

"Not long enough," Charlotte said. "Perry says he only makes each lease up for one year. That way, if anyone has a change of mind, no one is trapped for too long."

"That works," Sherry said.

"I love it here. We're so close to the Long Island Sound and the beach on one side. The perfect backyard for Mimi. We're only a few minutes from the center of Augustin too."

"I'd bet there was lots of interest in the cottage when it went vacant."

"Absolutely. Pep got lucky when he met Jarrod Colton last year at his food truck. I still can't believe their brief conversation led to us getting to rent this cottage."

"Have you heard any rumblings of the farm being sold?" Sherry asked.

"Nothing set in stone, have you?" Charlotte dropped another wet potato on the floor as she attempted to place it in Mimi's hand. "Slippery devil."

Mimi giggled as the misbehaving potato rolled across the floor.

"Thinking about certain clues Perry may have dropped here and there, maybe I should have picked up on what he intends to do with the farm. He waffles between how wonderful the farm is one minute and how he isn't sure he can manage the next. One thing is for sure. He loves the farm and is proud of his management skills. Maybe that's why he wants to record a year in the life of the farm, for posterity's sake."

"It sure sounds as if the idea is being explored. At least by his sons," Sherry said.

"Do you have concrete proof or are you sensing the mood has changed since Jarrod's death?"

"I wouldn't call the proof concrete. There was one hint that sparked my interest. Don mentioned a man rode with Jarrod to Long Island a couple weeks before he was murdered. Jarrod and the man had their heads together during the voyage. When they left the boat the man gave Don his business card. The man was a residential developer."

"Maybe Jarrod is investing in the man's business? He is a real estate agent." Charlotte was throwing out a scenario her questioning tone wasn't endorsing.

"That's a maybe. More likely it boils down to Jarrod testing the waters on selling the farm."

"That's a shame," Charlotte said. "Who was the developer? Anyone we know?"

"Harry Chan was his name."

"Harry Chan. Small world. A name from the past," Charlotte said. "If it's the same guy, we went on a few casual dates before I met Pep."

"His business card didn't specify where he worked out of. The cell phone on the card had a New York area code."

"The Harry I know did work in New York. He was getting his master's degree in urban and regional planning," Charlotte said. "It's got to be the same Harry Chan. Now I'm putting two and two together. He's been at the farm a few times since the spring. Good chance it's the same Harry Chan from Don's boat."

"Interesting. He's met with Jarrod at the farm?"

"Once I caught a glimpse of Jarrod showing him around. Another time Wellie was the guide. I said hello to Harry on those occasions. I knew he built a successful business but lost track of him over the years. Good for him. Not so good for the farm, although the Coltons could get a pretty penny if they sell out."

Sherry watched her niece rearranging the potatoes in order of size. Her thoughts went dark when she recalled Jarrod's murder had occurred yards from her precious niece. Were they in danger? Her heart would shatter if anything happened to her brother and his family. She sucked in a breath to calm her nerves. "Charlotte, you have more than a few connections to Jarrod and I'm getting worried for your safety."

"I'm sure plenty of people have connections to Jarrod and the other Coltons. Don't worry about us. That's my job to worry. If I ever had any notion I was flirting with danger, I'd be the first to admit it."

"My worry is if Jarrod's death has anything to do with the status of the farm's future," Sherry said. "Is Jarrod the only target of the murderer?"

"I haven't met with Perry since Jarrod's passing. I don't know if he has any idea who would be out to get his son and what that person's motives are. Is Jarrod's death a coincidence of timing?"

"The fact the property's future is in question, and a key management figure has been murdered, is too rich to be ignored." Sherry had read a book on the science of murder investigations and her takeaway was coincidences don't exist. Ray would steadfastly second that concept.

"I can see your hamster wheel turning." Charlotte tapped her temple with her wet finger. "What are you brewing up there?"

"That's funny. That's exactly what Don said last night when we were discussing Jarrod's murder. Nothing's brewing. Well, maybe something. Let's take the idea of a coincidence out of the picture. Why would Jarrod and Wellie be meeting with Harry Chan?"

"To get advice?"

"Maybe."

Charlotte handed Mimi another potato. The little girl was in toddler paradise building a potato tower.

"I have a meeting with Perry Tuesday. The day after Jarrod's funeral service. He's still interested in continuing the book project despite his family's loss. Of course, I am also, if he is."

"I should pay my respects at the memorial reception," Sherry said. "I didn't know him, but this town is so small it's nice to support a family you have even the slightest connection to."

"Pep and I will make an appearance. Maybe you can babysit while we go, then we trade off and you go to the reception," Charlotte said.

"Of course," Sherry said. "I'll put it on my calendar."

On cue, Mimi held up a fingerling potato in each tiny hand and began squealing with delight.

"She's another potato lover," Sherry said. She had a vision of the farmland covered in spec houses. "It would be a shame to lose Augustin's connection to its heirloom crop."

"I agree," Charlotte said. "Perry tells me the farm produces over twenty varieties of heirloom potatoes that can sell for a premium. He's got a good thing going if he and his family are on the same page about the farm staying a farm."

"Getting back to recipes, potatoes are a misunderstood breed," Sherry said. "People think they're a high-calorie food to avoid, but that's only the case if you've trained yourself to glob on butter, sour cream and bacon bits. Those are Perry's words."

"Those add-ons do sound worth the extra calories," Charlotte said with a laugh.

"Think about the method of cooking rather than the add-ons. That's the twist we're giving our potatoes to boost their flavor."

"I can't rule out the bacon bits," Charlotte said.

Sherry removed the bowl of fingerlings from in front of Mimi before replacing it with a smaller bowl containing a whisk. The toddler had no chance to protest the swap as Sherry demonstrated the whisk's ability to blend the bowl's contents: mayonnaise, Dijon mustard, olive oil, and Italian herbs. Mimi cooed with delight during the activity.

"Let's get back to work on the crunchy chicken nuggets and garlic-Parmesan roasted fingerling potatoes. The chicken thighs are cubed, if you wouldn't mind tossing them in Mimi's mixture," Sherry said. "I've cubed up about a pound."

"Where's the giant vat of hot oil to fry the nuggets?" Charlotte asked.

"These aren't fried. You won't believe how they're made," Sherry said.

"I know you. You're a kitchen magician. But chicken nuggets need to be crispy or they're chicken softies."

"Watch and learn," Sherry said. "First, we used the mayo and mustard blend Mimi whipped up to coat the chicken thigh cubes. The coating acts to adhere the breadcrumbs to the chicken while keeping the chicken moist inside the coating. Did I mention you won't believe how well this recipe works?"

"Seeing is believing," Charlotte said, issuing a challenge.

"Second, we need a bowl of panko breadcrumbs seasoned with some sea salt and pepper. You can get more creative with the seasonings, as you see fit. Sky's the limit. Just make sure you use only panko breadcrumbs for this recipe. Toss the chicken in the bowl of breadcrumbs and coat all sides. Next, we lay the coated nuggets across an oiled baking sheet, or Bernie would do quite well, and bake at three hundred and seventy-five degrees for about twenty minutes, or until sizzling and golden brown. It's so easy."

"Perfect," Charlotte said. "And the potatoes are ready to get roasted."

"Yes, they are. We've tossed them in olive oil, Parmesan, and garlic and they're ready to go in the iron skillet. The skillet gives them a fantastic browning. They come out like thick potato chips without the oiliness. Crispy on the outside, creamy in the middle."

"Won't the potatoes take longer to roast than the chicken?" Charlotte asked.

"See? You're already in tune with your inner cook. Yes, we put the potatoes in about fifteen minutes before the chicken. Potatoes are very forgiving and it takes a lot to overcooking them. But a word of caution, no one likes undercooked potatoes."

Chapter 12

The timer rang. The chicken was added to the oven.

"We have twenty-five minutes to take a walk," Charlotte said. "Would you like to see the other two cottages on the farm? They're as charming as ours."

"Sure," Sherry said. "Let's bundle up. It's chilly out today."

Charlotte's cottage was on the southern side of the Coastal Greater Tator Farm, as were the other two cottages. Charlotte explained that a divorcée was renting one cottage and the man with the plumbing issue, and his wife, were renting the third cottage.

Sherry held Mimi's hand to keep her on course. The toddler tended to weave from side to side on walks, doubling the distance covered, along with the time it took to reach any destination.

"Good morning, Madeline," Charlotte said as they passed the neighbor's house. Madeline was enjoying a cup of something on her whitewashed pillared porch. She was wrapped in a colorful blanket, seated on one of two twin Adirondack chairs. A woman who shared many of Madeline's facial features sat beside her. Madeline lifted her mug and toasted the trio as they approached.

"Hello. Must be visiting day," Madeline said. "My sister Lulu is here and Isaac's got a guest, also." She pointed to Isaac's parking spot. Two cars were parked in the small lot to the side of the adjacent two-story cottage. "Hi there, little Mimi. What a cutie."

"This is my sister-in-law, Sherry," Charlotte called out. Her attention drifted to Mimi, who was picking up her gait.

"Nice to meet you," Madeline said. "Did you hear I'm competing against you at the cook-off?"

"If you're also competing then it's true. That's great news, Madeline. Any hints on what you're making?" Sherry asked.

"Not African-Style Groundnut Stew. Hope you don't mind. I hounded Charlotte until she told me the title of your recipe. I'm making Colombian chicken, corn and potato stew."

"May the best stew win," Sherry said.

Mimi wasn't in the mood to stop and listen to adult small talk. She scurried away. Sherry threw Madeline and Lulu a hurried wave and trotted off to tail her niece.

"You didn't tell me your neighbor was in the cook-off," Sherry said when she caught up to Charlotte.

"Sorry. So much is going on it slipped my mind. I have no idea what caliber cook she is."

"The unknown of the other contestants is half the fun," Sherry said.

The group continued to the third cottage, which was tucked among a garden of tall ornamental grasses still holding on to their showy autumn tassels. The grass fronds towered over the little girl and the women hurried to catch up to her before she was lost behind the shrubbery. Mimi climbed both steps leading up to the front door. She touched the house plaque adorned with a large number three, posted beside the doorbell. She stood on her tiptoes and pushed the button.

"Mimi, no," Charlotte warned. "Don't bother them."

A man opened the front door. "Good morning, Mimi," the man said. "Have you come for a cookie?"

"I'm sorry, Isaac," Charlotte said. She leapt up the stair steps. "She remembers the delicious snickerdoodle you gave her last week. Now she's on to you."

"They're my favorite, too. Hold on one minute. My wife made a fresh batch a day ago." In the process of turning around Isaac ran into his guest, who was gathering up his coat. "Oops, sorry, buddy. Folks, this is Harry Chan, a friend of mine. He currently hails from Long Island but we're tempting him to move back to Augustin. Be right back with your cookie, cutie pie."

Sherry's mouth opened but she swallowed her words.

"Harry," Charlotte said. "How are you? You're getting to be a regular around these parts."

Mimi clapped her hands, awarding high praise for the return of Isaac. He had three cookies in his hands. He placed one in each of the ladies' hands, saving the biggest for Mimi. The glee on her face was enough to erase the awkward moment between the adults.

"Do you all know each other?" Isaac asked. "Charlotte, you may have seen Harry wandering around the farm on occasion. I introduced him to the Colton brothers and now I can't get rid of him."

"Thank you again for that," Harry said. "I do know Charlotte." His sights shifted to Sherry. "I'm not sure I've had the pleasure of making your acquaintance."

"Harry and I go back a ways," Charlotte said. "We had some good times, but in the end, we parted friends."

"We've never met. I'm Sherry Oliveri," Sherry said. She stuck out her hand and shook Harry's, then Isaac's.

"Sherry Oliveri," Isaac said. "Nice to meet you. I admit to seeing you around the grounds on occasion."

"Oliveri. Yes. As in Pep and Charlotte Oliveri? Sisters-in-law?" Harry asked.

"That's me," Sherry said.

"Isn't this a small world. Do you use your maiden name still?" Harry asked.

"I do because I'm not married. I was once, but he and I grew apart," Sherry said with a coy grin. "I do have a fiancé."

"Lucky him," Harry said. "Does he work here in Augustin? I'm always interested in building my network of contacts."

Sherry considered how to get the reply from Harry she sought. "If you've ever taken the commuter boat *Current Sea* from the Augustin Marina to Long Island, Don Johnstone was your captain. That's my man. If you haven't, you should try the water commute one day."

"Sure. Yes. I have. I remember him. I probably gave him my business card. He gave me a great feeling of confidence we'd arrive safely. I travel back and forth between Long Island and Augustin many times a month but I've only ridden the boat once," Harry said.

"I'm not much of a boat person. I prefer lounging on the beach to being out on the water," Isaac said. "The boat does sound like a perfect alternative to sitting in traffic. I'll give the *Current Sea* a try on my next trip to Long Island since I've met the captain's lady."

Sherry's unwavering gaze urged Charlotte to jump into the conversation.

"Harry, do you have business dealings with the Coltons?" Charlotte asked.

"Not formally," Harry said. He glanced in Isaac's direction. "I'm a developer and I want to be on their radar should they ever want to sell."

"It's a lovely piece of land," Isaac said. "The owner, now and in the future, is going to have to pry my hands off the cottage house key. I couldn't be more content here."

"Hah," Harry said. "There's nothing certain about the future. I do know that timing is everything and I thrive on good timing to get the best deals."

"Is that why you're here today?" Charlotte asked. "Is right now a good time to make a deal?"

"All pleasure today, no business. Despite his prickliness, Harry and I are friends," Isaac said with a laugh. "My wife left today to visit her mother and I'm taking the opportunity to try something new. We're taking a forty-mile bike ride around Hillsboro County. I hope I survive."

"How about you three? What are you up to on this crisp November day?" Harry asked. "Sherry, maybe you're taking a boat ride with your fiancé?"

"Sherry is kind enough to come over and give me cooking lessons. We have something in the oven as we speak," Charlotte said. "I think I'll wrap up what we cooked and offer it to Perry this afternoon. He might be too busy making funeral plans to eat properly."

"That's a wonderful gesture," Isaac said. "I've sent him some flowers."

"Is there any lead on who might have done this to Jarrod?" Harry asked. "I got a call from a Detective Bease. I can only imagine it's about the murder. I've scheduled a call-back for later today. I don't have much to tell him except I traveled to Long Island with Jarrod for research on a project. It must have been your fiancé who gave him my name. Or was it you, Isaac?"

"Could be either one," Isaac said. "Yes, I did mention you've had some meetings with Jarrod here at the farm. What was I supposed to do, lie? The detective asked me point-blank if he had any knowledge of anyone spending time with Jarrod here besides those who live on the farm."

"Thanks a lot, buddy. I thought we were friends," Harry said. "I didn't need to be brought into this."

"You have nothing to worry about, unless you've got something to hide," Isaac said. His tone was oddly playful.

"You're not implying anything untoward about my intentions, are you?" Harry asked. He sounded peeved.

"Want to explain what you and Jarrod were going to Long Island for?" Isaac asked.

"Research," Harry said.

"With Jarrod?" Isaac asked. "Interesting."

"I picked up on the word *research*. You know I'm a marine biologist and research is practically my middle name," Charlotte said. "What type of research did you do with Jarrod?"

"Are you an investigator besides being a research scientist?" Harry asked. "If you're not, I'd be careful asking questions that could spell trouble for all of us. Let's leave the investigation up to Detective Bease and his homicide unit. What is the quote? Too many cooks spoil the broth?"

"I'm not an investigator," Charlotte said. "I'm concerned the Coltons may get taken advantage of. Despite his gruff exterior, Perry is a passionate farmer. Money can talk loudly."

"Taken advantage of by me? No. Perry doesn't do anything he doesn't want to do," Harry said. "Charlotte, now would be a good time to give me some credit in the character department. I wasn't the world's worst boyfriend as I recall, and I've matured."

"You were hardly my boyfriend," Charlotte said with a chuckle. "We went on about five dates over a six-month period. To me that doesn't constitute a boyfriend. I'd give you a solid C-plus grade."

Harry's scowl was chilling.

"Harry's right, Charlotte," Isaac said. "I'd advise leaving the investigation to the professionals."

"Detective Bease is the best at what he does," Sherry said. "You can tell him all you know now, or you can wait until he discovers secrets on his own. Either way, he's very thorough."

Chapter 13

Sherry pulled her phone out of her coat pocket. They had seven minutes to return home to beat the oven timer. "Girls, we need to get back to the kitchen."

Mimi peered up from her seated position on Isaac's front porch. She had created a leaf collection that encircled her. She stood and kicked a hole through the circle to free herself.

"Sorry about the mess. Let me sweep the leaves away," Sherry said.

"Please, no. Mimi is welcome to bring nature closer to me any time," Isaac said. "What's on the menu?"

"Today's recipe features one of the farm's most spectacular products, the heirloom fingerling potato," Charlotte said. "Perry is so proud of his heirlooms."

Isaac pursed his lips. "Can he even still remember what his farm produces? I mean, I get the feeling it's all too much for him, especially now, without Jarrod. Liz can't be expected to take on her husband's role full-time under the circumstances. It took three phone calls and finally a face-to-face to get my plumbing issue resolved. I could have drowned by then."

Harry nodded stiffly. "You shouldn't speak poorly of the elderly or dead. Perry is one of a kind and Jarrod did the best he could. Charlotte, it's good to see you, as always. Maybe I'll be around more often, and we can talk about old times."

Sherry clasped Mimi's hand, and they headed back to Charlotte's.

"Did you all have a nice walk?" a melodic voice called out as they passed Madeline's cottage.

"We sure did," Sherry said.

"It was a little more dramatic than I'd hoped for," said Charlotte. Madeline didn't seem to hear Charlotte's muted reply.

"That's nice. Do you two have a minute?" Madeline said as she stepped off her porch and into their path. She waved her sister forward to join her.

"Maybe three minutes, tops, our timer is about to ding," Charlotte said. "We have a recipe in the oven."

"What are you two cooking?" Lulu asked.

Sherry mentally ticked off another minute as she listened to Charlotte relay the recipe. She repeated to herself how forgiving dark meat chicken and potatoes could be if left in the oven past the desired cook time.

"I have another quick question," Madeline said.

"Sure. Then our time's up," Charlotte said.

"I'll be fast." Madeline scoured the surroundings before returning her attention to Charlotte. "I saw you both talking to Isaac and his ubiquitous companion, Harry."

"That's right. Mimi bulldozed her way over to Isaac's house and we tagged along. His wife's snickerdoodles are to die for."

"Yes, well, be that as it may, I have some reservations about Isaac and Harry. With a murderer floating around the farm, none of us can be too careful. I can't trust anyone."

"I hope you can trust me," Charlotte said.

"I trust you as much as you trust me," Madeline said.

"What does that mean?" Sherry said under her breath.

"Lulu and I were discussing the men. We both agree you should be extra cautious around both. We all should be. You know Isaac was questioned by Detective Bease and Harry is next in line."

"Cautious?" Charlotte asked. "What do you mean?"

"And weren't you questioned by Detective Bease?" Sherry asked.

"Yes, but I didn't murder anyone," Madeline said.

"You think one of those two murdered Jarrod?" Charlotte asked. "I highly doubt that. I know Harry. He might be a ruthless businessman, at least that's how he pictures himself, but he's no murderer. He loves his pursuit of the dollar too much to sacrifice profit for jail time."

"And Isaac?" Madeline asked. "Do you know him well?"

"Not at all," Sherry said.

"And you, Charlotte?"

"Unless you knew him before you moved to your cottage, I know him as well as you," Charlotte said.

"Have you seen his interactions with Jarrod?" Madeline asked. "All he did was complain about his plumbing and cause a headache for Jarrod and Liz, who tried their darnedest to please him. Maybe Isaac got fed up with having leaky pipes one too many times."

"Detective Bease will get to the bottom of who killed Jarrod," Sherry said. She tried to temper her tone, but impatience was creeping in. "I'd sit on your speculations until they're proven fact."

Madeline spent the next moment seemingly inside her head. "Okay. I mean I don't think he is who he says he is. I've asked him so many times what he does for a living and all I get is a vague answer about investments and his ongoing search for opportunities. His latest answer is entrepreneur."

Lulu nodded. "What does that tell you?"

"Could be he's private," Charlotte said. "If he's sitting on an idea he isn't ready to share, he's also protecting his intellectual property. He has a right to that." She paused. "If someone asked me what I do for a living at this moment I wouldn't have a definitive answer either."

"Maybe I'm extra wary because a murder happened yards away. Isaac strikes me as someone who's hiding something," Madeline said. If she was hoping for someone to resolve her fears she was disappointed. Her mouth drooped to a frown when Charlotte announced the kitchen timer was about to ring.

"Time to move along. I'll talk to you soon when I have more time," Charlotte said with a wave. "And don't worry too much. Either of you."

"One more question," Lulu said as Sherry took a step toward Charlotte's house. "Is Detective Bease single? He's my type."

Sherry coughed as her throat constricted. "I'm not sure. If you're questioned by him you can throw in a question of your own." She couldn't contain a smile while pondering what answer Ray would come up with in response to Lulu's potential probing question.

"I could do that," Lulu said.

Sherry and Charlotte tossed a wave as they headed home.

"What *does* Isaac do?" Sherry asked when they were halfway to Charlotte's house.

"Isaac told me what he told Madeline. He's looking for the next best thing."

"What was Harry like when you were dating, or not dating?" Sherry asked.

"After two dates I knew Harry was someone I would never have wanted to be the father of my children. That was my litmus test for a lifelong partner. I wasn't going to put any more effort into a relationship going nowhere. Life's too short for that." Charlotte grasped Mimi's free hand. "Pep passed the test with flying colors."

"Is someone out there?"

The hair on the back of Sherry's neck prickled. "What was that? Do you hear that?"

"Can someone help me?" A deep muffled voice hailed the trio toward the potato storage building. "I'm stuck."

"Charlotte, hold Mimi's hand while I see what's going on. I can't tell if it's a friendly voice or what."

"Sounds a lot like Wellie," Charlotte said. "I wouldn't be too worried."

"Better safe than sorry. Let me go check." Sherry crept up to the building and called inside. "Are you there? Is that Wellie?"

"That's right. It's me. The handle has locked in place. Cranky old b—"

"Hold your tongue. There's a child out here," Sherry said with haste. "What do you suggest I do to get the doors open?"

"You need to smash the handle with something strong. My tools are back in the pickup truck. And the keys are in my pocket." Wellie groaned. "This day has gone from bad to worse. This is the last thing I need. I don't want to bother Dad. He's trying to rest today before we plan Jarrod's service."

"I know, Sher. I'll run back to the house. Take Mimi's hand." Charlotte skipped over with Mimi, who was catching on to the rhythm of a new game. The toddler giggled when she reached Sherry. "I'll be right back, sweetie. Auntie Sherry will play hide and seek with you. The man in the potato castle is hiding and we need to make sure we find him."

Charlotte handed off Mimi and sprinted to her house. She returned in less time than it took Sherry to explain to Charlotte where her mom went. Charlotte held up Bernie.

"The perfect all-purpose tool." A moment later the door handle lay in two equal pieces outside the double doors.

"Thank you, ladies. Now I know what my next task is," he said as he held up the two halves of the handle. "Looks like it can be resuscitated yet again, for a Band-Aid fix. I still need to fix the lock as well."

"Glad to help, Wellie. Stay safe," Charlotte said. "Sher, I emptied the oven before I grabbed Bernie. All is well."

Chapter 14

Charlotte's kitchen was blooming with the smell of roasted chicken bites and herbaceous potatoes. Sherry's nose told her the food was cooked well. She poked her fork into a potato for the final test. She blew on a steaming bite before nibbling the dark edge. Perfect.

"The potato skins are crispy. Inside is creamy and buttery. They need a sprinkle of sea salt, but I recommend letting each person salt their own. And these chicken bites are elevated fast-food nuggets that adults will enjoy as much as their kids."

"Thanks, Sher," Charlotte said. "I've learned so much from you. Pep's never going to let me out of the kitchen."

"Be careful what you wish for. When you took a leave from your job you said you wanted more quality time with your family. That always includes meals," Sherry said with a laugh.

"I'm warming up to the idea," Charlotte said.

"If you don't mind, let's call it quits in here. There are a few errands I need to run."

"Stick a fork in me, too. I'm done. Mimi needs some beach time. She loves the playground down there. We'll use it all winter until the snow clogs the slide."

"Let's tag-team the dishes and we'll make mincemeat out of the stack," Sherry said. She positioned herself in front of the sink and began scrubbing the bowls. She glanced up and caught sight of Wellie talking on his cell phone outside the window.

"I have a front-row seat to Wellie busy on a phone call." She watched as Wellie threw a wave to Madeline as she opened her car door. "There goes Madeline and Lulu driving away. I'm curious, does Madeline work outside the house?" Sherry asked.

"She told me she was in between opportunities. Her last job was at a store in town. Are you familiar with the landscape supply store and nursery called Landowne's. They're not too far from the Ruggery. She was in sales there, she said."

"Sure," Sherry said. "I buy my fall mums there every year."

"She left the job recently. She's lived on the farm for two years since her divorce. She told me in a moment of full disclosure she can afford the rent one year and it's too much the next. She said she should have taken her wealthy ex-husband for all she could, but since they had no children she opted to take nothing to be rid of him. She also told me Perry has been a very generous landlord, discounting the rent in times of cash shortages."

"Good for her, not good for the farm's bottom line," Sherry said. "I hope he grants you and Pep the same margins for what you can afford."

"Pep and I live within a strict budget so we know what we can afford. Our goal is to save enough to purchase a home soon. I know how tough that is for most people. At the same time, I don't want to haggle with Perry. The price he sets is the price we pay. That's only fair."

"Apparently not everyone has the same idea of what's fair. Good for Madeline that she can finagle a flexible rent deal," Sherry said.

"I did find it ironic that Madeline thinks Isaac has secrets. I've always thought she has secrets," Charlotte said.

"I wonder if her rent fluctuations set by Perry caused friction with Jarrod? He gives off a strict business guy vibe. He strikes me as someone who might not appreciate Perry's whimsical approach."

"There are lots of questions. Someone wasn't happy with Jarrod for some reason, that's what's clear," Charlotte said.

"Wasn't happy is an understatement. What if the same person isn't happy with Perry or Wellington? But what's causing the unhappiness?"

Charlotte lowered her voice as her gaze drifted in the direction of her daughter. "I'm trying to keep a brave face on for Mimi's sake but, honestly, I'm feeling more and more as if Perry might need protection from someone out there. I don't want to see him harmed."

"What about Wellie? Are you worried for his sake?"

"Wellie seems more able to handle himself in questionable circumstances," Charlotte said.

"Like getting locked in the potato castle? He needed us for that dangerous circumstance."

"Touché. He's young and strong and a serene character. Most of the time he's in control."

"It's you and Mimi I'm most concerned about," Sherry said.

"Maybe I'm too close to see the overall picture," Charlotte said.

Sherry glanced at Mimi then faced Charlotte. "You won't go sniffing around for answers with this little one in tow, will you? If there's something you see that's not right, please tell me or Detective Bease."

"I hear you loud and clear," Charlotte said. "It's just that the Coltons have been so kind to Pep and me. I hate to see this tragedy happen to them. I wouldn't mind if you dipped your toe in the investigation. You're so good at uncovering clues in murder cases. This one has a direct connection to the cook-off you're in."

"I was afraid you'd say that. I'll do the best I can but it's very early days. Jarrod had more going on than meets the eye."

Chapter 15

When the last dish was dried and Mimi had the silverware sorted on her high chair tray, Sherry gathered up her tote.

"Charlotte, I'll see you guys at the Local Farmers' Day on Wednesday. Many stores in town, including the Ruggery, are closing early to support the farmers of Hillsboro County and southern New England."

"We'll be there," Charlotte said as she hoisted Mimi out of her high chair. "I think Mimi is most excited about the parade prior to the cook-off. She has a new pair of overalls and the cutest flannel shirt to wear. She'll fit right in."

"I drove past the town green and there were already some parade floats being stored there. I even spotted a giant potato waiting to be inflated. Get a good seat for the cook-off if you can drag Mimi away from the parade. I'll wave to you," Sherry said.

Sherry gave Mimi their practiced aunt-niece hug, which they'd orchestrated over the past month. The pattern was a simple one due to the age of the younger participant—a hug, a twirl and a hand waggle. Mimi giggled when the choreographed maneuver was complete.

"Tell Pep hi when he comes back from serving lunch at the truck."

Sherry made her way to her car after goodbyes were said. She was lost in thought with the realization she hadn't spoken to Charlotte about the job offer she received via Patti. She rationalized it wasn't a job offer exactly, more of a preliminary screening interview with no strings attached. If she went forward with the process, accepting the invitation to interview, the chance anything would come of it was low. There must be dozens yearning for the television show's recipe creator position. The meat of Sherry's current résumé gave her a slim-to-none chance to win the coveted position. On the other hand, the experience of going to the next step in the process by putting herself out there was valuable. She'd share the news when the time was right.

Sherry reached for the car door handle while her mind was anywhere but on the present moment. A voice startled her, and she dropped her car key.

"Hi, again, Sherry."

Sherry turned to see Wellie walking toward her.

"I'm sorry I threw a wrench into your visit to your brother's house. Thanks again for rescuing me."

Wellie was dressed in his signature overalls and dragging a pitchfork. His footsteps were cumbersome under the weight of his mud-covered work boots. He leaned his tool against his shoulder and retrieved Sherry's key.

"Wellie, I didn't see you." She accepted the key from his gloved hand. "Thanks, and you're welcome. I was giving Charlotte some cooking tips."

"I could use a few lessons. My brother was a good cook. Dad's a lost cause in the kitchen," Wellie said.

"No one's a lost cause." Sherry softened her voice. "I didn't get a chance to tell you, I'm so sorry for your loss. I didn't know your brother beyond the time we spent here touring the farm. I wish I had had more time to get to know him now that part of my family lives here. You have my deepest condolences."

"I appreciate that," Wellie said. He lowered his head for a moment of reflection. When he looked up, he continued. "Charlotte's in good hands with a cooking teacher of your caliber. Word is, you're quite the accomplished cook. We were talking about the Oliveri family a day or two ago. My father boasts about knowing your father from the good old days and how your family is one of Augustin's true treasures. I hope the town thinks of our family in such lofty terms." He held his gaze on Sherry. "Despite the most recent occurrences."

"The Coltons are a treasure. Every farm in the county is important to Augustin. Yours is certainly the gold standard of heirloom potato producers. The town is so thankful for you and your family."

"Huh." Wellie sighed. "The costs of producing our gold are going up and we can barely make ends meet. The consumer's got to be willing to pay a premium for a potato. The profit fluctuations from year to year take a toll on our sanity."

"Maybe the uneducated consumer won't pay more right now, but give it time. Heirloom anything is a hot trend in the culinary world."

"That would be nice if you're right," Wellie said.

"I hear Coastal Greater Tator Farm is providing the potatoes for the Local and Vocal Farmers' Day cook-off. That's a win for the farm's exposure and a good opportunity to spread some potato wisdom."

"Yup. We are, despite Jarrod's passing. He would have wanted it. I like the way you think. Dad isn't sure the reward is worth the effort. He doesn't understand advertising in today's world is how to get sales. He's still living in the era when word of mouth was the method someone used to discover his quality potato."

"That's why the potato cook-off will be a great ambassador for you, not only to get your name on people's lips but also introduce them to the preferred choice of heirloom. Exposure and doable recipes will help get the word out." Sherry couldn't read the pout on Wellie's face for its meaning.

"Something's got to change. Do you know how much a new tractor costs?" Wellie's bushy eyebrows pinched together.

"I'd imagine quite a lot," Sherry said.

"And if Dad's on the decline, I'm looking at an expensive future of elder health care."

"Do you mind if I ask how long your dad has had trouble with his memory?" Sherry asked.

"It's a recent development. I think the increased workload at harvest time contributed to his memory loss. You know, stress can do that to a person. He was dead set against too many hired hands pitching in. He's getting paranoid everyone's trying to steal the farm out from underneath him. He's cutting off his nose to spite his face."

Sherry never liked that saying. The visual was cringe-worthy. "There are ways to reduce the stress. Have you considered hiring a full-time farm manager rather than trying to keep all the work between you and your father?"

"You sound like every other la-dee-da who thinks they know how to run a profitable farm. My brother thought his business plan was the answer to all our problems."

"A creative plan of succession is a smart idea actually," Sherry said.

She knew instantly the words hit Wellie like a ton of bricks. He squeezed his eyes shut. When he opened them the worry lines around his eyes were pronounced.

"I don't completely disagree. I thought Jarrod had the best intentions by introducing the idea of selling the farm for a simpler way of life. He didn't understand how hard it would be for Dad to pivot one-eighty degrees and put his feet up on an ottoman without a care in the world. Honestly, I didn't either. Dad wants to go down swinging, not be put out to pasture."

"I hope you don't sell out. The town needs your farm."

"Me, too. Problem is the town may need the money from the farm more than the harvested produce. That notion may have someone out for blood." The energy seeped out of Wellie's voice. "But money doesn't grow on trees and we're aware of being outdated with each harvest. The vultures are circling, and Greater Tator might be the lifeless carcass they're eyeing."

"Charlotte told me about her project with your father. That may be a way to educate the public about the importance of the farm's existence," Sherry said. "If nothing else it will help many generations of farmers."

"Huh. Jarrod was so dead against the two working together. He wanted to block any good idea that could prolong the farm's life. He only campaigned for his idea to sell off the land. That's it."

"Well. I'm sorry to sound harsh, but he's not here to stop the project anymore. Maybe after the dust settles the idea will blossom."

"I'd like you to be right. Jarrod's idea of selling out wouldn't have worked anyhow unless Dad signed off on it. That seemed as likely as me winning the lottery," Wellie said.

"If his name is on the title, your dad makes the decision unless there are other circumstances going on. That's the law. It's written to protect against bad things happening to good people."

"Then there's the journal Dad is writing with Charlotte. For what purpose, I don't know. He won't let me have any say in the matter," Wellie said. "Charlotte may regret getting involved."

"What do you mean?" Sherry asked.

"How do any of us know we're safe until Jarrod's killer is found? I don't feel safe. And Dad? How could he feel safe? Although he hasn't fully acknowledged Jarrod's passing has been labeled murder. That denial might be his best coping mechanism."

"Do you think Charlotte's in danger?" Sherry asked. She swallowed a gulp of air halfway through her question. The resulting cough brought tears to her eyes.

"I wouldn't want to be working closely with the man who's the face of Coastal Greater Tator Farm if someone is lurking in the shadows with the idea of shutting us down. Dad or I might be the next target. I'm watching my back day and night. Jarrod may have started the idea of selling off our livelihood, but someone has taken it to the next level on their own terms."

"Is that what you think? Someone besides Jarrod wants to shutter your business? For what reason?"

"Don't pretend you haven't heard whispers in town of how much better utilized this tract of land would be as beachfront mega-mansion plots versus a run-down potato farm."

"I've heard some rumors," Sherry said.

"I can tell you the original source of those rumors. Charlotte's friend, Harry Chan."

Sherry didn't like the fact Charlotte and Harry may be considered having any association. Not after hearing what the man was interested in. To what degree was Harry willing to take his desire to acquire the farm? Madeline's warning about Harry may be valid after all. And would Charlotte's work with Perry conflict with Harry's task at hand?

"I know he's a developer. I know he's been seen in talks with Jarrod, about what we may never know now that Jarrod's gone," Sherry said.

"Harry was playing both sides of the fence. He was working on Dad while working on Jarrod. He was covering all angles and that may have backfired."

"He rode my fiancé's commuter boat with your brother. I wonder if they were constructing a deal," Sherry said. "I ran into him an hour ago at Isaac's house. Is he the vulture circling the carcass you're alluding to?"

"He hasn't made a formal offer to Dad as far as I know. Dad can be tight-lipped these days. He's on the ball one minute, he's far, far away in his head another," Wellie said.

"That's too much pressure on your Dad," Sherry said. "Now with Jarrod's death on top of the uncertainty of the future, it's no wonder he's having trouble with his memory. Harry can't deal with Jarrod anymore. Maybe that situation will settle down."

"Harry's not giving up. He's ingratiating himself with Isaac now. That has me worried. I'm getting as paranoid as Dad."

"Which way are you leaning? Sell out or stay put?" Sherry asked.

"Someone who leans is off-kilter. I prefer to stay upright and let any decision happen when it's meant to be. In the end the money may be the deciding factor."

"Good for you. Personally, I don't think you should listen to the whispers out there. I bet there are lots of Augustinians who would fight for the farm's existence. It's part of the fabric of the town."

"I wish I could ignore the rumblings. I also wish I could take matters into my own hands and weed out those who are out to decide our future for us."

"What do you mean?" Sherry asked.

"There's a good chance someone's using devious tactics to drive us out." Wellie's words were laced with bitterness. "The pressure isn't going to disappear just because my brother is gone. I didn't just fall off the turnip truck, or in my case the potato tractor. And if we sold, do you realize how much would get eaten up by taxes? If someone is pushing us to sell, they're also pushing us into deep debt."

"Perry Wellington Colton? Who are you gabbing with?" a trembling voice traveled from the farmhouse's porch.

"Sherry Oliveri. She came to visit Charlotte and her niece," Wellie called back.

"Who?"

"Hold on, Dad. We can't be yelling back and forth all day."

"Why did he call you Perry Wellington? Is he mixing up your name with his own?" Sherry asked.

"Nope. That's my name. Perry Wellington Colton the Third. Same name as Dad and his dad."

"That's amazing," Sherry said. "You must be very proud to carry on the name."

"I'm not so sure. I've always thought the three names would sound better as a big-city law firm." Wellie raised his voice two octaves and delivered the words, "Perry, Wellington, and Colton Law Firm, how may I help you?"

Sherry laughed at Wellie's impression of a law firm receptionist.

"Having our names represent a law firm—hah! That's ironic. Dad hates lawyers. He always says he seals deals with handshakes the way it's been done for centuries between honest folks. Not with drawing up documents and contracts in a sterile office. No need to involve some fancy-schmancy middleman whose desire is to line his pockets with cash belonging to someone else. I'd have rather been named something with one or two syllables, not a statement name that conjures up images of trials and judges."

"Perry and Wellie are nice comfortable names," Sherry said in a near whisper.

Wellie turned back to where his father sat before returning his sights to Sherry. "I've got to go. Keep an eye on your brother's family, will you?"

Sherry shivered as the cold November wind reminded her to zip up her coat. "They love living on the farm. They'll be fine." Sherry wanted to put an upbeat spin on her statement, but instead the words stumbled over each other. "Will I see you at the local farmers' cook-off? I was lucky enough to make the final round and will be preparing my recipe Wednesday with Colton potatoes."

"Absolutely," Wellie said. "I'm bringing Dad. He's very excited about what the cooks will come up with using his harvest." The corner of his mouth lifted as he shuffled away.

Chapter 16

Sherry placed a call to Ray as soon as she returned home, even though Chutney took offense at not being walked. She knew what her dog had on his mind and scooped up the leash while she waited for Ray to pick up. She stepped outside while organizing her thoughts. Her mind was racing with concerns over Charlotte and her family's safety. Charlotte was committed to working with a man who may have the same enemies as his deceased son. How close was her brother's family to being in harm's way? How fast could Ray and his homicide unit find the killer? Not fast enough as far as Sherry was concerned. She drew in her breath to settle her nerves before Ray greeted her with a curt hello.

"Hi, Ray. You said you wanted to talk to me? Sorry it's a Saturday. Are you on duty?"

"I'm sorry someone died, but I have to work every day until I find his murderer."

"So, yes, you're on duty I take it," Sherry said. She glossed over his sarcasm with a touch of her own. "I have a few items on my checklist to go over with you."

"Really? Your checklist?" Ray sounded amused. "I'm ready. Shoot."

"Coastal Greater Tator Farm sits on land that is considered beachfront property. There isn't much of that left these days that isn't bursting with McMansions."

"Yes, go on," Ray said.

"Did you know the Colton offspring might be facing a huge tax bill if Perry were to pass away? Inheritance tax can be smothering," Sherry said.

"If Perry passed away there would only be one Colton, Wellington. You're saying he would inherit the farm. He would have to pay inheritance tax, yes. I am led to believe farmland falls under tax laws that incentivize the family to carry on farming." Ray had done his homework.

"By the way, is Perry Colton the name on the farm's title?" Sherry asked.

"I need to check that. If it is he may want to amend that at some point as he gets on in years. Makes handling paperwork easier if the elder gentleman passes away. My mother was more than happy to have my name on her house title in case of the unimaginable, which did occur eventually. You know what they say about death and taxes. No avoiding either."

"Yes, well, Jarrod was the son who wasn't interested in keeping the

Colton family farm tradition in existence, let alone being listed as an owner. He ran the idea of a sale past his father several times, Wellie told me. That kind of needling can go too far."

Ray sucked in a breath with such effort Sherry winced. She had struck a nerve.

"It's very early in the investigation, and while I always say the first forty-eight to seventy-two hours produce the most valuable information in an investigation, we can't project thoughts in people's heads to hurry the process along." He paused. "Why are you even giving this murder this much thought beyond the fact your brother and his family live on the Coltons' property? How well did you know the victim?"

"Not well at all," Sherry said. "The family's on my radar because they are the potato suppliers for my next cook-off, happening this Wednesday on the town's local farmer appreciation day."

"Bingo. A cook-off-related murder. No surprise there."

"I take offense at that," Sherry said. She also knew she didn't have a leg to stand on if Ray presented a rebuttal. He let her comment go unnoticed.

"You've answered my first question. The next question is, has your brother or his wife relayed any situations in passing, such as overhearing any Colton family squabbles on the farm, poor communication between the two siblings, violent behavior by Perry or Wellington Colton?"

"Pep and Charlotte haven't mentioned anything out of the ordinary. Why are you asking me, not them?"

"To get a different perspective. I'm following procedures."

"Charlotte said she spoke to you. She told me what she told you." Sherry's reply was half-hearted. She was holding back a few details, one being Charlotte's collaboration with Perry. She didn't want Charlotte drawn into the investigation too deeply if she herself hadn't mentioned the business arrangement. It was up to Charlotte to mention her side project with Perry if she saw fit to.

"Wellington Colton mentioned you and Patti Mellit took a tour of the farm the day before Jarrod's murder. What was that about?"

"Are you going to speak to Patti?" Sherry asked.

"She's on my list, yes," Ray said.

"You already spoke to Patti?" Sherry asked.

"Don't be defensive. I'm asking you to sift out possible witnesses, not to pin one of your friends to a wrongdoing," Ray said. "And yes, Patti was with you at the farm the day before the murder, so I debriefed her. Hers is another set of eyes on the murder scene."

"Patti invited me on a farm tour as research for an article she's writing on the potato farms of Augustin and Hillsboro County. All business. Isn't that what she told you?"

"She did," Ray said. "How about you? Did you see any behavior between the members of the Colton family you would categorize as hostile, edgy, aggressive?"

"Perry was a little hesitant when he first met Patti and me. He wasn't sure why we were there. Or he knew and it had slipped his mind. I'm sure he was warned we had an appointment to see the farm, but he gave the impression he was blindsided by our appearance. The brothers were considerate of their father's forgetfulness. Wellie was kind of prickly with Jarrod."

"Do you know why?" Ray asked.

"Under his breath, but loud enough to hear, Wellie sniped at Jarrod for not being around enough to be useful these days. Jarrod wasn't dressed for hands-on labor. No overalls like Wellie. I'd say farming isn't his thing and it was rubbing Wellie the wrong way. All families have these differences of opinion, interests, and abilities. I certainly don't have what it takes to run a food truck like Pep, or draw up artwork on rug canvases like my dad."

"But I'm certain Pep or Erno wouldn't murder you for not going into their line of work. Can we say the same about Wellington or Perry?" Ray said. "To be determined."

"Are they your prime suspects?" Sherry asked. Her thoughts went directly back to Pep's family's safety. Before Ray could respond, Sherry posed one more question. "What's your impression of Wellington Colton?"

"How is it you're asking all the questions when I'm the investigator?"

"I learned from the best," Sherry said.

"My impression of Wellington. First let me say impressions don't serve me well," Ray said. "Facts do. The fact is he's the elder son. Never been married. There's no doubt he's the primary caretaker of his father when his father needs attending to. He's carrying the mother load of the farm operations. During my interview with him he complained about the cost of bringing the farm into the twenty-first century. He's just lost his brother, his only sibling. They may have had differing opinions, but I'm sure there was love between them. If I'm forced to give an impression it's that he has the weight of the world on his shoulders. Beyond that, the evidence he killed his brother is, so far, inconclusive."

"I have a hard time visualizing Perry Colton acting out in a violent manner against his son," Sherry said. "I think he's a grumbly teddy bear trying to make ends meet in a world that isn't very appreciative of his efforts."

Ray took a moment to respond. "I respect your analysis of the elder man, but didn't you say you've only met him once?"

"You, too."

Ray grumbled. "I've talked to him four times."

"He strikes me as being a lot like my dad. Both will scratch and claw to save their family's legacy." Something caught in Sherry's throat, and she needed a moment to clear it. Ray jumped in.

"You're not the only one who feels strongly Perry Colton didn't have a hand in Jarrod's death."

"Are you talking about Charlotte?"

"That's right," Ray said. "Your sister-in-law came to Perry Colton's defense when I asked her whether he was fit to run such a big operation. I asked her because my conversations with him left me unconvinced he was."

"I don't think anyone could do the job solo. He would benefit from hiring a permanent extra hand outside the family. Charlotte's had a good rapport with Perry since she moved to the farm. I'd take her word over anyone's if she backs his good character."

"And her rapport with Wellington? Is that as good?" Ray asked.

"I don't think she has as much contact with him," Sherry said. "She saw Jarrod more, I'm guessing, because he collected her rent every month. He was the cottages' manager. If there was an issue, either Jarrod or his wife, Liz, would address it."

"The question of Perry's competency is a real factor in all of this. If Perry was deemed incompetent, with Jarrod out of the picture, that only leaves Wellington to run the show. I'm discounting Liz Colton as she'll have some decisions to make for her future. I didn't press Liz on her plans now that her husband is dead. I wouldn't be surprised if she doesn't fade out of the picture, leaving one more job for Perry or Wellington."

"From the small amount of time I spent with Perry, he appeared able to run the farm in bursts," Sherry said. "Small bursts."

"You might be projecting Charlotte's wishes onto the man," Ray said. "I didn't get the same warm and fuzzy feeling about his competency as you seem to have."

"What we don't know is what's going on behind the scenes," Sherry said.

"We?" Ray asked.

"You. I meant you and your team."

"There are many questions and we, meaning my team, are in the process of digging up the answers," Ray said. "I need to talk to Isaac Rowe, the man who lives in one of the cottages on the farm next to your brother. He and his wife, Fern, were not home when I was on the property talking to Pep, Charlotte, and the woman who also rents, Madeline Linzer. Fern Rowe is off the list as she's on an out-of-state visit to see her mother."

"I met Madeline when I was touring the farm with Charlotte. I was chasing my niece, so I barely got to say hello to her and her sister, Lulu."

"She's a talker," Ray said. "She bent my ear for about thirty minutes. My takeaway is she's a big fan of Wellington. She intercepted my questions about him and turned them into a showcase on his strength of character. As a matter of fact, she was so defensive of him it raised red flags."

"I know how much you like long answers to your short questions," Sherry said with a snicker. Ray didn't return the glee.

"She bombarded me with so many words I feel the need to re-interview her. Her story weaved back and forth and, in some cases, contradicted itself," Ray said. "I left the questioning unsure whether she knew nothing or knew so much she was hiding something." Ray stopped speaking and Sherry heard what sounded like a pencil tapping a table before he began again. "Patti told me something else."

"What's that?" Sherry asked.

"She told me, off topic, that she's arranged a job interview for you. You're in the process of deciding whether to proceed with the interview or scrap the idea of trying out for what seems on paper like the Sherry Oliveri dream job. She was concerned this murder might be disruptive to your decision making."

"She wants an answer Wednesday. The day of the cook-off," Sherry said. "When it rains it pours. A cook-off in four days, a job interview that could change everything, a murder, what else can come up?"

"So, you're going to interview for the position? Working at the prestigious test kitchen is an amazing opportunity. Think of all the recipe advice you could share with me."

Sherry hadn't seen Ray this excited since the day he announced his homicide unit won the annual grill-off against the Hillsboro firefighters.

"I need to make a list of the pros and cons for me, for Don, my father, and that's the short list. Right after we hang up."

"Was Patti on to something? Does this decision you have to make have any bearing on how you feel about the Colton murder case?"

Sherry's cheeks warmed. Her breath caught for a second and she had trouble forming her next word. "Wha-wha-what do you mean? What do the two have to do with each other?"

"Perry may be facing a farm with no heirs, and no future. At the same time, if you take a full-time job you would be leaving the family business run by your father, who, I estimate, is approximately the same age as Perry."

Sherry rubbed her forehead with the back of her hand. Ray was on to something that had been festering in her subconscious since Patti approached her with the opportunity.

All she could do to get through the conversation on a high note was to change the subject. "He's exactly Dad's age. Maybe you can come to the cook-off."

"Maybe," Ray said in a gentle tone. "Probably. Definitely, if you email me a copy of your winning recipe."

"Right after this, check your email. You should come to the cook-off. Under the guise of investigation research. The Coltons' farm is providing the potatoes the cooks will use. And, you never know what might happen at a cook-off. The pressure's high and the stakes are higher. Competition can breed bad behavior."

"Sounds like you're hoping something unsavory happens," Ray said.

"Not at all. I'm justifying any bad behavior in case it occurs."

"What's the prize? A lifetime supply of potatoes?" Ray asked.

"Not even close. First prize is an appliance package valued at two thousand dollars."

"Impressive. I'd like to go, schedule permitting," Ray said. "And, yes, history dictates, you never know what might happen at a cook-off. Bye."

Chapter 17

Sunday brought Sherry a day closer to accepting or refusing Patti's offer. She decided she needed another day of potato cook-off practice, rather than using yet another day to mull over the pros and cons of the new position. Cooking another batch of Speedy African-Style Groundnut Stew called for a trip to the grocery store.

Sunday mornings were typically quiet times to shop in Augustin. The hustle and bustle of customers didn't pick up until closer to lunchtime, and fewer people in the aisles meant more time to browse and compare options. Sherry's first stop was the produce section, specifically the potato bins.

"If I'd known you needed potatoes, I would have brought you as many as you need. Access to an abundance of heirlooms is one of the perks of living at Coastal Farm."

Sherry turned and found herself face-to-face with Isaac Rowe.

"Good morning, Sherry," he greeted.

"Good morning, Isaac. I would have gladly accepted your potatoes. And they would be so much fresher." Sherry lifted a small, sweet potato from a bin. "Charlotte recently mentioned one of the perks of renting on the farm is that she gets to dip into the potato storage bins."

"She's right. We count on them for dinner. It throws a monkey wrench into the mix if something stops me from collecting my prize. I remember one day I couldn't get the massive double doors of the storage building to open. I had a recipe for shepherd's pie waiting for me on our kitchen counter. My wife made me go find a pitchfork in the barn to try again. Then I was successful."

"How long have you lived on the farm?" Sherry asked.

Isaac stayed quiet longer than Sherry thought was reasonable. She watched as he screwed up his face while forming his reply. "I've rented for years. I met my wife after the first year, and it turned out my most attractive quality was living on the farm."

"Oh, I don't believe that," Sherry said, although she had no clue if she was right or wrong. "That was an amazing coincidence that you and Harry Chan are friends and he had a brief dating spell with Charlotte. Isn't it funny how life works."

"Very funny," Isaac said. "I wish I'd known your brother's family before I knew Harry."

"Why's that?" Sherry asked.

"That way Charlotte could have convinced me he's not a friend at all."

"I know he's a developer," Sherry said. "Must be hard to be off duty when you're always looking for the next best plot of land."

"That's not his main occupation. Harry's a career schmoozer. He hangs around the farm, and I invite him in for a chat every so often. But you're right, he's consistently on the hunt for the next big payout, no matter what the consequences. I considered riding his coattails for a while and drumming up some business for him. That proved harder than I imagined. He's on his own."

"Do you think he's interested in developing the farm?" Sherry asked. A woman alongside her cleared her throat as a subtle cue she was there to shop and Sherry was blocking access to the produce.

"I do. He's marking his territory every time he visits. He's sniffing around the Coltons like the vulture he is and they're his prey. I wouldn't trust him as far as I could throw him."

Sherry hummed a note of consideration.

"I need to get going," Isaac said. "Nice to see you. See you around the farm if you're visiting your brother."

"Okay," Sherry said. She was so surprised by his revelations she lost her train of thought and didn't give him a proper farewell.

"Harry's on the hunt. But how far will he go to get what he wants?"

"Did you say something to me?" the woman asked as she reached around Sherry for two potatoes.

"No, sorry," Sherry said. "I was talking to myself. I'm trying to remember my shopping list."

"Hah! I've been there," the woman said before loading up her cart with a bag of onions.

Sherry's mind wasn't on her recipe when she left the store with her sweet potatoes and chicken thighs. She needed to get home and find Harry Chan's business card. When she arrived home she unpacked her groceries before hunting down his card, then she dialed up his number.

"Hello? Harry? This is Sherry Oliveri. How are you?"

"What an unexpected pleasure," Harry said. The smooth lilt of his voice had Sherry convinced of his sincerity. "How may I be of service on this fine Sunday?"

"I hope I'm not bothering you on your day off," Sherry said. "I came across your business card when I was washing Don's laundry. I see that you're a developer and I had a question for someone in your line of work."

"Fire away," Harry said. "And no, you're not bothering me. I was reading the Sunday paper. Before you make fun of me, yes, I'm one of the last dinosaurs who loves the crinkle of paper newsprint in my hands."

That's ironic, Sherry thought. He calls himself a dinosaur yet has no qualms about destroying an ancient way of life, farming. "That's a perfect Sunday," Sherry said. "I'll be quick."

"Ready."

"My question has to do with the land my brother's cottage sits on."

"Okay, go on," Harry said.

Sherry pictured him straightening his posture as his voice gained volume. She heard a rustling of paper. He must have set the newspaper aside. "Let's say the cottage and associated land around it came up for sale. Since the land is part of a farm right now, who would set the fair market price?"

"Interesting scenario," Harry said. "My business concentrates on large-scale acquisitions that we transform into commercial properties or family dwellings. Those require a sizable parcel of land. You're talking about a chip off the farm. An acre, plus or minus, in the case of each cottage. I know because I've researched Coastal Farm. If Pep were interested—"

"Or Isaac Rowe or Madeline," Sherry added.

"Or Isaac or Madeline was interested in making an offer to the Coltons, they could possibly broker a deal with Perry Colton. In his current mental state, I hope they get a proper deal."

"I figured since you and Isaac are friends, you might have an inside track on any potential sales activity over there that might benefit Pep and Charlotte. They're in love with their small house and would snap it up if the price was right."

"Hah!" Harry laughed. "They'll need to get in line."

"So, if you don't have any input on a current fair price, do you know how Perry would go about setting the price?" Sherry knew she might be poking a bear, but she persisted. "If cottages are zoned residential, not farmland, they might be subject to heavy price increases as the land values go up and up. Beachfront is getting scarce, and the prices catapult with less supply. If the town gets involved, sky's the limit."

"You're right on target. I hope they have a pile of cash reserved because the value of that land is cha-ching." His imitation of a cash register opening was spot-on. "Your brother's best bet is to ask Perry Colton directly to hear what he has to say. Why not? And if they do, do me a favor and let me know?"

"Those are good ideas. Although you might be his most feared competition when it comes to purchasing the plot." Sherry laughed until she realized she was laughing alone.

"I didn't say I was purchasing anything. I said I researched Coastal. Don't put words in my mouth."

"Sorry. I just assumed the research was for possible purchases." She waited for a response that never came. "Thank you for sharing your business knowledge with me, Harry." She hadn't gotten the admission she hoped for concerning Harry's business association with Jarrod, if there was any. It did seem as though no deal had been struck by any parties. Maybe any potential land sale had nothing to do with Jarrod's murder after all.

"No problem. I'm sensitive to people not hearing exactly what I'm saying. I need to choose my words better, I suppose."

She balked at asking about Harry's relationship with Jarrod with this new revelation. The timing seemed off. She didn't want to raise concerns about her previous suspicions of activity between the two.

"Speaking of the farm, have you heard Jarrod Colton's service is private?" Harry said. "I'm disappointed only a handful of mourners can go. Invites only."

"That's interesting. Pep's family was hoping to pay their respects, and I would have, also. I'm glad you mentioned that. I wonder why that is?" Sherry asked.

"No idea. Well, some idea. I'm not invited either. I'm a bit surprised I didn't get the invite. I did know him fairly well," Harry said.

"Were you two business associates?" Sherry said gently.

"We've never done business together, but we've strategized. The timing was never right to pull the trigger, so to speak. He kept me on my toes, and I liked that about him. He was a tough nut to crack. Got that from his old man. Jarrod stayed one step ahead of trends. Like your friend's commuter boat. He saw the advantage of that mode of commuter transport as a wave of the future; pun intended. I would have liked to have worked with Jarrod. Things were heading in that direction, until we had a falling out. I know we would have resolved the problem in time."

"Is it anything you can talk about?" Sherry asked.

"I could, but I don't think I will. There are others involved and I'm not their mouthpiece. I was well on the way to smoothing the issue over and moving on, so that's all I'll say. The characters have changed, but that won't stop the process. Jarrod's untimely death may increase the chances of a resolution," Harry said. "Is there any other way I can help you? I haven't been your best resource so far."

Sherry tried one more time. "You've been quite helpful. Thank you. It sounds as if I might not see you around the farm anymore unless you have reason to visit Perry. He could probably use your business acumen to keep his farm afloat now that he'll be missing Jarrod's input. Even though you were in a bad way with Jarrod, would Perry accept your help?"

"I may have burned that bridge, too. Depends on Perry's mindset. The Coltons have a lot on their plate, and I came in with guns blazing. All that did was scatter them like scared rabbits. Timing is everything and I made a mess of it. Maybe I'll get a second chance. I'm nothing if not persistent. If that's all you need, I've got a lunch date."

"Don't be late on my account," Sherry said. "Thanks for your time."

"Say hi to Charlotte when you see her. Bye," Harry said before clicking off the call.

Sherry knelt and patted Chutney on the head. "Harry was at odds with Jarrod. And Isaac. And Perry. What was the conflict exactly?"

Chutney cocked his head while his eyes bore deep into Sherry's. She broke the dog's stare to check the time on her phone. In twenty minutes, she was to meet her father, his girlfriend Ruth, and Don for lunch. She didn't have time to change her outfit. They'd have to accept her Sunday casual comfort attire for what it was. Sweatshirt and denim.

Chapter 18

The last time Sherry dined at Shelly's Shorehouse more than a year ago the establishment was more paper napkin than white tablecloth. When she approached the dark wood entrance she saw that nothing had changed. The boat's docking ropes hung decoratively around the door. The window frames may have weathered but the seafaring ambiance projected on the exterior was the same. To complete the theme, an anchor was resting on a huge treasure chest to the side of the door. With minimal effort the owners of the Shorehouse had hit every note needed to convey the theme of the restaurant—surf-side shabby chic. Before she opened the door she vowed not to wait so long before she returned.

Don, Erno, and Ruth were already seated by the window overlooking the Silty Pretzel River. The sun was streaming in the window-lined wall. Patrons were illuminated against mahogany brown booth seats and tables. Three people Sherry loved with all her heart hailed her over to take a seat next to Don.

"Hi. I love this place," Sherry said. The others agreed. She sat among her family and scoured the menu. "Blackened cod sandwich and smashed hash browns for me. I'd go for the salad, too, but I don't want to overdo it."

"I'll have the same," Don said. "Let's split a seafood salad."

"I was hoping you'd say that," Sherry said with a smile.

"Me three," Erno said.

"I'm breaking the trend and getting a shrimp cocktail and wedge salad with extra bacon," Ruth said. She tucked a flyaway lock of silver hair back into its tidy bun. "Speaking of smashed potatoes, Sherry, I can't wait to watch you perform at Wednesday's cook-off. You can't go wrong. The Coltons grow the most delicious potatoes."

"How did you know they were supplying the potatoes?" Sherry asked. When Ruth screwed up her face, she regretted her question. Sherry's father's longtime girlfriend, Ruth, knew more up-to-date information than most Augustin citizens. That feat wasn't easy in such a tight-knit community, where everyone kept tabs on each other.

"My dear, Erno is one of Perry Colton's oldest friends. When I saw Patti Mellit's piece in the paper about the farm I was thrilled for Perry," Ruth said. Her tone reminded Sherry of something she had always meant to tell her father's girlfriend. She would have made a formidable classroom teacher with her ability to scold, correct, and teach simultaneously.

"We were in each other's weddings in the olden days," Erno added. "I went to his wife's funeral, and he went to your mother's funeral. We've been there for one another in the best and darkest times. I'm going to his son's service tomorrow."

"That was a private invite, wasn't it?" Sherry asked.

"That's right," Erno said. "If my buddy calls and wants me there, I'll be there."

"That's the best kind of friend," Don said. "When's the last time you saw your friend?"

"The last time I saw Perry was when I tweaked his deceased wife's rugs. That's a long time ago. All these years later we had a ten-minute conversation on the phone as if I'd seen him yesterday. He's a low-key guy. He made it very easy to give condolences, almost as if I were the one who needed comfort."

"I hope he's able to continue with the farm after the loss of Jarrod," Sherry said. "I heard many different things about where the farm is headed, not many of them good for the future of the land staying a farm."

"Perry mentioned Wellington is a help," Erno said. "He said Jarrod oversaw the management of the cottages and his wife assisted when needed. The couple doesn't live on the property. He wasn't sure how convenient it would be for Liz to continue to make visits, or even if she's interested. That made him a little sad."

"Too bad," Ruth said. "I don't want to go back to buying my potatoes from Idaho. By the time they reach Augustin I have no idea how old they are."

"It's complicated," Sherry said. "If Perry lets the farm go he'll have to pay a ton in taxes. Because of that, he'll be more than tempted to sell to a developer who'll pay top dollar. Even then, he'll have to construct some creative financial dealing to make much of a profit. If he passes the farm on to Wellington, that won't help either. Augustin may decide they want to collect exorbitant inheritance taxes."

"What's the point of passing the land down to his son if he'll be strapped with a wild tax bill?" Ruth asked.

"There's no good answer. I sure hope the pressure of all this didn't drive someone to murder." Erno shook his head. "Perry's my guy, but financial pressure on top of other stresses can put the lowest-key guy into a tailspin."

"Erno, you don't believe Perry would do such a thing," Ruth said.

Erno shrugged. "If there's one thing I've learned from Sherry's amateur sleuthing experiences, it's don't discount anyone until the final bell."

"Can we please order," Don said. "I'm starving."

"Good idea," Sherry said, although she was more than a little interested in what her father said.

Sherry broached a delicate subject after the three placed their orders. "Speaking of Patti Mellit, she has offered me an interesting chance to interview for a job."

"You have a job, dear," Ruth said. She dismissed Sherry's words with a toss of her hand. "Don't you have two or three others besides working at the Ruggery? The last I checked there are only twenty-four hours in a day and eight of those are for sleeping."

Sherry peered at her father, whose expression hadn't changed since she broke her news. "Dad, you don't seem fazed by what I said. It's almost as if you already knew."

Sherry glanced at Don and found her fiancé's sights were darting around the room, avoiding hers.

"Okay, I get it," Sherry said. "Someone has spilled the beans." She held her gaze on Don until he squirmed in his seat.

"Erno's my sounding board," Don said. "I wanted to know what his sage advise was. For me, not you. Should I encourage you to challenge yourself and make a change? Should I dissuade you to keep things status quo? Should I keep my mouth zipped?"

"Obviously the last choice was disregarded," Sherry said.

"Erno's known you forever and I've just jumped on board the Oliveri love boat. I don't want to mess up the voyage of a lifetime."

"Well, if you put it that way, how can I be annoyed with you leaking the news." Sherry kissed Don on the cheek. "What do you think, Dad? I get the impression Ruth might be voting for me to stay employed as is."

"You know I love having you work by my side at the Ruggery," Erno said. "You bring a certain je ne sais quoi to the store with all your various interests and pursuits. And Amber certainly loves having you there. I haven't mentioned this to her."

Sherry side-eyed Don again. His anguished expression spoke volumes. "Don, you told Amber, too? This isn't like you at all."

At that moment the server delivered their meals, giving Don time to formulate his answer.

"This is uncharted territory in our relationship. I don't know how I feel, to be honest. I needed a double dose of outside opinion. This sandwich looks delicious." Don took a bite of his sandwich.

"Dad, I'm asking you again. You gave Don some thoughts, how about giving me some?" Sherry said.

"Sweetie, I told Don what I'm going to tell you. It's a chance for something special. A position that not too many are as qualified for as you. I think you should go through with the interview and let the cards fall where they may. Don't overthink it at this early stage. Pretend it's like one of the murder investigations you've been involved with. Poke around, don't push, and let the answers come to you in time. Can somebody pass the tartar sauce?"

"That's what he told me," Don said. "Let the cards fall where they may, but play your hand. If only to keep from having regrets." He poked a crunchy browned potato with his fork and placed it in his mouth.

"Thanks, guys. I love you all so much," Sherry said.

"No need to get all mushy. In the end it's only a job. Speaking of the end," Erno began. He stared at his sandwich for a moment. "I know I just said let the answers come to you in time, but is there a way to hurry up and get to the end of Jarrod's murder investigation? Before Perry ended our phone call he asked for a favor. He's heard you are a seasoned investigator."

"He's heard that? Or you may have mentioned that?" Sherry asked.

"No matter, the subject came up and he asked if you wouldn't mind keeping one ear to the ground for any clues. He says he's at odds with Wellington over everything due to the uncertainty of who's lurking in the shadows."

"I'll keep my eyes open. The situation's getting complicated." She left the matter at that.

"He also mentioned a note he got that suggested he leave the farm as soon as possible," Erno said.

"What? He did? That's concerning," Sherry said. "What did the note say?"

"I've told you everything I know," Erno said.

"That ramps up the need for resolution a notch," Sherry said.

"Can I at least tell Perry tomorrow that you'll nudge Detective Bease along?" Erno asked. "That'll ease his mind."

"I don't know about the nudging part but there are some stones unturned I can check out." Sherry poked her food with her fork. "What if I find Perry has done something regrettable?"

"You'll find what you find," Erno said.

"You can't argue with that," Ruth said.

Chapter 19

After lunch Sherry and Don decided to pay Pep, Charlotte, and Mimi a visit. It was more a matter of Sherry making the decision to go and not giving Don a chance to decide otherwise.

"Shouldn't we have called first?" Don asked as he drove his truck down the lane to the farm's cottages.

"In this case the element of surprise might work in my favor," Sherry said.

"Whatever that means," Don said as he exited the car.

The afternoon air was crisp with ineffective sunshine struggling to cut through the chilly breeze. The perfect early November weather. Mimi was outside playing on her new swing set. Pep was seated at a nearby picnic table keeping a close eye on his daughter.

"Well, this is a pleasant surprise," Pep said as Sherry joined him.

Don greeted Pep in passing before taking a stance behind the stationary swing Mimi sat on.

"Hold tight," Don announced. "I'm going to teach you the art of swing pumping. You'll never have to rely on a pusher again. It's takeoff time."

Mimi screamed with delight.

"Are you hoping to channel some positive potato vibes for your cook-off?" Pep asked.

"A visit to the center of the local potato universe can't hurt. We were at lunch with Dad, and it's such a nice day we thought we'd extend the family visit to you guys," Sherry said. "Is Charlotte here?"

"Speaking of my queen, here she is." Pep stood up and lifted his arm, giving his wife a royal wave.

"I saw you out the window. How nice of you to visit," Charlotte said. "I was practicing my cooking lesson for dinner."

"How's it going?" Sherry asked.

"I've gotten through half the dicing. My hand is aching. I don't know how you do it. I'm happy to take a break."

Sherry raised her arm and flexed her biceps. The image was lost under her puffy jacket.

"I can't wait to try out my new skillet." Charlotte's sights drifted to the swing set. "Thank you, Don," she called out. He gave a thumbs-up. "What's new with you guys?"

"We had lunch with Dad and Ruth. They're doing better than all of us combined."

"I'm always happy to hear that," Charlotte said. "I can't wait for things to settle down here on the farm. We have investigators coming and going all day. I've spotted Detective Bease on the farm a bunch of times."

"Speaking of the investigation, Dad asked me to keep an eye out for any information that might crack the case," Sherry said.

"He did? Why is he asking?" Pep asked.

"For Perry's sake. They're old friends and have an unspoken allegiance to each other during hard times."

"That's right. By the way, that nugget of information would have been nice to know before I told the Coltons I would put potato toast on my menu if they considered my rental application with extra sensitivity. When I questioned Dad about why he didn't mention he knew Perry, he said, 'You kids have to navigate the world without my help. I'm not going to be around forever.' He said he knew I'd figure out a way to get noticed by the Coltons on my own merit."

"Sink or swim. That's what he taught us," Sherry said.

"You have to admit that in some cases the Oliveri name comes in handy. Either way, thanks, Dad," Pep said.

"How's Perry doing?" Sherry asked.

"I had a brief conversation with him yesterday. And we have a Tuesday meeting," Charlotte said.

"Were both meetings about the farm manual?" Sherry asked.

"Tuesday, yes," Charlotte said. "But not yesterday. That was the first Saturday of the month and that's when he deposits the rent checks, which he insists we write a paper check for. He doesn't trust electronic deposits. I can understand that. I dropped the check off with him since Jarrod is no longer with us. Jarrod would have gone door to door to collect the rent for his dad. On this go-round, Wellie drove Perry to the bank, another task that Jarrod did."

"Does Perry discuss this in his conversations with you about the farm procedures?" Sherry asked. "The rentals are an interesting aspect of running a profitable business."

"I have asked him about the cottages and their relation to the farm and, at the time, he referred me to Jarrod. I get the impression it's not his favorite side of the business, which I can understand. He may not have the drive to keep track of all that, along with the farm's comings and goings."

"Did Jarrod offer much information that was of use to you?" Sherry asked.

"He said something fascinating, but I wasn't sure how to interpret it. He said every month Perry apparently withdraws a cash amount after each deposit to keep on hand for emergencies. There's a one hundred percent chance Perry keeps a catastrophe fund under his mattress."

"How do you know that?" Sherry asked.

"There's also a one hundred percent chance Dad does, too," Pep said. "That's the way they grew up. Suspicious of banks, lawyers, big government, all those institutions that may not have the best interests of individuals in mind."

"One day I'll ask Dad if he has a mattress savings account," Sherry said with a laugh.

"In a conversation I had with Jarrod before his passing he expressed his admiration of his father's frugality, up to a point," Charlotte said. "Jarrod was afraid Perry reached the point he might be starving the farm of essentials. He thought he should stop reserving cash and start spending it or give up the good fight. Jarrod also expressed conflicting feelings about his dad's lack of trust of people who had his best interests in mind. He said the tension between family members had been building recently and his father's loss of memory only added to the dilemma."

"Sherry, I wish you could help me convince Charlotte to reconsider working with Perry. At least until this whole situation calms down," Pep said.

"I don't mean to pile on, Charlotte, but you should consider what Pep's saying," Sherry said. "A one-man operation can collapse under pressure like a cheese soufflé hitting cold air. No one wants him taking out his frustrations on you."

"I'll be fine as long as I don't rile him up with talk of the financials and cash flow," Charlotte said. "Perry could use some moral support right now, and I can see his eyes light up when we are discussing the farm procedures. Every walk we take around the acreage gives him a boost of adrenaline. If I didn't know any better I'd say the cure for his cognitive issues is to stay engaged in what he loves. Yes, he may have some under-the-weather days, but we all do. What he needs most is to accept the fact that he needs another helping hand besides Wellington."

"Actually, in October Perry was feeling poorly. He stayed home and had Jarrod and Liz take the rent checks to the bank," Pep said. "That's a good sign. He had a backup plan. It seemed to work for him. The check was cashed and withdrawn from our account as per usual."

"Does that mean Jarrod had a power of attorney if he were able to withdraw cash from Perry's account to hide under his mattress?" Sherry asked.

"Not sure, but it makes sense if he does," Pep said.

"I can ask him at our next meeting," Charlotte said. "I'll have to present the question delicately so as not to raise his ire."

"Perry's certainly a creature of old-fashioned habits," Sherry said.

"Dad's that way, too. Dad's come around in a few ways by leaps and bounds," Pep said. "For example, I wouldn't be surprised if he changes the hinges on the Ruggery's back door soon. Those hinges are a hundred years old, and I could hardly open that door last time I was at the store. He might even bring his Rolodex of customer information into the modern age of computers soon."

"Let's not go overboard," Sherry said. "I'll believe that when I see it."

"If Dad can modernize, there's hope for Perry," Charlotte said. "He'll be a lot more comfortable in this day and age if he throws in a few advances that'll help the farm run more efficiently."

"That might be a tall task. Perry follows routines religiously. He's quite a character. He's proudly boasted more than once he hasn't broken routines in years. Being sick wouldn't keep him from completing the rent check deposit ritual if Jarrod wasn't his substitute depositor," Pep said.

"Is the rent check made out solely to Perry?" Sherry asked.

"Ours is," Pep said. "That's what he mandated. In October, when he was sick, we asked if we should make the check out to anyone else for convenience's sake. He was having a bout of vertigo and couldn't lick it. He emphatically said no."

"Even Augustin Bank, who treats their customers like family members, wouldn't let Jarrod withdraw funds for Perry's under-the-mattress savings if his name weren't on the account," Sherry said.

"Wellie must also have power of attorney, which isn't a bad idea in case of emergency. With Jarrod gone now, any banking emergency would have to be cleaned up by Wellie," Charlotte said. "Yesterday, Wellie was Perry's driver. I offered to drive him. I wasn't sure how well he felt. Perry declined, saying he needed Wellie to meet with the farm's banker. I imagine they were setting him up to assist Perry. Just a guess."

Sherry's focus shifted from Charlotte to an approaching woman.

"What a nice family gathering," Madeline said as she carried a bulging tote bag toward the picnic table. "The beauty of a shared driveway is never missing a visitor siting."

Chapter 20

"Nice to see you, Madeline," Sherry said. "How's everything?"

"Nice to see you, too. I wouldn't say everything is hunky dory. I'm not happy with what's going on around here. Everything is a bit too exciting these days. I'm hoping peace and calm settles back in soon."

"I know what you mean," Charlotte said.

"I'm not sure you know the half of it," Madeline said. She rolled her shoulders, adjusting her bag. "While the handsome Detective Bease is focusing his attention on who killed Jarrod Colton, he should be paying attention to what's going on behind the scenes that may have contributed to the murder taking place."

"I think that's what the investigation is trying to achieve," Sherry said. "Have you told the detective all you know?"

"He didn't take me seriously," Madeline said. "I could tell. I might not be the clearest at recalling the details, but if you listen closely my words have worth."

Sherry recalled Ray suggesting Madeline needed to be re-interviewed because of her rambling delivery. Sherry wasn't about to share that information.

"Detective Bease also interviewed me, Pep, and Isaac," Charlotte said. "I'm sure he got the information he needed from all of us."

"Hah! That's a joke. Isaac is to blame for all this."

"All this?" Charlotte asked.

Madeline sighed. "Do I have to spell it out for you? Jarrod's murder. He may not have done the deed with his own hands, but Isaac put the idea out there in the universe when Jarrod crossed him."

Sherry wanted Madeline to continue without getting bogged down with the peaks and dips her narratives tended toward. She softened her tone and hoped her next question could be answered in a few words. "How did Jarrod cross Isaac?" No, that wasn't specific enough. Sherry attempted to rephrase her question. "I mean, how did Jarrod cross Isaac to the extent Isaac wanted Jarrod dead?"

"You know he and Jarrod were scheming. I told you. They walked around the farm with their computers and made notes on several occasions. I told Detective Bease as much. He looked at me like I was out of my mind, but I'd wager a pretty penny I'm right." Her response did little to shine a light on Isaac's possible motive.

"Are you being a tad judgmental, Madeline?" Pep asked. "Don't place blame where it doesn't belong. Isaac seems like a nice fellow. People walk around farms. He might have been helping Jarrod get a grip on the farm's harvest. Without evidence you can't say their scheming led to murder."

"Huh," Madeline scoffed. "You're on Isaac's side. I can see that. He probably frequents your food truck to stay on your good side. And you, Charlotte. I've seen you plenty of times with a notepad, transcribing whatever Perry's telling you." Her attitude was growing prickly, and Sherry was uncomfortable with her tone.

"Is there any specific reason you feel so strongly about Isaac having a hand in Jarrod's death?" Sherry asked. "Pep's right. Taking notes isn't a reason for murder."

Madeline shifted her tote from one arm to the other. "Sure, there is. Isaac could have lent me a huge hand and he chose not to. I'd even go so far as to say he backstabbed me."

"You're laying out some serious allegations, Madeline," Sherry said. Her frustration level was rising with this woman, who may or may not have valuable information. "At the same time, I'm having a hard time following what Isaac has done to you exactly, or Jarrod, or what Jarrod did to Isaac."

"Ugh. Why is everyone so dense? Am I not speaking English?" Madeline asked. "Isaac was tight with Jarrod, who was tight with Harry Chan. I was on my way to being tight with Harry until the three of them blocked me out. That led to them locking horns, which I was a witness to."

"Who locked horns?" Charlotte asked. "Harry, Isaac, or Jarrod? All three? And you were the cause?"

"Okay, so, let me back up to where things went sour. When I was first introduced to Harry Chan, we had chemistry. It was obvious. What other reason would he be coming around to the farm so often for? I was the only single girl on the property. He went out of his way to seek me out. Unfortunately, he was often accompanied by Isaac or Jarrod. You know, every guy needs a wingman to provide confidence." Madeline paused as if seeking confirmation. None came.

"Take my word for it. I know men. Time passed and Harry's advances stalled. He started talking more about business than romance. He was very interested in how I was able to pay such a low rent for my beautiful house. I think he was jealous I had a way with men, including Perry and Wellington Colton." She paused again. No one chimed in.

"Early one day about three weeks ago, Isaac and Harry were in a shouting match so loud I stormed out of my house to tell them to stop. Did either of you hear it?" She eyed Pep and Charlotte.

They shook their heads.

"A moment later I saw Harry walking from Isaac's house across the common green space, pumping his arms. Isaac trotted behind him gesturing with his arms overhead. Meanwhile, Jarrod, all dressed up in his business suit, comes from another direction with his hands cupped around his mouth, issuing orders. They reminded me of a pack of wolves celebrating a kill or scrapping over carnage portions. I watch a lot of nature programs."

"But what were they scrapping over?" Sherry asked. "If you don't know, can this be considered relevant at all?"

Madeline took a pause for the n-teenth time. When she rejoined the conversation her voice was calm. "Properties. That's what they always fought over."

"Why do you say you were backstabbed by Isaac?" Sherry asked.

"I just told you. Isaac was Harry's romance wingman. I was the prize and so was my cottage. Isaac also knew I was Perry's favorite tenant. He and Harry thought I could persuade Perry to sell one of them my rental. The romance fizzled. Isaac played me for a fool, but he got his in the end. Odd thing was Jarrod hounded me about the cottage, too. He asked me to vacate several times. Since Perry wanted me to stay, I'm still here."

Sherry exchanged glances with Pep. "More likely Perry wouldn't sell to Harry for other reasons. I'm sorry you were caught up in all this, but I'd be careful what you say in speculation. There's more here at stake than dating failures."

"The investigation hasn't proven a dispute over properties was the motive for the murder," Charlotte said. "Did the fight you witnessed continue for very long?"

"No. Liz Colton entered the scene, and the predators scattered. A drop of estrogen diluted the testosterone overload. Jarrod and Harry got in the car with Liz just as Wellie walked out onto his porch. I went over and had a word with Wellie. I probably shouldn't have done that because Wellie took off in his pickup truck. Almost looked as if he were tailing them but I know his pickup truck could never catch that gold sedan Jarrod and Liz drive. I've been in the truck and it's more show than go."

"You're telling all this to Detective Bease, I hope," Charlotte said.

"Most of it. Who wants to hear about a lost love? Harry doesn't know what he's missed out on. We could have been so good together. I even had our house décor picked out even if we were only renters together. But time stands still for no one. I've moved on." Madeline dismissed the potential for any more details with a flip of her free hand. She skulked away, leaving her audience anticipating what they might have heard next.

"Well," Sherry said. Her mouth dropped open. "I didn't see that coming. She's moved on."

"All that arguing over the purchase of bits of the farm is only theoretical," Pep said. "I don't know why they even bother to put in all that negative energy. The cottages aren't for sale. I know because I asked Perry. We'd be first in line if one came up for sale."

"It does seem like part of the puzzle is missing," Sherry said.

Chapter 21

"Sher, the countdown has begun for the cook-off. How are you preparing?" Pep asked.

"Nothing different. I've cooked the recipe a few times and I'm happy with the results. There are the usual uncertainties I have with any cook-off. I'm not sure what appliances the venue will provide us with. Probably a small stovetop and oven to accommodate different types of potato recipes. The challenge will be to get the potato cooked through in the allotted time."

"How long is the cook-off?" Pep asked.

"We get ninety minutes from start to plating. That's plenty for me. I can easily keep the stew warm until serving time. The flavors only get richer as the stew sits."

"What are the prizes?" Charlotte asked.

"I'll tell you," Pep said. "We have a huge banner hanging over our food truck location near town hall listing all the festival competitions and what's up for grabs. Let's see, there will be a chicken trick competition, and the winner gets two hundred and fifty dollars. There's a biggest winter squash contest and the winner gets the same amount. What else?" Pep tapped his forehead. "There's a Ninja course for the brave, a painted pumpkin contest for the artistic, and last but not least, a potato cook-off with the grand prize of two thousand dollars or two thousand dollars' worth of appliances for the culinary magicians."

"That's a big prize," Charlotte said. "How do you not get nervous? On top of the cook-off, you're due to tell Patti Mellit whether you want to interview for the North-Eats Test Kitchen job the same day. That's a lot on your mind."

"You know about that?" Sherry said, as if she was found with her hand in the proverbial cookie jar. "I would have told you two sooner if I'd known I had a leaky confidante. I've kept the matter close to the vest to keep my wits about me. I may have made the mistake of telling you-know-who." She gave a head tilt in Don's direction. When Don saw all heads turn his way, he gave a jovial wave. Mimi waved from the swing.

"You discovered the leak. Don told Dad and Amber, and so on and so on," Pep said. "No pressure, we're happy for you whatever you decide."

"Thanks. I'm as excited as you all are to hear my decision. I need to get through the cook-off first, then I have a few hours to make up my mind. I have some more to talk to Don about. His input will help me."

"I hear my name," Don called out as he and Mimi made their way over at toddler speed.

"All good things are being said," Pep said. "We're talking about what's going on in Sherry's mind. There's more action in there than on the turnpike during rush hour."

"If you get any insight, be sure to fill me in," Don said with a laugh.

Across Pep's backyard a spirited voice caught Sherry's attention. "Is that Isaac?" Sherry pointed to the cottage door that was propped open by a man. "No, I think that's Harry Chan."

"And that's Liz," Charlotte said. "If she doesn't get that plumbing issue cleared up she's going to have to make some financial compensations for Isaac as reparation for the inconvenience. We had to do a load of his dishes when his kitchen sink backed up again yesterday. He didn't want to ask Liz or Perry for help in their time of mourning, but I guess he was forced to."

Sherry recalled Isaac's, then Madeline's, comments concerning a falling-out with Harry. They must have worked out their differences. "Do you have any chronic issues with your house? Plumbing, HVAC, all the stuff happy homeowners optimistically believe will endure long after the mortgage papers are signed?"

"Knock on wood, no problems," Pep said. "Do you guys want to come inside? It's naptime for Mimi." He motioned to Don to bring Mimi over.

"No, thanks," Sherry said. "I think we'll head home."

"Whatever the boss says," Don said. "See you at the cook-off."

As they walked back to the car, Sherry mentioned Isaac's opinion of Harry. "He says Harry's a schmoozer, out for the next big deal, and not a good friend. Yet, there was Harry at Isaac's house just now."

"Men do dumb things. They pound their chests, mark their territory in unusual ways, and two seconds later go out for a beer with their declared enemy. What can I say?" Don said.

"Well, you've cleared up any misconceptions I may have had about the state of men today," Sherry said before she burst into a fit of laughter. "And that's why I love you dearly."

"Aw, shucks," Don said. "Glad to be of help."

"You're getting to be a fixture around here, Ms. Oliveri." Sherry turned and spotted Perry ambling away from his tractor. "Any daughter of Erno is welcome on my farm."

"Thank you, Perry," Sherry said. She stepped aside to showcase Don. "Do you remember Don Johnstone?"

"Hah," Perry said. "I guess you've been listening to my sons, who claim I have no memory left. To tell you the truth, I don't remember Don. Have we met?"

"Maybe not," Don said. "Nice to meet you in person. I've been hearing so much about your wonderful farm from Pep, Charlotte, and Sherry. It's nice to put a face to the name."

"My fault thinking you two have met," Sherry said. "Dad speaks of you in such glowing terms I forgot we haven't known you as long as he has. His stories of your friendship are very touching."

"He's been an important part of my life," Perry said. "Even if we don't see each other for years we pick right up where we left off. That's true friend-ship."

Sherry nodded, leaving the comment to sweeten the air for an extra moment.

"Can I ask you something, Sherry?" Perry said.

"Of course."

"At the Ruggery, has anyone in your family ever made a business decision they regretted? One that could jeopardize the future of your business?" Perry asked. The sorrow in his voice touched Sherry. She wanted to clutch his hand for support but reconsidered when Perry continued. "If someone hadn't killed Jarrod, I would have considered doing it myself after I found out what a fool he's taken me for all these years. I, too, may have made the biggest mistake of my life recently."

Sherry met Don's eyes, which were wide with concern. Sherry was at a loss for words.

"Forgive me," Perry said. "I didn't mean that." Perry shifted his gaze to his tractor. "Poor Ruby is the innocent victim in all of this." He smiled. "I love the name Charlotte gave my rusty friend."

"Do you think Jarrod was murdered because he made a bad business decision?" she asked hastily. "Or does your mistake have something to do with Jarrod's death? I'm trying to understand what could have ignited such anger against him."

"I'm getting that impression. I think Jarrod got the good name of Colton in a heap of trouble and I'm left to pick up the pieces. I got a threatening note left on my porch rocker this morning and it's the third one.

Chapter 22

"Can we see the note? Do you have it with you?"

Perry plunged his hand into his cargo pants and pulled out a crumpled piece of paper. "Take a gander for yourselves." He displayed a small square of paper and held it up to eye level.

The bright red ink formed block letters. *We're not going anywhere. You go.* Sherry read the words with a skeptical intonation.

To Sherry's surprise, Don jumped into the conversation. "That's so cliché. Couldn't the writer have put a bit more effort into the message's meaning? Sounds like a lazy threat to me."

Sherry was taken aback by Don's approach to Perry's concern. His spin on a situation out of his comfort zone could backfire, but she was willing to play along. They needed to keep Perry engaged and in a receptive mood.

"The wording is awkward, and the conveyed intent is less than threatening," Sherry said.

"Perry, this was written by an amateur who's making a half-hearted attempt to get a rise out of you. I wouldn't lose a minute of sleep over this," Don said. "Okay?"

"Well, now I feel better. Thanks, Don. If you're not worried, then I'm not," Perry said. "I haven't shown anyone but you two and I've only mentioned the notes to Erno. I don't want to muck up the waters Detective Bease is trying to swim through to find Jarrod's murderer."

"I would have thought you told the detective after finding the first note," Sherry said. She beckoned Don's opinion with a glare.

"I agree with Sherry," Don said. "Even if these notes are a sidetrack. They need to be documented."

"Even if I seem guilty by association?" Perry asked.

"What do you mean?" Sherry asked.

"I told you I think I made a very big mistake when it comes to the future of the farm. I can't say any more than that, but whoever wants me off the land seems to know how to get me to go. Someone knows I may have made a deal with the devil. That's all I'm willing to say."

"If you like I'll talk to Detective Bease on your behalf," Sherry said.

"Sure. Tell him I forgot about the notes. That excuse is working a lot for me lately."

Again, Sherry glanced at Don. She wanted to ensure Perry's comment registered with him.

"Sherry, your father says you are the best amateur sleuth east of the Mississippi. Do you have a take on what's going on around here?"

"Dad did mention he spoke to you. I think you should take some precautions, despite what Don says. Maybe don't walk into places like the potato storage building without a companion? That's my recommendation until Detective Bease can figure out who killed Jarrod. I told Dad I'd help in any way."

"You're busy. You have a cook-off coming up," Perry said. "What day is that again?"

"Wednesday. You're going, aren't you?"

"Sure. I'll be there. Do you want me to bring the boys along?" Perry asked.

Sherry winced when Perry slipped into the dark hole of his dwindling memory. Was he forgetting he only had one live son?

"Please, yes. There might even be a ceremony honoring the Colton farm and Jarrod at the cook-off. You both should attend," Sherry said.

"I don't want anyone fussing over me," Perry said. "Do you need your paper back?" He held up the square of paper.

"It's not mine, but sure," Sherry said. She took the paper from Perry and closed her hand around it before bidding him a good day.

Sherry decided she didn't have to run through her recipe again after all, and the remainder of Sunday was spent taking a walk around the nature preserve on the north side of town. While November didn't present plants at their finest, Sherry was still able to point out plants she could identify as edible. Don was quick to explain he trusted what was sold at grocery stores more than her newfound foraging skills. After an hour of conversation and exercise, Sherry's stomach was rumbling. They drove into town and got two bar seats at the newest restaurant in town, Harvest. Sherry ordered a chardonnay, and Don ordered a locally brewed ale.

The drinks were handed across the bar top at the same time a woman walked up beside Sherry. Don stood and gave the woman a hug.

"Sherry and Don," Patti said. "Two of my favorite-est people. I saw you come in. I'm sitting over there." She tipped her head in the direction of a table across the room. "I'm eating with three of the cook-off sponsors. They're fascinating foodies who love to shop and cook local. They're giving me so much fodder for my festival articles. I can't believe my luck."

"Once again, let me repeat," Sherry said, "you have the best job in the world."

"Oh, stop it," Patti said. "It's only a great job because of people like you, who do the most interesting things with ingredients, and I get to write about it." Patti shifted her sights to Don. "You're interesting too, Don."

"Thanks, Patti," Don said. "I try."

"I won't bug you about the job interview decision, but on another subject, I'm wondering about whether there's been any progress finding Jarrod Colton's murderer?"

"I'll let you two handle this while I study the menu," Don said as he sat down.

"I'll put the case in perspective for you. Remember the bins full of potatoes inside the potato storage building?" Sherry asked.

"Of course," Patti said.

"Well, the number of directions this case could go in is about equal to the varieties of potatoes we saw in the Colton harvest," Sherry said.

"That doesn't sound like a recipe for a fast resolution." Patti lowered her voice, which, if she was worried about being heard by others, wasn't necessary because the restaurant had begun piping in music that was a bit too loud for Sherry's taste. She had to lean in to hear Patti. "I'm no amateur sleuth but I have a feeling about Wellington Colton. I realize they were very kind to show us around the farm and all, but he was so frustrated with Jarrod."

"I agree. There was discontent when we were on the farm. But it's another level of anger to go from a verbal lashing to all-out murder. Wellie has the reasons to go after his brother, but did he?"

"Maybe at the cook-off we'll get a better indication of who had such a problem with Jarrod," Patti said.

"The situation is one more thing to think about come Wednesday," Sherry said. "It's getting crowded up here." She massaged her temple. Sherry peered over at the table Patti indicated was hers. "Do the sponsors seem fully on board with the local farm theme?"

"Absolutely. One man is the marketing director of Nutmeg Foods, the umbrella company of so many wonderful regional boutique foodie stores."

"Yum, I love that. Puts a premium on what was otherwise undervalued with the consumer, like anything heirloom."

"The other man is the head of the Northeast Restaurant Association. Can't get more influential than that. Each of them is also kicking in some surprise prizes, so stay on your toes."

"That's exciting," Sherry said.

"The third sponsor is a big one. And an unusual one. The woman is the head of a large northeast real estate company whose grip reaches all over the tristate area and up the New England coast. She's hardly taken her eyes off her phone since we've been here. Kind of annoying really."

"Real estate brokers are always on call," Sherry said.

"Her company is the largest east of the city, although I'm sure she'd show you the city properties if you're willing to pay the price."

"Does she have any fingers in the food world pie in some way?"

"Her company, Down Home Realty Group, specializes in upscale housing with a water view, although to talk to her you immediately get the impression she'd sell you anything, anywhere, if you're willing to do the deal immediately. She's a tough cookie. Is that a good enough food connection?"

"Tough cookie? It's a stretch. Good for her. I look forward to trying to impress her with my recipe. I'm not in the market for a luxury home on the water but enough people are. That should keep her in business for a long time. I'm intrigued with her selection as a sponsor."

"Let's just say she campaigned hard for the spot, and when push came to shove it was easier to choose Down Home rather than fight the pressure." Patti shrugged.

Sherry glanced at Don. He was tugging her coat as if he were a neglected child. "My man is giving me the signal to sit. I'll see you soon, Patti. Have a good dinner."

Chapter 23

Sherry was slated to open the Ruggery Monday morning. She would be working solo. Erno was attending Jarrod Colton's memorial service and Amber wasn't coming into the store until after lunch. Monday morning openings were Sherry's favorite. The store had been shuttered since Saturday afternoon and the musty, earthy smells of the abundant lamb's wool stash intensified in the two-day sealed environment.

Sherry unlocked the front door and was enveloped with the signature scent of the Oliveri craft. She took a deep breath and smiled with satisfaction. At her feet, Chutney's nose twitched incessantly as he was bombarded with the earthy must. Sherry's mind wandered to the border collie she and Chutney had recently passed on the sidewalk. She imagined the Ruggery's Monday morning scent of intense lamb's wool might send the dog, whose instinct was to react to sheep, over the edge. She mentally put introducing a border collie into her store one Monday morning on her bucket list. The scenario might make a wonderful advertisement if she filmed the scene. Sadly, time was running out if she was leaving the store for her next opportunity. In the meantime, she was entertained watching Chutney, whose instinct tended toward running endlessly with no particular purpose except to practice a zoomie exercise. He pranced from room corner to room corner taking in the variations of smells.

Sherry hung up her puffy coat and settled her purse behind the sales counter. She turned the thermostat up a few degrees, as was the order of business every Monday morning. Erno promised he would one day invest in a timing device to raise the store's temperature half an hour before opening time and lower it at closing time. One more step to conquer to bring the Ruggery into modern times. She returned to the sales desk to organize her day. There she found a note from Amber spelling out a customer order for pickup Monday morning, dated the previous Saturday. Mrs. Jeffrey would like three skeins of navy blue yarn. The darker yarns required careful collecting. If they weren't from the same dye lot the difference in the hand-dipped colors could be evident. It wasn't impossible to match yarns from different dye lots, but it took a well-trained eye and natural light from the window to get it right. Sherry was up for the challenge.

She set out for the supply closet with the hope she had a trio of navy yarn skeins from the same dye lot number. She got lucky and found the last three from the previous week's shipment. No sooner had she located the yarn than the front doorbell chimed, indicating she wasn't alone anymore. She hustled out of the storage closet cradling the lamb's wool. In walked Ray Bease.

The first thing Sherry noticed was Ray had updated his wardrobe since she last saw him. She liked what she saw. He had swapped out his crinkled khaki pants, overcoat adorned with unspeakable stains, and clodhopper black leather shoes with frayed laces bound up in knots. Now he was looking slick and youthful in his fawn-colored corduroy pants, camel hair overcoat, and trendy black slip-ons with contrasting white soles. The crumpled fedora he donned on the ill advice of someone trying to help him convey the look of a dedicated detective was nowhere to be seen. In its place was a fresh baseball cap with a HHU logo. Ray appeared rested and years younger than their previous face-to-face months ago. No wonder Madeline's sister displayed interest in the man.

"What's your secret to eternal youth, Ray?" Sherry asked. "You age backward every time I see you."

"Good morning to you, Sherry. You've just made my day. I hope I don't ruin yours." Ray removed his hat to reveal a receding hairline. If that was the only visual indication he was in his early fifties he was doing a great job living his best life.

"HHU? What does that stand for?" Sherry asked as she tracked the hat he placed on the sales desk.

"Hillsboro Homicide Unit," Ray said.

"I should have figured that out," Sherry said. "It's good to see you. To what do I owe this in-person visit?"

"Two reasons," Ray said. "The first is to wish you good luck in your upcoming cook-off. I know luck has little to do with your success but sometimes luck comes in handier than talent."

Sherry laughed at the truism.

"And the second reason is to discuss a few things about the Jarrod Colton murder, if you have a minute." Ray scanned the store. "Are we alone?"

"Amber's not working until after lunch and Dad is going to Jarrod Colton's memorial service this morning. No customers yet. I expect Harriet Jeffrey within the hour to pick up her navy blue yarn. If you'd lend a hand we can make short work of balling the yarn up for her." Sherry handed Ray a skein of wool. "Settle down on a stool and have at it." She laid her yard down on the sales table and undid the knot indicating the beginning of the yarn. "Watch and learn."

Sherry gave Ray no choice but to follow her lead. Once the yarn was wound overtop itself the balling process was only a matter of keeping any twists and tangles from occurring until the end of the yarn was reached.

Sherry was pleasantly surprised how intently Ray committed to his task. "You're hired."

"I've got the hang of this," Ray said. "Now, let's see how good I am at multitasking. I have a few questions for you." He peered up from his hands and away went the tiny ball of yarn, only in its initial stages of development. When it hit the floor the unthinkable happened. The entire ball unwound into a straight line of yarn. "Are you kidding me?"

"Back to the drawing board," Sherry said. "Don't feel bad. Multiple unwinds are a rite of passage."

"Ugh. I'm not giving up that easily." He reorganized his material and started over. "Okay. I'm not going to look at you while I talk so don't be offended."

"Good idea," Sherry said.

"I was going to make an appearance at Jarrod Colton's memorial service, but I was notified it was private and was denied. Officer Sedgeman and Trooper will be on duty, patrolling the periphery of the church. You remember Trooper, our K-9 Unit sergeant, right?"

"Of course. Wait, Trooper is a sergeant? Dogs can get promotions?"

"The highest honor for our hardest workers," Ray said. "In case Hillsboro County got a second dog for the homicide unit we wanted he or she to know who's boss."

Sherry nodded. "Makes sense."

"Anyway, Officer Sedgeman and Trooper were assigned to patrol the service perimeter because the Coltons are involved in an ongoing murder investigation."

"Have there been any threats against the service or the venue?" Sherry asked.

"No. Why would you ask that?"

"My dad mentioned Perry received a note that told him to get off the farm. Not an overly aggressive note, more like a suggestive note," Sherry said.

"A suggestive threat?" Ray said. "That's a new one."

"I have it with me. Look." Sherry set her yarn on the table in front of Ray. She stood and found the note in her coat pocket. Ray absorbed the note's content.

"May I?" He held the note up.

"Of course." Sherry watched Ray store the piece of paper in his notebook.

"Why didn't Perry tell me about the note?" Ray asked. "He knows Erno?"

"Perry said he forgot." She said the words but not with conviction. "Dad knows Perry well. Perry reached out and invited Dad to the memorial service."

"Your father got an invitation to the private service?"

"He did. Dad and Perry Colton grew up together and have maintained a presence in each other's lives. They've been there for each other, especially in the hard times," Sherry said. "I'm only just learning of their connection now, after all these years. Augustin is a tight community. Those two are the best example of how loyal the residents are to each other."

Ray broke his rule of not looking at Sherry while he was winding his wool. "Good friends support one another through thick and thin. Your dad is amazing."

"I agree," Sherry said.

"My question to you is, have you spent much time with the other renters of the Coastal Greater Tator Farm cottages?" Ray's handling of his yarn grew slow and deliberate.

"I hadn't until all this commotion happened. I've made more trips over the past week than since Pep and his family moved to the farm. I want to see what's going on over there. I'm worried for Pep and his family. I wanted to see for myself whether they're safe. That's when I've run into Isaac and Madeline, the other renters."

Ray stayed quiet as he twirled the last of the yarn around the ball he formed. "Nailed it."

Chapter 24

"Good job. Thanks. Harriet will be thrilled when I tell her the chief homicide detective balled up her yarn. Puts some great provenance into the rug she's hooking."

"What's the woman's rug theme?" Ray asked. "I might as well know what I've contributed to."

"A rooster ruling the roost. It's beautiful. The blue yarn will make up the border, which matches her living room decor. She will be married thirty years next year and this is her tribute to her husband. He was a chicken farmer until they married. She thinks he continues to pine away for the olden days of a simpler life."

"That's kind of bittersweet, isn't it? Is her husband happy? What if she said to him, 'Sorry your dream of a chicken-filled lifestyle got taken away from you after our wedding vows, but here's a rug instead'?" Ray asked.

"I'm not a marriage counselor. I'm just a manager at an artisan rug store my family is beyond happy to own and maintain."

"Would you give up the store for your intended?" Ray asked. He rolled the completed ball of yarn across the sales table toward Sherry.

"Don would never ask me to do that. How about you? Would you give up your detective work for the One?"

Ray studied his ball of yarn. "Do I have to decide right now?"

"Not unless you're really in that situation. Are you?" Sherry asked. She imagined Ray and Lulu walking down the aisle. She blinked away the image.

"No, but I have played the storyline over in my head once or twice. It's not an easy question. I'm very used to working with facts, and the facts would be tinged with emotion. That's uncharted territory for me."

"I may have opened Pandora's box by mistake. Let's put a pin in the subject until need be." Sherry extended her hand. "I'll be there for you, like you've been there for me. Promise." She shook Ray's hand.

"Deal," Ray said.

"Any other questions about the farm or the renters?"

"The investigation's focus currently is on those who spend time on the farm or live there. That's the reason for my question to you. About the other renters. They'd have knowledge of, and access to, the tractor the body was found entangled in. The engine was running, so either someone knew how to turn it on or it was inadvertently left on and proved a convenient disposal unit for the body."

"Wellington would know all that," Sherry said. "By the way, don't you need a key to turn on a tractor? There can't be too many keys to the big machinery floating around the farm for any walk-on to use."

Ray tipped his head but didn't tip his hand. "Continue."

"Wellington has motives to want his brother dead. Protecting his father's interests and ultimately his own financial well-being, for one. He was angry with Jarrod and that was on full display at the marina the day he tried to chase down Don's boat. There were lots of witnesses."

"Okay. Is there anyone else you think is an obvious suspect? Perry, for example," Ray asked.

"I'd hate to think Perry would go to such measures. On paper he has reasons to want Jarrod to side with him to save the farm. I wouldn't think Perry was thrilled Jarrod's ambitions were heading in a different direction."

"Yup," Ray said.

"Jarrod was meeting with Harry Chan, who is a developer. The possibility a business deal went awry is out there. What the meetings entailed isn't perfectly clear. Obviously, developing the farm is a charm on anyone's bracelet. Harry's, especially. If he were all hyped up thinking the deal was done and it collapsed, maybe anger turned to rage."

"Maybe, possibly, and not perfectly clear tells the tale of where the investigation is," Ray said.

"Circling back to Perry, he said to me he thinks he's made a bad business decision. He wouldn't elaborate."

"Noted. And the renters? Madeline and Isaac?" Ray asked. "They are technically in business with the Coltons. Could one of them be the murderer?"

"There's a thread missing in Madeline's involvement in the murder. I wonder if she had more of an issue with Jarrod than she's letting on. Jarrod had a tight association going with Isaac Rowe and Harry Chan. She lists Harry and Isaac as having crossed her in more ways than one. Even though she didn't clearly name Jarrod as someone she'd prefer dead, she said she wouldn't be at all surprised if one of those two men did." Sherry paused as her face screwed up with a sour expression. "You were spot-on about Madeline. She was all over the place as she was explaining her relationships to me."

"Chan and Rowe? What did she say to you about them?"

"The two men were very involved with Jarrod, business and otherwise."

"Yup. That's no secret. And their relationship to one another?" Ray asked. "And please skip the part where Madeline has a thing for Harry Chan."

"Harry, Isaac, and Jarrod are frenemies. They work, play, fight, and make up. The common denominator for all four of these people seems to be the influence they could have on the future of the farm."

"Would you include Madeline on the frenemy farm suspect list?" Ray asked.

"I would," Sherry said. "Not necessarily as strongly as the others. She provides more in the way of background noise than anything else. I do get the feeling she would run interference for Harry Chan if he were guilty. Especially if he returned her unrequited love."

"Would you label her a busybody?" Ray asked.

"Busybody, yes, which may be helpful in the long run if she knows more than she thinks she does."

"I see."

"A side note: her sister, Lulu, thinks you're a catch."

Ray's eyebrows shot halfway up his forehead. "Thank you for that information. I will give it the consideration it's due. Let's stay on track here."

The corners of Sherry's mouth turned up as her friend fought to stay stoic.

"The issue is, would any of them kill for a stake in the farm property? Is that even a possibility given the ownership rights? And why was Jarrod the one who was murdered? It's Perry's farm. It is, isn't it? You'd think Perry would be the target of the murderer, if it's the land they're after and the title was in his name," Sherry said.

"Perry Colton is the owner. That information is something anyone can find out with a simple public records search, yes. Financial complications set in when Perry passes away and the inheritor of the farm must pay taxes. Exorbitant taxes. No one's laying out money right now, but the fact is a huge prize—or booby prize—is looming if the farm changes hands. Something's not adding up. Is the prize just the farm?" Ray asked.

Sherry made a mental note to double-check the farm's ownership. "It's a big prize. On one hand, if Perry were deceased and there was no plan of succession for the farm, the remaining kin would have to pay a pretty penny in taxes to take over. On the other hand, if the sale were done while he was alive, a developer would pay him quite a lot."

"Still taxes," Ray said.

"Perry would be in control of the transaction. He could retire under his own terms, even if the government swooped in and collected a chunk. Or, on one more hand, he may figure out a way to keep the farm, much to Jarrod's dismay."

"Jarrod has no say in the matter anymore. Perry isn't necessarily worth more alive than dead if what you've spelled out is really the case," Ray said.

"But why kill Jarrod if the farm is the prize? Jarrod was murdered and the status of the farm remains the same. Perry's the owner."

Ray grumbled as if he were having trouble digesting what Sherry was saying.

"I have mixed feelings about Perry, on several levels. On one hand—" Sherry said.

"No more hands, please. Just state the facts."

"Maybe the prize isn't the farm in and of itself. Maybe the prize was winning the battle over the farm."

Ray grumbled again. "Go on."

"Perry has his reason to be annoyed with Jarrod."

"Annoyance doesn't equal murder in most cases," Ray said.

"I'm empathetic to Perry trying to save the farm. His sons were making that task very difficult, if not impossible."

"You realize you've placed the light of suspicion on both Wellington and Perry?"

"I do. I'm observing your reactions," Sherry said.

"Don't waste your time trying to get a rise out of me," Ray said. "I don't react."

Sherry smiled.

"Are you sure, and I mean one hundred percent positive, Perry would rather have the farm limping along with minimal outside help, as is, than sell out?" Ray wasn't posing a question so much as issuing a challenge for her to back up her assertion with facts.

"Well, maybe not one hundred percent. Would anyone in their right mind not be tempted to sell out if the price was right? Makes me wonder about the bad business decision Perry said he made. That may be the missing puzzle piece."

"I'm thinking out loud now. That's not the same as speculation, mind you. You're spinning a tale of a father who was being pressured by his sons to make a move that would really benefit them financially in the long run. If

Perry isn't on board with the sale and Jarrod pushed and prodded one too many times, could Perry have snapped? Or did he begrudgingly sign on, only to immediately regret his decision? He certainly knows how to run the tractor that tangled Jarrod up."

Sherry shivered as the visuals revealed themselves. "So does Wellington."

"I don't know much about farming. The coast of New England isn't traditionally farm country, is it?" Ray asked. "Is their farm all that profitable for all the effort it takes to deliver some potatoes to the local grocery stores? The Coltons may have fifty beautiful acres by the sea, but in terms of a highly productive small farm, you can't make a silk purse out of a sow's ear. Even I know that."

"How do you think the Native American people survived so long before their lifestyles were so savagely interrupted by foreign explorers? They farmed crops on the coast to go alongside their collected seafood bounty. The settlers settled where they landed, inland and shore points. They made it work for them. Farmers are a resourceful lot."

"True," Ray said. He checked his phone. "Thank you for the history lesson."

"Has the final determination been made on the cause of death for Jarrod? Was the contact with the tractor what did him in? And how could he have ended up in the prongs without help?" Sherry winced when she finished her questions. Too many unsightly images were crowding her brain.

"There's been a holdup from forensic surgeons. The cause is not always so cut and dry, no pun intended. In his case we're looking at two definite reasons he didn't survive, but we need to know which came first. In a case such as this I'm not willing to provide details until the facts are verified. You understand?"

"I understand."

"We'll be in touch. Oh, and what's the latest on the cook-off? What time should I be there?"

"Are you coming for business or pleasure?"

"A bit of both. I'd like to see the cook-off action all the way through to the awards ceremony."

"In that case I'd suggest getting a seat by one thirty, Wednesday afternoon. The cooking begins at two."

"Are the Coltons attending?"

"I know Wellington will be there. He told me as much. I hope Perry comes to see what we can do with what the farm produces. Somebody may have to remind him of the event that morning."

"That's up to his son. Very good," Ray said. "That's all for now."

"Where are you off to?" Sherry asked. She wasn't expecting a direct answer since he was on duty. She was testing the waters on how far into the inner circle of Ray's investigation she'd pried herself.

"I'm going back to the farm for a word with Madeline. After our initial conversation I was able to narrow down some questions. If I'm more selective with the questions, maybe her replies won't wander. I know a little about directing the conversation with people who love to touch on every distant point in response to a simple question." Ray winked.

"Hey. I know you can't be referring to me. And my answers don't wander so much as explore uncharted realms."

"See? You're doing it again,' Ray said with a sly grin.

Ray's attention left Sherry as he scanned the showroom. "The place smells like a slice of Scotland this morning. Earthy and woolly. It would be funny to let a border collie loose in here and watch him search for the source of the smell. They do love sheep."

"Brilliant minds think alike. Goodbye, Ray," Sherry said. She held up the ball of yarn Ray wound. "Thanks for your help."

It wasn't long after Ray left the store the balls of yarn were hand-delivered to Harriet Jeffrey. Harriet was thrilled that the chief homicide detective of Hillsboro County had a hand in rolling her yarn. She threatened to save the yarn in a special place rather than use it for its intended purpose. As an alternative, Sherry cut off a segment of a yarn thread and put it in a tiny gift box. That was a first for Sherry and amused her as much as it brought joy to Harriet.

Hours later, Amber and Bean arrived at the store with a tuna fish salad sandwich on a buttery croissant for Sherry. The salad was made just as she preferred it, with celery, scallions, capers, mayonnaise and Dijon mustard. Amber knew her so well. Sherry set up an impromptu picnic setting at the sales table to celebrate Amber's surprise lunch delivery.

Chapter 25

On her way downtown, Sherry planned to stop at home to feed Chutney. She debated driving the scenic route home to view the forecasted waves pushing onshore, their height boosted by a full moon. A storm that was brewing out at sea would compound nature's show. The more direct route would take her by town hall. The Augustin newsletter she edited and formatted for the mayor's office wasn't due until after the cook-off, so there was no excuse to drop in at Mayor Drew's office. Instead, she had another reason for visiting. The issue of inheritance tax needed to be explored. The town's tax office may provide the answer she sought. She could drive the scenic route another time.

Sherry parked her car next to her friend Kat's sporty convertible in the municipal parking lot next to town hall. Kat was the mayor's office manager but had yet to score a coveted parking spot near the building's entrance.

Kat's was the first office Sherry and Chutney visited when she entered the cavernous building that housed Augustin's governing body.

"Hi, Kat," Sherry said. "I'm missing our outdoor tennis so much."

Kat's attention rose from a stack of papers. "Hi, Sherry. I miss it, too. We're going to have to take up snowshoeing if we want to spend time together."

"Okay. I'm willing," Sherry said.

"Hold on one second," Kat said. She pulled out a desk drawer and retrieved a biscuit. "Here, boy." She handed Chutney his reward for visiting her. "Okay, back to you. It's not newsletter time yet. Is there something else I can do for you?"

"Do you have a minute to introduce me to someone in the tax records department who might answer a few questions for me?" Sherry asked.

Kat stood and walked around her desk. "Right this way. Miss Cammie is the one you want to speak to on all matters tax-related."

The tax department was down one flight of stairs and through a dimly lit hallway. Sherry carried Chutney and followed Kat into a room filled with seated men and women, whose scowls advertised impatience. Kat waved her forward.

"Shouldn't I wait my turn?" Sherry whispered as they entered the office suite. She avoided eye contact with those seated as she passed through the waiting room. She could have sworn she heard a sigh and a grumble before entering Miss Cammie's office, the focal point of which were countless filing drawers.

"No, no. This is an emergency. Plus, Miss Cammie is going to thank me for your visit. You saw the state of the people waiting to see her. Your shining face is the beacon of happiness she's been hoping for. Unless you have a complaint. If you do, then have a seat," Kat said. She challenged Sherry with a wide-eyed glance.

"No complaints here. Just looking for information," Sherry said with a forced smile.

"Kat, what can I do for you?" Miss Cammie asked. She was a stout woman in a flowy dress and flat functional shoes. Her hair, partially held at bay by a scarf, sprang playfully in every direction. The multiple step stools parked in front of the file drawer stacks must get plenty of use, judging by the older woman's lack of height. Sherry soon discovered that any shortage of height Miss Cammie may suffer from, she made up for in attitude.

"Miss Cammie, this is Sherry Oliveri," Kat said. "She has some general tax questions for you. All time-sensitive, and they should be treated with the utmost discretion." Kat checked her phone as it buzzed. "Mayor Drew. Gotta go. You're in good hands, Sherry. Stop by my office before you leave. Thanks, Miss Cammie. I owe you one." Kat dashed out of the office.

"Yes, you do," Miss Cammie said with a hearty chuckle. Miss Cammie let loose a hissing whisper. "Every case is an emergency to that youngster. Nice to meet you, Sherry. Cute dog. Would you like a seat?" She pointed in the direction of a chair alongside her desk. "I wouldn't say no to taking a seat for a minute. I'm in constant motion. Believe it or not, following the paper trail is faster than a computer search. I step up and down these stools all day like I'm doing a stair climbing machine at the gym, which is something I should do more often, obviously."

"Sure, let's sit," Sherry said, avoiding Miss Cammie's comment about her fitness level. "This won't take long." After both women sat down, she continued. "I have a friend I'm trying to help. He owns a farm. My friend is over seventy, staring retirement in the face and considering a succession plan for his kids. I mean his remaining child."

"Let's save some time here. Is your friend Perry Colton?"

Sherry's mouth dropped open. "How did you—?"

"You're not the first to come in to inquire about that property. Coastal Greater Tator Farm on Beachside Avenue. It's a trending topic. What's your friend's question?" Miss Cammie held up air quotes as she posed the question.

Sherry went silent. The fact others had inquired about the farm's tax implications meant what? Was a potential buyer out there gathering information? Did a family member visit town hall on a fact-finding mission concerning putting the farm on the market? Was that person Jarrod or Wellie Colton, or possibly Harry Chan?

"Sherry? Your question?" Miss Cammie pointed toward the waiting room. "The natives will become restless any minute. And full disclosure, I take job discretion very seriously. I never give out names of citizens who come see me or share the reason for their visit. Just as I won't be giving your name out no matter how many times a certain Detective Bease asks me for names."

"Detective Bease was in?" Sherry asked, with full expectation of a solid reply.

"Were you listening to me? You seem distracted. Pay attention. I said I don't talk about others who I meet with." Miss Cammie checked her watch and began tapping her foot as Sherry formulated her question. "The people waiting outside my office aren't genies, here to grant my ongoing wish to live my best life in Florida. Those folks want to reduce their local taxes to nil while magically increasing the town's services."

Sherry took an extra moment to gather her thoughts. Miss Cammie was throwing her for a loop, and she didn't want to forget her purpose. "My question is about taxes on the state and federal level. Namely, inheritance taxes on farm property. Let's say it's a very pricey chunk of land akin to the size and value of Coastal. Coastal is a hefty parcel featuring coveted beachfront land on one of the four sides of the nearly perfect rectangle."

Miss Cammie's smirk was distracting Sherry's attempt at disguising the evident facts behind her question.

"Beautiful fifty-five acres of land in a perfect location. A blessing and a curse. Pricey at today's valuation," Miss Cammie said. "That's a problem if the inheritors can't afford the taxes that are inevitable if the land loses its farm status. The law may also be changed at any time to include farms at a higher tax rate. With those threats looming, no one is safe from Uncle Sam."

"With that incentive disappearing, who'd want to own a farm these days?" Sherry asked with a sigh.

"May I continue?"

"Sorry," Sherry said.

"I'm lumping state and federal in together to give you the big picture. It's a worst-case scenario if it's a profitable farm, which includes the value of equipment and buildings."

"Almost worth not upgrading," Sherry considered out loud. She drew a pinched expression from Miss Cammie for the interruption.

"The taxes put the recipient in a tough spot. Come up with the huge amount due or sell out to cover what's owed. That's why someone came up with the saying two things you can't avoid are death and taxes. Unfortunately for the Coltons, the two eventualities have collided. May Jarrod rest in peace."

"Selling out is the only way around the taxes?" Sherry asked.

"Let me be clear. Again, please listen closely. There is no way around taxes. The obligated party must find the payment. And, I might add, if Augustin ever decides to increase taxes on farms, whether they change hands or not, that law could be amended in Augustin's favor." Miss Cammie shifted in her chair. "Anything else I can do for you?"

Sherry clinched the muscles in her jaw to thwart her desire to ask for names of who else had inquired about Coastal.

Miss Cammie's time had expired along with her patience. She stood. "No? Good. I have folks waiting. Nice to meet you, Sherry, and good luck in future cooking competitions."

"Oh, you know about my hobby?" Sherry asked with a sheepish grin.

"I know you have to pay taxes on your winnings, and you've done so through my office," Miss Cammie said. "You'd be surprised the things people must pay taxes on. Yours is one of the happier storylines. Have a good day."

"Thank you, Miss Cammie," Sherry said. She nestled Chutney in her arms and let herself out of the office.

While she may not have gotten the specific answers she was hoping for, Sherry left the town tax department with the sense she was on the right track. She made her way back to the mayor's office.

"Sherry, mission accomplished?" Kat asked. She reached in her desk drawer and handed Chutney another biscuit.

"I'd say mission ongoing. There's more work to do," Sherry said.

"I hope you're not having tax issues. I wouldn't wish that on anyone," Kat said.

"No. I'm just double-checking the laws. Can't be too careful."

"Are you excited about your upcoming cook-off? The news is all over town you made the finals," Kat asked. "Our office is closing early Wednesday and we're all going to be there to support the event. I'm obligated to remain unbiased, but I'm on team Sherry for the win."

"Thanks. Yes, I'm very excited. Pep and Charlotte live on the Coltons' farm, which is the potato supplier for the cook-off. Their heirloom potatoes are a work of nature's art."

"Potatoes are kind of boring, aren't they?" Kat said. "My mom's mashed potatoes were like the pasty glue I used in kindergarten. I lost my taste for the dull side dish at a very young age."

"I'll wager that you'll change your mind if you taste the recipes," Sherry said.

"Challenge accepted. Speaking of the Colton farm, Mayor Drew called me into his office a few minutes ago to issue a press release that the Local and Vocal Farmers' Day would be presenting an honorary postmortem award to Jarrod Colton in thanks for his contributions to the town's farming culture."

"Interesting. I wonder whose idea that was?" Sherry asked.

Kat curled her finger, encouraging Sherry to lean in. "A man named Harry Chan called the office with compelling reasons for the award. Mayor Drew couldn't say no. Funny thing is when we reached out to Perry and Wellington Colton to be a part of the ceremony, they said they'd get back to me. You'd think they'd be all in."

"There's so much going on in their lives right now. They might be feeling overwhelmed."

"We had to construct a ceremony plan as if they weren't participating, just in case they don't. I'm sure the community is behind the honor whether Perry and Wellington have a hand in it or not.

"What were Harry Chan's reasons for the ceremony?" Sherry asked. "If you don't mind me asking."

"I don't mind one bit. Let me think," Kat said as she rifled through her stack of papers. "Here it is." She lifted a paper up to eye level. "He said Jarrod Colton's work salvaging heirloom seed potatoes was the reason they were the festival's choice of potato for the cook-off. He said Jarrod was modernizing the farm without sacrificing its contribution to keeping Augustin a throwback town. And he said Jarrod took the notion of local to the next level by forfeiting an easy profit and instead celebrating a deal with a handshake."

"What does any of that mean?" Sherry asked. "Seems kind of wordy and circular, while not saying much at all."

"You'd know," Kat said. "You're the newsletter editor. You know when there is meaning in something and when there's none. To me it sounds like

Jarrod forfeited a business opportunity in favor of keeping the farm a farm."

"That's not what I gathered. Jarrod isn't behind the farm's success. Perry is. And why has Harry Chan taken on the role of the harbinger of the farm's good tidings?"

"I can't fully explain Mr. Chan's motivation. Our office liked the positive message being conveyed. I only hope Jarrod Colton is worthy of the honor. Too late now. The festival schedule's been printed, and Jarrod Colton is being honored whether he deserves it or not."

Chapter 26

Sherry arrived home from town hall and, after feeding Chutney, went straight to her computer to begin a search. She scrolled around the Down Home Realty website with the mindset she was interested in purchasing one of the cottages situated on the Coastal Greater Tator Farm. If she really were in the market she would compare prices to comparable properties around town, especially near the shore. She had to consider what price would be reasonable to offer the owner, Perry Colton. The total acreage would come into strong consideration if he were interested in selling a chunk of his property to the right buyer. That was the number she searched for first. Ray told her the farm consisted of fifty acres. Miss Cammie told her fifty-five acres. That's a large discrepancy considering the hefty price of beachfront land.

When she put in Charlotte's cottage address the property was listed as "not on the market." She tried Madeline's, then Isaac's. She got the same results. They did have their own addresses, rather than the farm's Beachside address, which Sherry found interesting. If the small plots of land weren't zoned as farmland they would be convenient to sell.

Sherry changed the address in the search box to the farm's Beachside Avenue address. A quick scan of the site confirmed fifty acres was the correct acreage after all. Not fifty-five, as Miss Cammie specified. The cottages must make up the difference. Sherry got the impression the dissolution of the farm may be in progress to everyone except Augustin's tax department.

Sherry clicked back to the website's home screen. On a whim she clicked on the Hillsboro office of the company, the closest branch to Augustin. A bright smiling group of portrait pictures filled the screen. Among the real estate agents listed on the page's bottom row was a familiar face, Jarrod Colton. Obviously the website hadn't been updated recently to reflect his passing.

She picked up her phone and made a call.

"Miss me so soon?" Ray asked.

"Of course, but until we meet again I wanted to confirm something you said that went over my head at the time."

"Shoot," Ray said.

Sherry heard muffled voices on Ray's end of the phone.

"Are you there?" Sherry asked.

"Sorry, I stopped at the grocery store because I want to make your recipe tonight and I don't have chutney."

Sherry's heart warmed. "If you have any questions while you're making it, please call me."

"Will do. It's one of the most interesting recipes I've ever read. What do you need?"

"You said Coastal Greater Tator Farm was fifty acres. Is that right?"

"Yes." Ray spoke in a hushed tone. "One pound of boneless, skinless chicken thighs, please." He raised his voice. "Chicken thighs are so much less expensive than breast meat. And so much more flavorful. Does everyone know that?"

"If I'm not mistaken, I taught you that," Sherry said.

"I'll give credit where credit's due. Yes, you did. And where is the chutney in this store? I've looked in the jelly and jam aisle and no luck. The butcher has no idea. There's no one else in sight to ask."

"It's in the international section. America hasn't embraced chutney as mainstream yet. The ginger and mango stewed up in a jelly throw people off. They don't know what they're missing."

"Hah, I agree," Ray said and laughed.

"About the farm," Sherry said. "Where did you come up with fifty acres? I thought it was a bit larger than that, if we include the cottages."

She held her breath in anticipation of Ray scolding her for probing him with a question directly related to the murder investigation. He had told her, ad nauseam, that he held his cards close to the vest when it came to sharing the progress of an ongoing investigation. Rightly so. If he revealed something prematurely the course of the case could be altered in favor of the perpetrator. Her hope was their recipe banter had softened his mood, and he would be willing to answer her question.

"Augustin Town Hall has a pending, or more accurately frozen, application for Connecticut's farm preservation program, signed by Perry Colton. The exact acreage was marked down as fifty acres. A helpful woman at the office said the application was incomplete and set aside until further notice."

"Miss Cammie," Sherry said. "She told me fifty-five acres. I wonder why the discrepancy?"

"Probably because to the Augustin tax department the Coltons' own fifty-five acres. To a real estate agent who may have access to the existence of a pending application, they can only work with an acreage number based on its selling significance. A farm is a farm, the extra five acres are housing lots. Does this have relevance to the murder?"

"There's a chance it does," Sherry said.

"I should know better than to question the tangents you set off on, but don't you think you're nitpicking with the acreage count?" Ray asked. "Excuse me, can you show me where the mango chutney might live? Thank you. You were right. It's in the international section."

"My favorite aisle."

"You haven't explained how the acreage discrepancy relates to the murder investigation," Ray said.

"I'm working on the connection."

"Sherry, I could listen to you ruminate all day or I could get something done. I think I'll choose the latter. I'll talk to you soon." Ray clicked off.

Sherry's phone buzzed to notify her she was receiving a text. She didn't recognize the incoming number, and her contacts didn't attach a name to the texter.

Please check your email for cook-off paperwork. Please email back when signed and notarized in the next 24 hours.

"Nothing like needing a fast turnaround. The cook-off's in two days." She scrambled to find the email on her laptop. She printed out the necessary forms, put her coat back on and hoisted Chutney into her arms. "Time to go see Vivienne at the bank."

As she drove downtown, Sherry counted her lucky stars. Vivienne, Augustin Bank's vice president, was always more than happy to notarize Sherry's cook-off documents. Sherry was welcomed with the woman's beaming smile when she walked through the bank's automatic doors.

"I was wondering when you'd come in," Vivienne said. "I read your name in the paper this morning as one of the potato cook-off finalists. You always need your legal documents in order, in the likely event you win a prize."

"You know me so well," Sherry said.

"Please have a seat. You know the drill. I need ID and bank card. Help yourself to a butterscotch candy."

"Don't mind if I do."

"And here's a treat for my favorite pup." Vivienne reached in a glass jar at the side of her massive desk and secured a dog biscuit. "For you, young man." She fed Chutney the treat, which he promptly crumbled across the beige office carpet.

"Can you tell me what your recipe is for Wednesday or is it hush-hush?" Vivienne asked.

"I haven't been told not to tell so I'm happy to share. It's Speedy African-Style Groundnut Stew," Sherry said.

"I've never heard of that. Hah, I guess that's the point. What's a groundnut and what makes the recipe African? And isn't there supposed to be a potato featured in the recipe?" Vivienne asked as she jotted down Sherry's Connecticut license number in her notary logbook.

"Thanks for asking. I'm surely going to have to answer that question when the interviewers come around to my cook station. Now's my chance to practice my answer." Sherry straightened up her posture and cleared her head of interfering thoughts. "Groundnuts are peanuts. Peanuts grow in the ground, although they are not nuts at all. They are legumes, which are the family of plants that produce pods."

"Wait, wait, wait," Vivienne said. "I have a suggestion you can take or leave. Every day I deal with folks who are speeding through life with no interest in anything but hearing the pertinent facts. You're getting too technical with your answer. Your audience is foodies, not botanists. If you get into that amount of detail while you're trying to cook, your chicken is already burned." She lowered her voice. "And you might lose your audience."

"You're right," Sherry said. "Let me start over. A groundnut is a peanut. Groundnut stew is very popular in West African countries and beyond. My stew's richly flavored with ginger, peanut butter, and a hint of fruit. My version features local heirloom sweet potatoes and chicken. It all comes together with the magic of a few shortcuts. Fast, full flavor in every bite."

"Perfect," Vivienne said. "My mouth is watering."

"Thanks, Vivienne."

Sherry watched Vivienne record the last of Sherry's information before pushing the cook-off papers across the desk. Sherry signed and returned the papers to Vivienne's side of the desk. Vivienne cosigned them and used her notary embosser to officially proclaim the papers signed and legalized.

"Good luck, Sherry. I'm hoping to get to the cook-off on time. Anything else I can do for you?"

Sherry squared up the papers while organizing her thoughts. "I have a banking question."

"That's my specialty," Vivienne said with a laugh.

"Let's say, God forbid, my dad begins to show signs of cognitive decline. He might have trouble with his memory, forgetting things, losing his place in a conversation, that sort of thing."

"Oh, no. I'm sorry to hear this."

"No, no. He isn't doing any of those things, I'm just presenting a scenario." Sherry reassessed her scenario when she realized she may be putting her father in a bad situation because he was the bank's customer, and they might question his ability to make crucial financial decisions. "Bad example. Dad's cognitive abilities are stronger than all of ours combined."

"You're beginning to lose me," Vivienne said. "So, we're not talking about your father?"

"No, absolutely not. Let's say it's the owner of a valuable business."

"Like the Ruggery?"

"Yes, but definitely not the Ruggery," Sherry said with a note of agitation. "Let's say, um, since I'm in the potato cook-off and the local supplier is Coastal Greater Tator Farm, the senior Colton, Perry, who owns the farm, is waning a bit mentally. He may ask for someone to help him with, let's say, signing checks and legal documents. I wonder if you know if Perry Colton has given power of attorney to any of his sons, or both? That would help me sort out my friend's dilemma. She's in the process of making that type of decision."

"Of course. I know the answer to your question about the Coltons. They are one of our oldest customers. By the way, so is your father. And as such I could never give away their private information without their consent." Vivienne paused and seemed to study Sherry's reaction.

Sherry wasn't surprised by Vivienne's reply so much as disappointed. She thought she had built a level of trust with Vivienne, but she was wrong. In the end they were banker and client, not confidantes. Sherry uncrossed her legs to stand. "You're right, I shouldn't have asked."

Vivienne cocked her head toward her shoulder. "I could, though, paint you a broad-brush picture of a hypothetical bank customer whose son came into the office with a power of attorney document accompanied by his father, who's not cognitively impaired so much as suffering from a rotten bout of vertigo and was having trouble moving about. A hypothetical lawyer had drawn up the papers and it was all legitimate and aboveboard, as the documents noted. The papers were signed willingly, and the signatory understood what he was passing along to his son."

"So, my friend could sign deposit slips and make account withdrawals if she has a similar power of attorney, given to her under a similar set of circumstances?" Sherry asked.

"Absolutely. He or she could deposit, withdraw, and even spend as that person sees fit, all in the name of someone else. Let's hypothetically say the temporarily impaired customer was a creature of habit and always deposited, then withdrew, a small amount with each deposit cycle, that pattern would remain unbroken. The respectful son was instructed to act on the father's behalf to continue the ritual. The good faith rule applies that the person or persons with the new power do good in the name of the other. It's not guaranteed but I must accept the signed document for what it is." Vivienne nested her hands together on the desk when she was done.

"On behalf of my friend, thank you." Sherry stood, as did Chutney.

"I hope your friend puts her newfound knowledge to good use. Possibly in an investigation of some sort." The sly smile on Vivienne's face told Sherry she knew just what she was up to.

"She will," Sherry said as she left the office.

"Oh, and if your friend has other concerns about the future of valuable land plots, she may want to make a visit to my first cousin, Cammie Kulwich, at the land records department in town hall. That woman knows more about every inch of Augustin than your father's friend Ruth Gadabee, who is the self-proclaimed chief Augustin historian."

Sherry's struggle to mask a snicker failed. "Miss Cammie is your cousin? Augustin really is a small world. She's amazing. I need to go visit her with questions. And you are spot on about Ruth, bless her heart." She left Vivienne's office with a sense she had moved a step forward.

"Chutney, I think we can fit one more errand in while we're out and about. Tomorrow is a workday, all day. It's our last chance before Wednesday to get some answers."

Chapter 27

Tuesday's alarm went off way too early for Sherry's liking. She was in the midst of a dream slash nightmare where someone was chasing her with an oversized iron skillet and the only thing stopping her demise was hiding behind a massive farm tractor. At that point she realized, to her further dismay, she was entangled in the machine's harvesting forks. She was exhausted when she woke up to the incessant buzz of the alarm.

"Glad you woke up," Don said. "I was about to shake you. You were grunting and saying unintelligible words." He placed a mug of coffee on the nightstand. "I could hear you from downstairs. Bad dream?"

"Terrible. The kind you can't wake up from."

"I'll meet you downstairs. My first trip got canceled because of the storm brewing this morning. Ice, wind, sleet pellets. Too much for the *Current Sea* to handle. Should clear up by the afternoon. Let me come with you to the Ruggery. I never get a chance to make an appearance. I'm sure Erno can assign me a task."

"Your weather bad fortune is my good fortune," Sherry said. "I'll be down in a few."

When Sherry and Don arrived at the Ruggery they were greeted with a banner draped above the sales counter wishing Sherry good luck for the next day's cook-off.

"Amber is so thoughtful," Sherry said. She sent off a text thanking her co-manager for her well wishes. "It's going to be hard to keep my mind off the cook-off all day. I keep running through the steps of the recipe."

"You've prepared it a hundred times, right?" Don asked as he hung up his coat. "I know because I've eaten it eighty-nine times." He waited a beat. "And loved each bite."

"Thanks."

"That darn sleet's dripping all over the floor. Is there a towel in the kitchen?" Don didn't wait for Sherry's reply. "Be right back."

The miserable weather combined with the hangover of last night's nightmare left Sherry feeling uneasy. The fact Don and Chutney were with her at the store was a comfort, but she wondered why she needed any. Her anxiety was charged most likely by the cook-off being less than twenty-four hours away. That had to be it. The decision that was due after the cook-off was muddying the waters as well. The perfect distraction came when she found a note from Amber on the sales counter listing customer needs to be met for the day.

"I'll leave the towel behind the counter. We're going to need it every time the door opens." Don pointed to the store's front door, which was shuddering with each gust of wind. "Kind of creepy. I'm glad I'm not out on the Sound."

A moment later the door opened and, as Don predicted, the sleet rained in sideways.

"Hi, Dad. You never enter through the front door. Why now?" Sherry said.

Erno pulled down his coat's hood and splattered water in all directions. "Good morning, all. I couldn't get the back door open. Don, I'm glad you're here. I'll need your muscles to unjam the back door hinges. After the storm we may need to change them out for ones from this century. Time to modernize."

"Maybe you're not Erno Oliveri after all, sir," Sherry quipped. "My dad would never use the dreaded word *modernize*."

"Meet the new me," Erno said.

"Okay. We'll see how long that lasts. How was Jarrod Colton's memorial service?" Sherry asked.

"The service was a mixture of sadness, surprises, and secrets," Erno said. He hung up his coat while Don dabbed at the puddles that accumulated where Erno walked. "Sadness because Perry's son passed away too soon. Jarrod and Liz had no children to carry on their legacy."

After a pause, Erno continued. "Maybe that's a reason the legacy of the farm was important to Perry. No sign from Wellington that he'll settle down with someone and have children."

"Was Perry the one who organized the service?" Sherry asked.

"Liz took care of all the arrangements, Wellington told me. Liz felt Perry wouldn't be up to making any decisions at this time and I agree. He was very mellow during the service and only showed signs of life at the reception."

"That's sad. What were the surprises?" Sherry asked. She held Amber's note in her hand as she waited for her father to recall yesterday's events. She gave him ample space to express himself. He was touched by the funeral, judging by his solemn tone.

After a moment Erno said, "The reception attendance was a bit bigger in number than the service, but only by a few."

"Where was the reception?" Don asked.

"There was a brunch buffet back at the farmhouse Perry and Wellington live in, which changed the mood to more of a celebration than a send-off. Potatoes galore. A surprising amount of food."

"Really? In what form?" Sherry asked.

"There was a scalloped potato dish, a cold potato salad, tiny potatoes halved and topped with a wonderful white fish salad. Red potatoes, I think. There was also an interesting casserole, like a shepherd's pie. I'm still stuffed." Erno rubbed his belly. "I didn't even eat breakfast today because I'm still full."

"I guess that all makes sense, but surprising if you think about it. Jarrod wasn't super into the farm remaining a farm. Maybe the menu was a subtle message of some sort," Sherry commented.

"There was also a professionally drawn-up ad about the cook-off on the table," Erno said. "That was a surprise, I'd say."

"Who joined the reception that wasn't at the church service?" Sherry asked.

"I met one lady named Madeline, who said she lived on the farm and wanted to pay her respects. And a man named Isaac said the same. Maybe Pep and Charlotte should have stopped in," Erno said.

"I think they were told it was a private event," Don said. "Right, Sher?"

"That's what I heard, too. Anyone else?" Sherry asked.

"I spoke with a man who said he was Jarrod's colleague at a real estate agency in town. Jarrod joined the team within the past year, he said."

"Was his name Harry Chan?" Sherry asked.

"No, it was Kyle something. The man admitted he didn't know him well, but Jarrod was already making a name for himself for his initiative in seeking out potential sales. Kyle wanted to come as a rep from the agency to support the family. Nice guy." Erno paused. "I did meet a Harry. Every introduction was brief because Wellington asked me to keep an eye on Perry and decide if I thought he was getting overwhelmed, code for out of touch with reality."

"Harry Chan?" Sherry asked.

"Good chance that was the last name. He was kind of a slight fellow with a mustache and a hairstyle that defied gravity. He was with the Isaac fellow and headed straight to Wellington and Madeline after we were introduced."

"Did Perry ever reach the overwhelmed stage?" Sherry asked.

Erno shook his head. "Not even once. You'd never know he's rumored to have, shall we say, signs of mental aging. For a guy everyone wanted to get a word in with, he was as sharp as a pair of rug-trimming shears."

"Good for him," Don said. "Maybe the rumors are wrong. Wouldn't that be nice."

"How are Wellington and Liz holding up?" Sherry asked.

"I wish you could have been there, then I wouldn't have to go through your twenty-question inquiry," Erno said with a ring of irritation.

"That was the last question, Dad. Then we need to get to Amber's to-do list," Sherry said in an effort to change the souring mood. "I'm trying to take the temperature of those left to run the farm."

"Okay. Let's see. Oh, right. This is where the secret part comes in," Erno said.

"Lucky I asked," Sherry said. She wagged her finger to emphasize the relevance of her full inquiry.

"Throughout the morning Wellington was quiet but attentive. He told me not many people know how much Jarrod's death will change things. Then Liz and the Harry fellow came into the conversation and Wellington changed the subject. That's what I call a secret."

"And the subject never came up again?" Sherry asked.

"Nope," Erno said. "Liz chimed in and said how nice Pep and Charlotte were and how happy she was to have them living on the farm property. The moment was lost."

"The question is, will the farm still exist without Jarrod, and did his murder have to happen for that secret to come to fruition?" Sherry asked.

"That's your specialty, figuring all that out," Erno said. "Can we get to work, please? Don, follow me. No sense waiting for this storm to end. Time has come to see if you can get these ancient hinges to cooperate. That's a lot simpler than reframing the door panel."

"The eternal question," Don said. "When is the right time to say good-bye to something useless."

"The time is now," Erno said. "Grab a screwdriver."

"The matter might not be that deep," Sherry said to Don. "But I like your analytical thinking. You're going to need towels if Dad insists on working on the hinges during the storm."

"Let's strike while the iron's hot. Oh, I almost forgot," Erno said. "Perry gave me a bunch of leftovers on my way out yesterday. I brought some containers to share for lunch." He gestured toward a paper bag resting by the coatrack.

"All those potato dishes will give me good vibes for the cook-off," Sherry said. "I can't wait to try them. Thanks."

"I'll put the bag of potato goodies in the refrigerator for later," Erno said. He and Don left Sherry at the sales counter.

A jarring rattle drew Sherry's attention to the door. Why was she on edge? It was only a passing storm, nothing unusual for November in New England. Tomorrow the storm would be history, as the weather was predicted to be calm and chilly. As the question swirled in her head the door swung open. She jerked backward as the door chime hit a shrill note. The doorframe smashed into the wall, propelled by the wind.

"I'm sorry. The door ripped out of my hand. It's unbelievably windy out there."

Chapter 28

"Good morning," Sherry said. The rush of cold wind sent a shiver crawling down her spine.

"Did I hear the door slam with the wind?" Erno called out as he walked in from the kitchen. "Do those hinges need changing, too?"

"Good morning, Mr. Oliveri," the man said. He was bundled in a rain-splattered black down parka. He was wiry in stature and carried himself with assurance as he approached Erno with an extended hand. "Isaac Rowe. We met yesterday at the Colton farm. I wasn't exactly invited but I had an overwhelming urge to extend my condolences to the family."

"Hi, Isaac. Nice to see you again. I'm happy to see you took me up on the offer to come by the shop. You sure picked a doozy of a day to be out." Erno joined Sherry at the sales counter. "This is my daughter, Sherry."

"Yes, we met at the farm on a separate occasion. I served her a home-baked cookie." Isaac's chuckle was as hearty as a man twice his size.

"Can we show you around the store?" Erno asked.

"That would be great," Isaac said.

"Sher, would you mind? I'm working on a hardware problem in the kitchen."

"Hardware, as in computers?" Isaac asked. The amazement in his tone brought a smile to Sherry's face.

"Son, before computers there was the original hardware," Erno said. "In this case, brass hinges that need replacing." He winked and returned to the kitchen.

"Your dad was a hoot at Jarrod's service yesterday," Isaac said. "He regaled us with stories of his long-ago past with Perry. Perry brightened up every time Erno spoke. They must have a deep friendship."

"That's my dad," Sherry said, pride driving her smile. "Was there a large showing at the reception?" She knew the answer, but Ray's words concerning gathering different perspectives rang in her ears.

"Quite small. Like I said, I wasn't invited but felt the tug to stop in. What could it hurt, except for the fact I wasn't counting on Harry being there. I should have known he'd worm his way in. You can't trust that guy as far as you can throw him. He's my friend one day and gives me a punch to the gut the next. I wasn't happy he thought he was close enough to Jarrod to attend his funeral service."

"Funerals are very personal affairs. You felt one way, he felt another. I wouldn't harp on anyone else's motives for being there but your own."

"Motives. That's the understatement of the year," Isaac said. "Heck, I wouldn't be surprised if he ended up being Jarrod's murderer."

Sherry grimaced. "He seems like a nice person. He's an old acquaintance of Charlotte's. I certainly hope he's not a murderer." The day was getting worse by the minute. Sherry felt a headache coming on.

"I shouldn't have said that. I'm just so angry with him. Anyway, please, show me around. I'd love to surprise my wife with a rug from the Oliveri family store. I hope I can afford your goods. Business has been slow lately." Isaac lifted off his dripping knit cap.

"We have all price ranges and rug sizes. Not to worry," Sherry said.

As they toured the store, Sherry got the impression Isaac wasn't fully engaged in her tutorial. She wasn't either. Her wish was to delve further into Isaac's comment about the possibility Harry murdered Jarrod. The timing had to be right, so she continued educating him on the hooked rug business. She couldn't help but notice, each time she showed him a different collection he scanned the rugs in haste before redirecting his attention toward the kitchen. After the winter-themed oval rugs were examined, he spoke.

"Is your dad coming back into the showroom?"

"I could go get him," Sherry said.

"I wouldn't mind," Isaac said.

Sherry went to the kitchen to find her father. She found him managing Don's removal of an offending door hinge. "Dad, Isaac Rowe would like to see you."

"Me? Really? Okay." Erno set down the screwdriver he was holding and followed Sherry into the showroom. "Yes, sir. Have you found something you like?"

"Every rug is special," Isaac said. "I need some time to figure out where we'd put one. If I come home with the wrong subject matter or color, my wife will think I'm not in tune with her decorating style. In the meantime, may I have a word with you?" His gaze shifted to Sherry, who stood her ground. She was interested in what Isaac had to say to her father.

"At Jarrod Colton's service yesterday, there was talk of change at the farm. I was interested in whether you're privy to any information about what the future holds for the lovely piece of property?" Isaac asked.

"With all due respect, why should Dad relay any of his private conversations to you, Isaac?" Sherry asked before her father could speak.

"That's putting him in an awkward position."

Isaac's mouth dropped open. His gaze left Sherry and found Erno. "Sir, I'm only asking because I think Perry Colton is in a bit of trouble. All thanks to Jarrod's misdeeds. You might have some inside information since you appear to be his close friend."

"That's not a valid enough explanation," Sherry said. "There's a murderer on the loose and I don't want my dad's name attached to any false information out there."

"What, exactly, have I done to deserve your mistrust?"

"For one, several people have said they've had a falling out with you. Harry Chan for one. My brother's neighbor and yours, Madeline, also said as much. That's two opinions and there might be more. I believe where there's smoke there's fire. I don't want you to come between my father and his longtime friend just to satisfy your need to, well, I don't know what your need would be."

Isaac lowered his head and paced in a small circle. When he reached his original position he raised his head. "Erno, did Perry mention to you that he made a deal with me to buy the farm's cottages and the associated five acres? It's a confidential deal we made that is pending approval by the town's many boards. There's a ton of red tape wrapped around farmland sales, even the smallest parcels of land, especially for development. There isn't much of that type of land left and the town doesn't want to lose what's left."

Erno groaned, a noise Sherry only heard him produce when something was deeply troubling him. Her worry was he put himself in harm's way by reuniting with Perry during such a volatile time. When his scowl untwisted, Erno cleared his throat. "Yes, and no. We had a friend-to-friend talk about life in the golden years. Plans for his career were central."

"Perfect," Sherry said. "You don't have to say anything else, Dad."

"He didn't confide in you that I was his choice to purchase the properties? We have a binding agreement thanks to a gentleman's handshake we made years ago." The frustration in Isaac's tone translated into a crack in his voice.

"The notion of a handshake deal never came up. You might be living a pipe dream, son," Erno said.

"My lawyer has everything documented," Isaac insisted. "He promises me a handshake will be binding when the boards approve everything. Despite what Jarrod and Harry have said about who gets the deal done."

"You'd better pack some patience, son, if you're hoping Augustin's boards will approve the sale to anyone with development plans. It's going to be a long, harrowing ride for you, at best."

"My plan wasn't to develop the Coltons' farmland," Isaac said. "I only wanted to buy the cottages and spruce them up a bit for sale. No harm in that plan, right?"

"Nope," Erno said. "Especially since all I hear from my son, Pep, is that he lucked out with one of the cottages that isn't having infrastructure problems. Sprucing up the houses sounds good and necessary."

"Sherry? Do you see me in a different light now?" Isaac asked.

"I reserve judgment," Sherry said. "What were you hoping Dad would tell you he had discussed with Perry yesterday?"

"I think the holdup on the sale of the cottages has more to do with Jarrod's murder than anyone knows," Isaac said. "Jarrod had his own idea for the farm, although, I wasn't the one he was making plans with."

"How long have you and Perry had this handshake deal going?" Sherry asked.

"Years."

"Why has he continued to rent the houses out if he knew they'd be selling?" Sherry asked.

"Because it's not a done deal and he needs the income," Isaac said. "Unfortunately, things are moving along at the speed of cold molasses. At the same time there are others hovering around trying to insert themselves in the proceedings. Not to mention, Perry comes and goes mentally. As time marches on I can only see that situation getting worse. I may lose my connection to the deal if he drifts too far away. Then the developers may swoop in."

"How is your relationship with Harry?" Sherry asked.

"He knows I'm very interested in the farm cottage plots. We've talked about it many times. His minimal knowledge of my deal with Perry is another matter. He's constantly inserting his intention to buy a cottage, should they ever come up for sale. Unfortunately, he's seen me one too many times bending Perry's ear. I think Harry knows what's up and he's cut me off in hopes of keeping me out of the inner circle. I might even go so far as to say he might be threatening Perry to sell out to him instead of me."

"Perry didn't mention anything like that specifically but did say someone was going out of their way to make him feel uncomfortable," Erno said.

"It's Harry. Now that Jarrod's out of the picture Harry needs to establish a new connection to the farm. I have a ninety-nine percent certainty he's placed notes in strategic locations that Perry will find. The notes contain carefully chosen words in hopes of nudging Perry off the farm. I'm guessing Harry has every intention of playing both sides and acting as hero and saving the day, so Perry is beholden to him."

"Do you know it's Harry writing the notes or are you just hoping, because you have a vendetta against him?" Sherry asked.

"I have some evidence," Isaac said. "This morning Wellington was checking on the state of the cottage driveway to see if there was any need for a salt de-icer application. Fern and I saw him out the window and she insisted I go outside in the raging storm to see if he needed any help. When I got to the driveway pavement he had slipped on some black ice and was down. Madeline was at his side, helpless. I hoisted him up, which was no easy task. He's not a small man and the footing was abysmal. He was okay and I helped him back to his house. On our way we passed Harry leaving the farmhouse in his car. Wellington was just as surprised as me to see Harry had stopped by to check on Perry so early in the morning. Anyway, there was a note on the door, drenched in sleet. How could it have not been Harry who left it on the door? If he didn't, why hadn't he removed it from the door to give to Perry?"

"What did the note say?" Erno asked.

"We brought it inside and it said something like, *Sell out before it's too late*."

"Doesn't the person who is leaving the notes know that in order for the farm to sell, especially to a developer, it has to run the gamut of Augustin board approvals at the very minimum?" Sherry asked. "You can't rush these things. Threatening the outcome won't help and may complicate the process if another investigation is launched to find the source of the notes."

"Perry said something that rings true now," Erno said. "He said, 'there are two types of people in the world. Those that are out for themselves and those that are out for others.'"

"And how does that relate to the threats and Jarrod's murder?" Sherry asked.

"What if the notes were written to have the opposite effect? You know, to slow down the process to a standstill," Erno said. "Slow down the Coltons making a move. Has anyone considered that? They may have been written by someone who is out for others, not themselves."

"If that were true and the thought of scaring away potential buyers is on someone's mind, do the mild threats have any connection to Jarrod's murder or should they be ignored?" Isaac asked.

"The notes are a distraction," Sherry said. "Unless I'm way off."

"I don't think you're way off," Isaac said.

"Do you think the uncertain future of the farm got Jarrod murdered?" Sherry asked.

"It must be a factor. Everything changed when Perry fell ill recently. After that, Perry's memory began to slip on numerous occasions and concern for his long-term capability was on the table. It was at that point I think our deal may have leaked out. Both Jarrod and Harry turned on me and that must be the reason why." Isaac began to pace back and forth in front of the sales desk. "It's making sense now that I've spelled out the timeline."

"But how did Jarrod get himself killed?" Erno said. "And how much danger is Perry in?"

"Perry should take the notes seriously. You said it. Perry's in some trouble and Dad's his friend. This needs to be solved," Sherry said.

Chapter 29

"I think it's in everyone's best interest to get this investigation ramped up. Don't you have a cook-off tomorrow? You need to concentrate on winning. Did you know Madeline's one of your competitors?" Isaac asked.

"I did," Sherry said. "Nice to have a friendly face on the cook-off stage with me."

"I'll see you there," Isaac said. "I'll be rooting for the Coltons' potatoes."

"They'll be in everyone's recipes," Sherry said. "Very diplomatic of you."

"I need to get a move on. I'll report back to my wife about the gorgeous rugs I saw. She'll be thrilled. Thank you for your time. Both of you," Isaac said. He shook Erno's hand before setting out into the storm.

"He seems like a nice man," Erno said. "Why were you so hard on him?"

"I wasn't hard at all. I can't help feeling he's deeply involved in the cause of Jarrod's murder. No one is off the suspect list," Sherry said.

"Maybe what you're feeling is born of pressure and stress," Erno said. "Let's get busy and get your mind off what you can't control."

Sherry fell silent. Erno might be right. The cook-off was less than a day away. A decision that could change her life was due in the same time frame. The rumbling in her stomach wasn't due to hunger, unfortunately. The feeling was more of an acid buildup due to the current uncertainties. The unease about what lay ahead at the cook-off was a contributing factor. So many people associated with Jarrod Colton would be in attendance. Whether the gathering was more than a cooking competition or not, she would try her best to push life's distractions aside for the ninety minutes she constructed her recipe Wednesday.

The Ruggery's front doorbell chimed and brought Sherry out of her thoughts. A couple made their way inside, out of the barrage of icy pellets.

"I'm sorry, we're ruining your floor," the woman bundled in a rain-stained down coat said. "My coat's no match for Mother Nature today."

"Come on in and get warm. I'll hang your coat up," Sherry said. When the woman pulled down her hood, Sherry recognized the face Patti had pointed out at Harvest restaurant.

"Thank you. I can do it." The woman removed her dripping coat and found an empty hook on the coatrack. "You're going to run out of hooks." She laughed and extended her hand. "My name is Abby Cranwell. You must be Sherry Oliveri."

"Yes, I am. Nice to meet you."

"I brought my husband with me to your lovely shop on the recommendation of Patti Mellit. Today was a great day to visit because all my real estate clients have canceled on me due to the dangerous roads." She turned her gaze toward her husband, who had made the choice to sling his coat over his forearm and carry it rather than hang it up. He appeared quite a bit older than his wife. "Hon, this is Sherry Oliveri. Sherry, this is my husband, Tony."

With greetings out of the way, Sherry gave the couple the option to browse on their own or take a guided tour. Abby chose neither.

"Before we move on to choosing a rug, I'd like to get some business out of the way," Abby said.

Sherry didn't like the sound of that but presented a brave face nonetheless. "Sure."

"You must have learned from your friend Patti I'm a sponsor at tomorrow's cook-off. As such, we'll keep all talk of the cook-off off-limits," Abby said.

"Of course," Sherry said.

"Hon, I'm going to take a gander across the room. The demonstration setup looks fascinating," Tony said. "I'm going to try my hand at hooking. Maybe it's the hobby for me. You keep suggesting I take one up to stay out of your hair." He sauntered off to the canvas tacked to a wooden frame on the other side of the store.

"I knew he'd love it here," Abby said with a smile. "He's the craftiest one in the family. Now that he's retired, my mission is to keep his mind engaged."

"That makes me very happy," Sherry said.

"I worked with Jarrod Colton at Down Home Realty," Abby said.

"Okay," Sherry said. She wasn't sure where Abby was leading her, but she was all ears.

"I was questioned early this morning, by phone, by a Detective Bease. He had questions about what Jarrod was like to work with, his demeanor on the job, that sort of thing."

"Background information," Sherry added.

"Right. I told him Jarrod was a work in progress and had made some mistakes in his first months at Down Home. He was aggressive in seeking out sales, to the point of turning off potential customers. This region is low-key. People want to make a connection before doing business. Family-run businesses are more the norm in Augustin than franchises and big box stores.

You know what I mean. I can already feel that vibe here in your store."

Sherry nodded.

"I matched your name, Oliveri, from the list of cook-off finalists to a last name on Jarrod's sales leads listing left to me after his passing."

"I shouldn't be on anyone's real estate sales list currently. I'm not in the market for a new home," Sherry said with a shrug. "And neither is my father, Erno."

"A Pep and Charlotte Oliveri," Abby said.

"My brother and his wife. Yes, they might be looking, although I'd categorize it as a soft interest at this moment. They're saving up first. People like to attend open houses to see what's out there. I'm sure they've done that."

"You're right, they have. They were on another list as well. A small list. A list of people who had contacted Down Home to file a complaint against Jarrod."

"This is the first I've heard of this," Sherry said. "My brother is renting a cottage on the Coastal Greater Tator Farm. Owned by the Coltons. Are you sure they had a problem with Jarrod, rather than Down Home? Maybe they signed up with an agent and realized there was a personality clash. That must be the problem."

Abby shuffled her feet as if she were growing impatient with Sherry's guesswork.

"No. I'm certain it was a complaint against Jarrod Colton, specifically. The entire office is advised when an employee is called out."

"I wouldn't think Jarrod causing a ruckus with his renters would work in his favor. I'm assuming it had something to do with his business methods? What else could the problem be?"

"Apparently Jarrod, on the unauthorized behalf of Down Home Realty, was relentlessly dogging your brother to break his lease. Pep called our office manager in Augustin and told the company to leave him alone, specifically Jarrod."

"Why would Jarrod pressure my brother? It's not Jarrod's cottage property to sell or rent anyway. The name on the land title is Perry Colton. I know because I inquired. Jarrod has no right to act on his father's behalf."

"Unless Perry Colton asked his son to," Abby said.

"That's true but doubtful. From what I gather, Perry likes the farm as is. He may sell the cottages at some point to pay for farm improvements, but there's a ton of red tape involved in that process." Sherry pictured the handshake between Perry and Isaac. If Abby wasn't aware of a gentlemen's agreement to sell a parcel of Coastal farm, Sherry wasn't going to be the one to spill the beans to a woman she barely knew.

"You don't have to tell me," Abby said with a sigh. "The bureaucracy babble is a nightmare for us real estate agents. That land is pure gold, minus the potatoes. It's also well-known the land is bound up in a process to assign a preliminary hearing concerning rezoning some, or all, of the land. Moving the process forward is about as easy as moving a mountain. That process was started way before Jarrod even became a real estate agent." She laughed with caution. "Hah. It's probably the reason he got his license so he could cash in on his family's land."

Sherry saw no humor in Abby's reference. What Abby seemed to not know was that Jarrod most likely had power of attorney and that could be as good as having his name on the land title. Jarrod may have been a renter's broken lease away from selling out. Her brother, Pep, was putting a stop to it. "Good job, Pep," she whispered.

"Long story short, I hope I didn't get your brother in trouble. And I hope Detective Bease doesn't have the slightest suspicion about your brother having anything to do with Jarrod's murder. I mean, I basically gave the detective a reason your brother might be mad at Jarrod."

"Mad, annoyed, bothered, maybe. Mad enough to murder him? I don't think so," Sherry said. "Seems to me there were others with stronger motives to kill him rather than my brother's minor grievance."

"You mean like Jarrod's own father when he found out Jarrod was going behind his back?" Abby asked. She didn't wait for an answer. "What I'm here for, besides what I've already mentioned, is to let you know if you ever hear of your brother being interested in breaking his lease, would you mind contacting me? I'm not going to act on Jarrod's behalf and try to convince Perry to sell out, rather the opposite."

"What do you mean?" Sherry asked.

"My parents were farmers in the Midwest. They were coerced off their land by a wily developer when I was in my teens. Leaving the bucolic life on the farm scarred me. My parents never adjusted to a new lifestyle and their happiness faded away. I want the Coltons to leave or stay on their own terms. It's personal. That's why I wanted to be a sponsor in the potato cook-off."

"What do you suggest is the right way to go about ensuring Perry maintains control? It might already be too late."

Abby sighed. "I'm afraid that might be true. Tomorrow is the cook-off. The farm's time to shine. All we can do is support them. No matter what, the

Colton potato will be in a winning recipe and that's a good start."

"If Jarrod was pressing my brother to give up his rental, is it right to assume the other two renters were getting the same treatment?" Sherry asked.

"The person who would know that best is Liz Colton, Jarrod's wife. She didn't work for Down Home, but she made several visits there, especially at lunchtime. I talked to her many times in the Augustin office while she was waiting for Jarrod to wrap up a meeting."

"She'll most likely be at tomorrow's festival, maintaining a brave face and representing her husband," Sherry said. "Another person I might get a chance to talk to. No wonder my head is beginning to spin."

"I'm sorry. You have so much on your plate. I wish I had brought you more information rather than more complications. I don't know if Jarrod's murder has an association to his business practices."

"Honey, I found the perfect rug," Tony called out from across the showroom. "And I hooked a rainbow in four colors."

"I better strike while the iron's hot," Abby said. "I'm not sure he's seen the price tag of your wares." Abby made it to her husband's side at a good clip. She turned back to Sherry. "It's perfect and so is Tony's rainbow!"

• • •

"Who's ready for a lunch of potatoes and more potatoes?" Erno called out from the Ruggery's kitchenette. "I'm unwrapping the goodies as we speak."

Sherry made her way to the kitchen to see what was on the menu.

"Here's your hairpin, Sher," Erno said. He held out a gold clip adorned with an enamel mosaic. "Very pretty."

Sherry examined the hair accessory. "I wish it were mine but it's not. Where'd you get it?"

"The Coltons returned it from your farm visit. I forgot Wellington put it in the lunch bag."

"Not mine. Must be Charlotte's or Mimi's," Sherry said. "How about Fern Rowe or Liz, or Madeline?"

"Now you're getting out of my comfort zone," Erno said. "Wellington asked me to ask you if it was yours and I'm doing what I'm told," Erno said. "It was found mashed in the mud at the farm," Erno said. "Wellington cleaned it up for you."

"I'm surprised it survived with all the heavy machinery traffic," Sherry said.

"Well, do you want it anyway? No one is claiming it," Erno said. "Hold on to it, and if someone comes looking for it we know where it is."

Sherry combed her fingers through her hair and inserted the clip to hold back the strands that would normally scatter across her face. "How's this?"

"Well, look at Miss Fancy Do," Don said as he set down his tools. "Looks great."

"Another memento from the potato farm," Sherry said. "Let's get back to work. Inventory's not going to happen by itself."

The rest of the day went smoothly due in part to the inclement weather limiting the number of customers. As the time ticked closer to closing the shop she developed a nagging need to put a period on one more item concerning Jarrod's murder before she shifted gears to the cook-off.

"Dad, I'll lock up after I make one call. See you at the festival tomorrow. Will Ruth be with you?"

Erno tugged his arm through his coat sleeve. "Ruth has stated in no uncertain terms that if I'm more than three minutes late picking her up in the morning she's going to the cook-off without me. She wants a seat in the front row, and she wants you to win. Does that answer your question?"

"Sure does. See you both there." She blew her father a kiss as she scrolled through the recent call listings on her phone. She clicked Ray's number as she watched her father shut the front door. She trailed him, turned the lock, and flipped the *Open* sign to *Closed*.

"Hi, Ray. Hope all is well."

"Good afternoon. What can I do for you?" Ray asked.

"I had a chat with Abby Cranwell today. She came to the store."

"The woman from Down Home Realty. Yes. I've spoken to her. She's a brave soul to go out in this weather."

"I agree," Sherry said. "She wanted to tell me Jarrod Colton was dogging Pep in an effort to get him to break his lease. Supposedly so he could sell the cottage out from under his father." Sherry paused for Ray's reaction but was met with only silence. "Ray?"

"Yes?"

"What do you think about that?"

"You're regurgitating the conversation I had with her," Ray said.

Sherry winced as she visualized Ray's description. "I wanted to add that while Jarrod was doing his share to vacate the cottages so he could do whatever with them, Pep wasn't at all angry with Jarrod."

"Pep communicated with Jarrod's office he would like Jarrod to ease off. That's the mature way to get things done," Ray said.

"You didn't come away with a feeling Pep may have murdered Jarrod?" Sherry asked.

"Not in the least," Ray said.

"I don't think Perry Colton and Jarrod were on the same page with what Jarrod was trying to execute. Abby Cranwell, the woman from Down Home, has the same feeling."

"Interesting."

"Jarrod had power of attorney for his father," Sherry said.

"So does Wellington," Ray added.

"Both do? Why is Perry handing out power of attorney to everyone?" Sherry considered out loud. She didn't give Ray time to respond. "Has the cause of Jarrod's death been verified by your office? I haven't seen a public statement."

"The results are in. My office was advised to withhold any release until after tomorrow's festival in respect to the family. Also, for security reasons. My officers will be roaming the grounds of the convention center, some in uniform and some in plain clothes. There's a consensus any announcement on the murder weapon might inflame the suspect. We don't want him or her to take further action if he sees Jarrod and the Colton family being honored."

Chapter 30

"Can you tell me the cause of death?" Sherry asked.

"Yes," Ray said.

"Really? Even before the word is made public? I expected more of an explanation about the investigation proceeding through its paces and me having to wait patiently for the steps to fall in line.

"Two reasons I'm telling you. One is, I'm going to ask you to hold the information to yourself until I give you the go-ahead. The second—" Ray paused and cleared his throat. "There's a good chance this could be the last time we work together. By work together I mean I'm in charge and you offer some practical tips that often help my unit get the job done. Now you're on your way up the career ladder and you won't be so much at my disposal."

"Did your voice just crack?" Sherry asked. "Ray, I never knew you cared so much."

Ray blew out a forceful exhale that brought a broad smile to Sherry's face.

"I hear a smile of satisfaction," he said.

"Yes, you do," Sherry said. "I'm glad you trust me and appreciate me."

"More for your cooking expertise but I'll take the help on this investigation too, if you're offering. I admit I'll miss you when you're gone."

"No one said anything about going," Sherry said. This time her voice faltered. "I have twenty-four hours to make up my mind. Even after that, there are no guarantees they'll consider me beyond the preliminary round of interviews."

"They'd be fools if they didn't," Ray said.

"Thanks, Ray. Are you trying to avoid telling me Jarrod's cause of death with all this complimentary chat?" Sherry laughed with a gentle kindness. Her friend was being particularly vulnerable, and she didn't mind it one bit. Sherry heard the rustling of paper through the phone. "Still using pen and paper rather than your computer tablet, I hear."

"The tablet's battery died. That never happens with pen and paper."

"Good point."

"The report reads, Jarrod Colton was found at five fifty-five in the morning by Wellington. He summoned the Augustin Police Department. First on the scene was Officer Troy Sedgeman and Sergeant Trooper. They met Wellington at the sight where he found Jarrod entangled in the fork prongs of a potato harvester that was attached to a running farm tractor."

"Ruby."

"Ruby?" Ray asked. "Who is that?"

"Ruby is the name of the tractor, christened by my sister-in-law, Charlotte. The tractor is so rusty it appears red in many spots. She thought the name was fitting."

"Well, Ruby didn't do Jarrod in," Ray said.

"But I thought—" Sherry began. She immediately realized her mistake in admitting she'd made a premature assumption. When was she going to learn?

"The fact is Jarrod found himself among the prongs, but none had pierced him in a life-threatening way. He was already dead. He died of blunt force trauma to the back of the head. The weapon was a pitchfork that was found leaning up against the potato storage building. It had Jarrod's blood, hair, and clothing fibers on the fork."

Sherry cringed at the image Ray described. "Poor man. Where was the tractor located?"

"Very close to the potato storage building. It was parked within feet of the double doors."

"I saw Wellington with a pitchfork the day I stopped by the farm," Sherry said.

"Were you there to do some investigating?" Ray asked.

"No. To give Charlotte a scheduled cooking lesson."

"I see," Ray said. "So, you saw Wellington with a pitchfork." He said the words slowly and deliberately.

"I did. Pitchforks are farm tools and useful in all sorts of ways. Hay collecting, removing stones from the soil, even making burrows for seed planting. We use them at the Augustin Community Garden all the time."

"I see."

"How long had Jarrod been dead when Troy arrived on the scene?" Sherry asked.

"The coroner's window of time of death is between midnight and five in the morning. It all occurred in the dark of night," Ray said. "Except possibly moving the body."

"How far was the body moved?" Sherry asked.

"There were muddled drag marks feet from the building, close to the tractor."

"That could have been another use for a pitchfork."

"Or tractor," Ray added. "Someone was good at blending in footsteps with the dirt path. Any obvious indentations in the almost fully frozen dirt were tricky to spot. But that's what Trooper's good at."

"Jarrod's not a big man," Sherry said. "But, there's something to the term *dead weight*. I tried to drag a futon mattress from one bedroom to another recently and it was almost impossible. It was so unwieldy. I couldn't get a good grip anywhere. It couldn't have been more difficult if it had anchors attached to the corners."

"You're comparing a corpse to a mattress?" Ray asked.

"Luckily, I've never had to move a corpse so that's the closest reference I could think of."

"I'm really going to miss you," Ray said.

"I doubt it."

"The chief is trying to call through," Ray said. With that, he clicked off.

"Goodbye," Sherry said to no one listening.

Chapter 31

Sherry had just finished putting together a Caesar salad when Don came in the house from a visit to the marina. Like hers, his winter coat was soaked through. He tossed it in the dryer for thirty minutes on the extra-duty cycle before joining Sherry.

"What did you do at the marina this afternoon? You couldn't possibly have launched the boat," Sherry said. "If you did, don't tell me. I don't want to picture you battling the elements."

"I didn't launch. I did some maintenance and cleaning. Boring but necessary. Now I'm ahead of the game. Tomorrow will be dry and sunny so it's back to business as usual. The plan is to head over to your cook-off as soon as my runs are complete. Try not to win until I get there." Don gave Sherry a bear hug. "Tomorrow's a big day."

"It is. I'm trying to keep my eye on one prize at a time."

They sat down after Don helped himself to a beer. Sherry poured herself a glass of chardonnay.

"Smells like roast chicken," Don said.

"I'm cooking chicken strips for the Caesar salad. I miss my iron skillet. That's what I would have used to get a nice brown edge on the chicken. I'll replace that workhorse as soon as I get a minute to shop."

"How is Charlotte liking her iron skillet? What did she name it again?" Don asked.

"Bernie. I hope she likes it as much as I did. I know she's already used it once, but not for cooking. We had to use it to rescue Wellington from the potato storage building on the farm. The door handle is so old it locked him inside. Charlotte ran home, retrieved the skillet, and whacked the locked door handle right open."

"That's using some ingenuity," Don said. "Did the skillet survive?"

"Sure. Those things are so heavy-duty they can take high heat, be used as battering rams, and still serve up a delicate stir-fry in an instant." Sherry laughed at the image she created of Bernie's many uses.

"Need help with dinner?"

"No, thanks. Tonight is a one-bowl wonder."

Sherry returned to the kitchen after she emptied her wineglass. "Charlotte had a work meeting with Perry Colton today," Sherry told Don. "The project they're working on must be coming along. I wonder if Jarrod's death will affect the content at all?"

Sherry brought over the chicken Caesar salad and took a seat.

"You said the sons may not even be mentioned in the manual. I was thinking about that whole situation. Wellington could have been angry at Jarrod for working outside the farm, leaving him and his aging father to fend for themselves. How can you fault Jarrod for spreading his wings?"

"I agree," Sherry said. "It wouldn't have been impossible for Jarrod to find a replacement for himself on the farm. In the long run the investment in a new farm hand would be worth it. Perry was the roadblock to that happening. He's stubborn about keeping the farm as is."

"What does your gut say is the motive?" Don asked.

"Before his death, whether Jarrod worked the farm or not, in the typical sequence of events the sons would one day inherit the farm. Then comes the decision. Should Jarrod and Wellington try to make do while facing a huge inheritance tax if Augustin imposes one? And if the land isn't passed down as farmland, rather as developable land plots, is that the death nell for the last potato farm in Hillsboro County?"

"That may be the Coltons' preference," Don said.

"In that scenario, Jarrod wanted to be the point man behind the sale. At least that's how it seems. I'm getting the impression Jarrod wasn't being aboveboard and honest with his family about his intentions. I don't think he was being honest with Harry Chan, either."

"How do you mean?" Don asked.

"When Isaac's handshake deal with Perry came to light, those two became the chosen ones Jarrod needed to side with. He may have shut Harry out of the dealings at that point."

"Messy," Don said. He speared a chicken strip. "Do you think Perry had already verbally sold the cottages?"

"Yes."

"Perry, you devil," Don said.

Sherry studied her plate as she positioned her fork. To form the perfect bite, she needed a salty anchovy morsel, some Parmesan-laden romaine, and a homemade crouton. Scooping with her fork, rather than spearing, was the way to go. After she savored the flavor burst on her tongue, she continued.

"Here's what we know. Jarrod may have gone behind his father's back to consider selling off some of the rental properties. Abby Cranwell, a manager at Down Home Realty, where Jarrod worked, confirmed as much. Pep, too. Oh, and you said you saw a handshake between Harry Chan and Jarrod on your boat. That happened right after Wellington attempted to storm the *Current Sea*. And right after Madeline saw a kerfuffle between Jarrod, Isaac, and Harry. Had everyone discovered Jarrod was attempting to go solo on a juicy deal of a lifetime?"

"I can't imagine the sale would go smoothly when Perry and Wellington discovered Jarrod's intentions," Don said.

"Peeling one more layer back, how motivated was Jarrod to help the farm with the cottage sales, rather than cash in for his own profit? Had he proposed the sale to his father as a way to save the farm and been rebuffed? Maybe his father misunderstood his good intentions. Dad did say Perry said some people are only out for their own personal gain. Did he mean his own son?"

"And Wellington? What does your suspect radar say about him?" Don asked.

"On my trip to the farm to cook with Charlotte, I ran across Wellington holding a pitchfork. I just found out from Ray a pitchfork was the murder weapon. The body was then moved to the tractor, maybe to stage an accident."

"The clues are presenting themselves. Would you mind scooping me some seconds?" Don asked as he held out his plate. Sherry obliged with a heaping spoonful of salad. "Don't skimp on those yummy croutons."

"Yes, sir," Sherry said. She cherry-picked some croutons from the bowl and arranged them artfully on Don's plate.

"Do you think the murderer will be at the cook-off tomorrow?" Don asked.

"What a question! Are you trying to make me nervous?" Sherry said with an insistence that left Don smiling. "There's a good chance he or she will be."

"There will be plenty of suspects, that's for sure."

Chapter 32

Wednesday morning bore no resemblance to the day before, weather-wise. The sun was shining, and the cool breeze was gentle. The month on the calendar could easily be September rather than November. Don's departure at the crack of dawn was a good sign the day would be a dry one. Sherry was relieved she didn't have to layer up beyond a cardigan and her light down coat before heading to the convention center. The red plaid flannel shirt she put on was warm enough for an indoor activity. She secured her VIP parking pass, gave Chutney an extra treat, and headed out the door.

"Good morning, Sherry," Eileen called out from across the road. "You don't need it, but good luck today. I'll be seated as close to the front as possible. Would you be a doll and wave to me so my friends give me credit?"

"Okay, Eileen. Will do. Wear something bright so I can spot you," Sherry said.

"Thanks, dear. My friend Gigi's daughter is in the cook-off. She eats so many potatoes she's beginning to resemble one," Eileen said. "Her name is Lola. Her boyfriend is on the police force. His partner is Officer Sedgeman, who is your friend Amber's boyfriend. He was on call the morning of Jarrod Colton's murder. Isn't it a small world?"

"Yes, it is," Sherry said. Her wish to not have the subject of Jarrod's investigation come up before the cook-off was not granted. "See you soon." Sherry tossed her neighbor a wave and headed to her car before Eileen could elaborate any further.

Sherry received a call from Charlotte while on her way to the convention center.

"I wanted to wish you luck in case we can't talk before the cook-off," Charlotte said.

"Thanks. I'm going to need some luck. Potatoes can be transformed into so many different recipes I'll have my hands full making my recipe shine."

"I'm so excited for you."

"I have some things to talk to you about later if you have a minute. Investigation details I'm trying to iron out. I'm concerned about Perry's safety and yours and Dad's. The more we know, the faster Jarrod's murderer can be found and put away."

"I'd appreciate that. Things are looking murky in the whole situation. I have some items for you, too. I won't distract you with them now."

"Did you meet with Perry yesterday?" Sherry asked.

"I did and it was eye-opening to say the least," Charlotte said. "And I'm not talking about the notes for the farm manual."

"Is Perry coming to the festival?" Sherry asked.

"He said he was. In his words, he 'wants to see for himself how his farm is affecting the community.'"

"He said that? How can we interpret his words?" Sherry asked.

"Now's not the time to try. Wellie was going to drive his father, but he has an errand to run this morning. As far as I know, Perry recruited Liz to drive him. I'll offer if I hear he needs a lift."

"Liz? Good. Jarrod will have a nice contingent to accept his honor. I'll see you all there," Sherry said.

"Absolutely," Charlotte said. "You've got a huge fan club coming to cheer you on."

Sherry arrived at the Augustin Fairgrounds and Convention Center with plenty of time to spare. Her VIP pass got her access to a convenient parking spot. She had no supplies to lug into the cook-off arena; instead she carried an empty canvas tote to be filled with any miscellaneous memorabilia she might purchase or be gifted, as was always the case at festivals and cook-offs.

Her first task was to find a bite to eat for lunch before scoping out the exhibits.

"Sherry, over here," a voice called out. Sherry turned and saw Patti waving to her. "Want to help me find some lunch? You have about two hours until your cook-off, right? I can show you where the venue is located so you feel settled."

"Hi, Patti. Sure, that would be great."

"I need a book of tickets and then we're set," Patti said.

The duo trekked across the huge space to an indoor pergola serving as the ticket table. Either side of the structure was decorated with bales of hay, milk canisters, and various metal farm gadgets. The ambiance was coastal and agricultural. The amazing transformation of a cavernous generic convention floor into a farm festival gave Sherry the shot of adrenaline she needed to put some pep in her step. Flannel was the garb of the day. Men, women, and children were all sporting solids and plaids in the soft durable material. Sherry had made a lucky guess on her clothing of choice.

The ticket line was moving at a good clip, and they procured admission in no time. Sherry was on the VIP list, ensuring her admission fee was waived. The ticket saleswoman dressed in flannel recommended a lunch at the booth specializing in brisket bowls.

"Shouldn't we eat at Pep's truck?" Patti asked when they were out of earshot of the recommender.

"He's not working today. His sous chef has the flu, and Toasts of the Town is shut down for at least three days. Personally, that sounds optimistic to me. Charlotte may have to jump in the truck kitchen if his absence goes on too long."

"Pitfalls of running your own business," Patti said. "In that case I would love to try a brisket bowl."

Before the women found their lunch they headed to the far end of the massive convention space. There they found a stage set up with ten ovens, recipe preparation tables, and several aproned men and women traversing the stage with pots and pans in their hands.

"This is where the magic's going to happen," Patti said. "They're in the middle of setting up. How exciting."

Sherry drew in a deep breath. "The organizers don't get enough credit. Most cook-offs do such a wonderful job making the event appear seamless when I know it can't possibly be. Many thanks to all the behind-the-scenes people."

"Sherry Oliveri?"

Sherry's attention left the stage and found a short stout woman waving in her direction.

"Hi, Miss Cammie. I was getting a sneak preview of my cook-off digs." Sherry extended her arm toward Patti. "This is my friend Patti Mellit. Augustin's finest culinary mind."

"How are you, Patti? Long time, no see," Miss Cammie said.

"You two know each other?" Sherry asked. "Patti, have you had tax issues?"

"Bless her heart," Miss Cammie said. "Patti has been preparing her mother's taxes for a decade since her father passed away. I lend her a hand whenever she asks."

Patti gave Miss Cammie a hug, which was no easy feat considering their height differential. "Miss Cammie's the best."

Learning about the softer side of Miss Cammie's hard exterior was a welcome revelation.

"Miss Cammie, I wasn't aware your cousin was Vivienne at the bank. She recommended you if I had any tax questions."

"And I would recommend Viv for any banking-related issues," Miss Cammie said.

"She's always so helpful when I need to get something notarized," Sherry said.

"Are you doing double duty today? Cooking off and gathering information to crack the Jarrod Colton murder case?" Miss Cammie asked with a sly grin. "This is a much better place to go hunting rather than the tax record department. You've got all the characters right in front of you."

"What do you mean?" Sherry asked.

Miss Cammie pointed to the cook-off stage where Perry, Wellington, and Liz were inspecting the table housing a mound of various shapes, colors, and sizes of potatoes. The trio was smiling and even shared a laugh as Perry constructed a potato pyramid on the preparation table. "The question is are they as happy working together as they appear."

Sherry waited for Patti to follow up. She didn't have to wait long.

"So, the rumor's true. The end of the farm may be near?" Patti asked.

"I wouldn't say too near. Augustin bureaucracy can drag their feet with the best of them. Many a landowner has tried and failed to get approvals and variances passed for changes to be made to their properties. The writing is on the wall, though."

"Miss Cammie, do you know if a business deal can be done based on both parties shaking hands? I mean, is that a legal and binding way to get a deal done?" Sherry asked.

"Yes, it is. With some exceptions. Let's say one of the parties passes away. If the deal was never documented in writing, the deal's off. For the sale of land between parties the handshake deal might be considered a promissory beginning to a deal, but a written contract must eventually be drawn up to be legal. In the world we live in these days, it's best to have the most ironclad form of contract there is. A handshake deal is a genteel approach to sealing a deal but naive in the end."

"Miss Cammie knows what she's talking about," Patti added. The admiration in her tone was evident.

"Aside from real estate sales and other high-value transactions, if both parties agree, then the deal has been done. If intervening parties have other documents that override the handshake then there's trouble. That's all I know. From that point on, the legal route is the way to settle any disputes. That's where the friction can tear the involved parties apart. Enough said."

"Scoping out the competition?" The voice at her back startled Sherry. A man dressed in another variety of flannel shirt approached.

"Isaac, how are you?"

"Pretty good," Isaac said as he kept his gaze trained on the stage. "Look at those Coltons admiring their wares."

"I'm happy for them," Sherry said. "They could use some good fortune."

"Hah," Isaac said. "They wouldn't know good fortune if they ran over it. Otherwise, things would be a lot different around the farm. Good luck today." He walked away.

"Everyone has their opinion, it seems," Patti said.

"I want this investigation over with so there's an end to the unease," Sherry said. "My family is involved, and I don't like it."

"Miss Cammie, we were heading to the brisket bowl for lunch. Would you like to join us?" Patti asked.

"I may not look the part, but I'm a vegetarian. No brisket for me. I was going to check out the grilled cheese booth. I'll see you both at the cook-off. Enjoy your lunch." Miss Cammie strutted away.

"She said a lot without naming names," Sherry said.

Chapter 33

"C'mon. The line's getting longer." Patti pointed out the line of people leading up to the brisket bowl counter. Getting to the line was easier said than done. Crossing even the smallest portion of the convention center was difficult as the crowd numbers increased. On their way, Sherry was shouldered aside by a woman pushing a stroller. A moment later, two teenagers texting, rather than watching where they were going, spun her sideways after grazing her. She reminded herself the festival was for a great cause and any annoyance that came from the smothering crowd should be overlooked. Lost in thought, she was dangerously close to causing a head-on collision.

"Hi, ladies," a cheerful voice said. Unlike half the milling crowd, the woman was not dressed in flannel except for a flannel-ish scarf wrapped around the neck of her coat.

"Hi, Liz," Sherry replied. "I saw you up on the stage with Perry and Wellie. You three looked as if you were having fun. Do you know my good friend Patti Mellit?"

"I'm a huge fan. I read all your columns. You and I share a meal every time you publish."

"That's a lovely way to put it. You have made my day," Patti said. "How do you and Sherry know each other?"

"Liz is a Colton," Sherry said.

"Yes, of course." Patti whacked her forehead. "I haven't seen you in such a long time." Patti turned to Sherry. "Liz was a freshman when I was a senior at Augustin High. One of my best friends was her senior buddy, as they were called."

"Right," Liz said with a chuckle. "So long ago. Ugh, so much has happened since the good old days."

"I'm so sorry for your loss," Patti said. "Call on me any time you need something. Sherry has my number."

"That's so kind of you. Thanks," Liz said. "The past week has been a blur. I'm still reeling. I wouldn't be here if it weren't to support the family. I'm not really in a festival mood. I'm so numb that I've lost track of Perry. I'm supposed to be his companion all day. He's so in and out of sorts he can wander in any direction before I can count to ten. I'm running around like a chicken with its head cut off trying to find him. Have either of you seen him?"

"I saw him around the cook-off stage with you," Sherry said. "Maybe he's still there with Wellington. He's in safe hands with his son."

"I wouldn't be so sure of that," Liz said. "Wellington doesn't always have his father's best interests in mind."

"Times are stressful. I'm sure Perry's front and foremost on his son's mind," Sherry said. "I have some extra time before the cook-off. Would you like us to canvass the area for Perry if he's not with Wellington?"

Liz nodded. "Thanks for the offer. I'll find him. I'll circle back to the stage and make sure Perry's okay. So far he's having a cloudy memory day at best, and he might not remember where he is and what he's here for."

"I know there are police officers and undercover officers patrolling the grounds. I'd mention to them you've lost sight of your charge."

"Good idea. I don't want to sound off any alarm bells, but it's been about ten minutes since I've seen him. I better get a move on. See you at the cook-off." Liz walked away at a fast clip.

Sherry got her bearings and located the line she'd momentarily lost that led to the brisket bowl vender. She couldn't help but notice the vender next to the brisket was a local frozen yogurt supplier for Pep's food truck. She had often forgone his truck's specialty, topped toasts, for a frozen yogurt topped with granola and seasonal fruit. The idea of the fresh treat made her mouth water.

"Are you coming?" Patti asked. "You seem lost in thought."

"I most certainly was," Sherry said with a laugh. "I have food on the brain."

"Excuse me. Aren't you Sherry Oliveri?" a woman in a flannel shirtdress and winter boots asked with breathless enthusiasm.

"That's her," Patti said.

"I won't take up much of your time. I want to tell you how much you mean to my daughter." The woman grasped Sherry's hand. "My Sara is at the middle school where you give occasional lessons. She's not only obsessed with gardening now but also with growing our food."

"What a compliment," Sherry said. "I couldn't ask for a nicer sentiment."

"I have one more. She says she wants to be you when she grows up and compete in cooking competitions. And do lots of volunteer work."

Sherry's reply caught in her throat. After she took a breath she thanked the woman again and vowed to continue the conversation with Sara at her next school visit.

"That was special," Patti said. "Do you get that sentiment often?"

"I'm much more comfortable giving thanks than receiving thanks," Sherry said. "Sara is a sweet girl."

After a lunch of saucy shreds of brisket served over rice, Patti and Sherry went their separate ways. Patti wanted to explore every food offering while Sherry wanted to take a seat and gather her competitive thoughts. Navigating through the building crowd was taking its toll on her patience. The air in the convention center was warming thanks to the combined body heat of the growing crowd. Sherry was tiring.

She made her way back to the other side of the floor and found a welcoming row of empty seats. A few moments seated might bring her a second wind. The vantage point gave her a panoramic view of the festival. Around her, children were screaming with joy, parents were chasing loose toddlers, and couples were meandering from exhibit to exhibit. She checked her phone for the time. She was due backstage in twenty minutes.

"Are you hiding in plain sight?"

Sherry raised her sights from her phone to see Perry standing next to her. "I guess you could say that," Sherry said with amusement. She scanned the area and saw no sign of Liz accompanying her charge.

"Mind if I have a seat next to you?" Perry asked. He sat before Sherry could answer. "I passed Madeline on her way to the stage. I didn't know she was a good enough cook to compete against the likes of you."

"Anyone is," Sherry said. Her modesty was on full display. "Are you participating in the honor for Jarrod?"

"I'm expected to, yes." Perry lowered his head and studied his hands. "It's no secret my sons and I are at odds. When my own son sabotages my best intentions, what am I supposed to do?"

"Can I ask you a personal question?" Sherry asked. Her tone was gentle, although she raised the volume of her voice as the festival was growing loud.

"Sure."

"You're not at all cognitively impaired, are you?"

Perry raised his sights and met Sherry's gaze. "Not in the least. You're one great detective."

"I'm not a detective at all. I have a father who values his friendship with you, and I want to help sort this out if I can. I need your help, though. I need you to trust me and be straight with me."

"Under one condition," Perry said. He held his gaze on Sherry's eyes.

"Name it," Sherry said.

"You have to go along with the idea out there that I'm losing my marbles."

Of all the conditions Perry might name, having Sherry bend the truth was one she wasn't comfortable with. "Perry, I—"

"That's the condition if you'd like my help," Perry said.

"Do you agree, I'm helping you as much as you're helping me?" Sherry countered.

"I do. Is it a deal?" Perry extended his hand.

Sherry accepted the deal and shook the farmer's calloused hand.

"Do you want to hang out and people watch with me for a few minutes?" Sherry asked.

"No, thanks. I heard from a concerned Augustin police officer that Liz is on the lookout for me. No one thinks I can browse around on my own and not get into trouble. I told him I'd find her on my own rather than have him escort me back to her. I better honor my word." Perry tipped his head and told Sherry he'd see her at the cook-off.

Chapter 34

Time flew by as Sherry tallied up the families she hadn't seen in ages who were enjoying the festival. Many were former or current Ruggery customers. If she caught an eye a wave would come her way. It wasn't long before the time had come to return to the cook-off stage.

Back at the stage each cook was greeted by a woman who handed out a logoed apron and general logistical instructions. Sherry took her position at the third of ten ovens as she was told to do. She greeted Madeline, who manned the oven next to her. Each of the ten cooks was assigned a small prep area station beside their oven and stovetop. Sherry's nerves were on alert because she had no way of determining whether all her necessary Speedy African-Style Groundnut Stew ingredients were accounted for. She found with relief that the pots and pans were visible across a long table behind the contestants. With no other options in sight, she assumed the labeled paper bags lined up across the back of the stage must be the ingredients.

The stage was raised so she had a good view of everyone. The viewing audience was provided at least twenty rows of folding chairs and those seats were nearly filled. The side aisles were lined with spectators, as was the area behind the seats. Sherry scanned the packed audience. She was able to pick out Ray Bease, Erno, Ruth, Charlotte, Pep, Mimi, and many other familiar faces. There was no sign of Don. He must have run into a schedule glitch. That wasn't a problem so much as a disappointment for Sherry. The others' smiles eased her nerves but did little to squash her main concern: why no cook had any supplies at their stations.

A generous round of clapping began when a woman, who Sherry recognized as a local talent who made it big in Hollywood and was often pictured in the *Nutmeg News*, strutted across the stage. The woman stopped in front of the microphone stand.

"Good afternoon, everyone. I'm Gina Cousins. Welcome to the Local and Vocal Farmers' Day Potato Cook-off."

The audience cheered. The energy Sherry received from their enthusiasm elevated her excitement another level.

"Today you will be treated to a rare display of creative talent by ten home cooks who have beaten out hundreds of others to make the final round of the cook-off. The cooks will be showcasing Coastal Greater Tator Farms potatoes in an original recipe they have created for the competition. I grew

"

up in Augustin and had plenty of their potatoes over the years. Mashed, scalloped, roasted, baked, and hash-browned. Do me a special favor, audience, on the count of three, please call out your favorite way to prepare a potato. One, two, three."

The response was deafening. All ten cooks burst out in laughter, momentarily breaking the tension that hung in the air. Gina knew what she was doing. She held up her hands to quiet the crowd.

"This is a potato-loving people," Gina announced. "Now, back to business. The cooks will have ninety minutes to prepare the recipes we will be handing them." She held up a thin stack of papers. "Yes, they need to read the recipes before preparing them. That's the twist."

"Why does there have to be a twist?" Madeline whispered to Sherry. Sherry shrugged. She had no idea why there had to be a twist.

"You may be wondering why our ten cooks don't have any pantry items or cooking implements at their ovens. I bet they are wondering as well. We are throwing them a curveball."

Sherry couldn't contain a groan. At the same time, many other cooks shifted their weight from foot to foot, bowed their heads and puffed out their cheeks.

"In my hands I have ten recipe sheets. Each cook was asked to bring their personal copy with them today as well. Any notes were allowed so long as they fit in the margin. That way the cook's comfort level may be higher."

"Phew," Sherry whispered. She glanced down at her copy of her recipe, margin notes included.

"What they don't know is they will not be cooking their own recipe, but rather their neighbor's."

The cooks shared expressions of wonder.

"Pardon me a minute while I hand out the designated recipes to the wrong cooks. Yes, you heard me correctly. Sherry Oliveri, you will be cooking Madeline's recipe and Madeline, you will be cooking Sherry's. You two are now team number one. And so on, down the line. Five teams, ten recipes. You will want to give the person with your recipe your personal copy as well to reinforce the proper execution of your recipe. Remember, your recipe is now one of two recipes your team is preparing. Teamwork makes the dream work. May the best team win. The prize money will be doubled and there will be two winners, as a team, not one. When I finish handing out the recipe sheets our fantastic helpers will bring over your ingredients and cookware. You're in charge of grabbing your utensils because I know personal preferences are strong."

Sherry exchanged glances with Madeline, who appeared as shocked as anyone. "We can do this," Sherry whispered.

"Cooks, we'll take a few minutes and sort out supplies, deliver them, and answer any last-minute questions. Same ninety-minute time limit, start to plating. Remember, you aren't cooking your own recipe. You are cooking your teammate's. A recipe you have never cooked before, let alone read. Read the recipe from start to finish before you begin. It would behoove you not to try to micromanage your partner at the expense of your own recipe preparation. Use your time wisely."

"The days of the traditional cook-off are over," Sherry whispered to Madeline.

"Let's do this. It's worth a full kitchen of appliances."

Gina had one last word. "Maybe you've figured out by now the themes here are teamwork, executing good recipe skills, and a celebration of our local farmers. If potatoes are the centerpiece of each recipe you cooks have nothing to worry about. The judges will reward the team who can stretch their skills the farthest. Good luck to you all. No matter what, the local farms are the winners."

The cook-off began minutes later with the boisterous proclamation, "Let the cooking begin."

The first surprise came when Sherry read the sheet with Madeline's recipe printed on it. The recipe was not for Colombian chicken corn and potato stew, as Madeline had mentioned at the farm days ago. Sherry directed her gaze in Madeline's direction and was met with an apology.

"I wanted to impress you, so I made up a fancy description for my recipe," Madeline said. "Who knew we'd end up teaming up together? It's my first cook-off. I was afraid you'd laugh at my concept. I'll never tell you a white lie again."

"Don't give it a second thought," Sherry said. "Twice-Baked Potatoes Three Ways sounds amazing. I can't wait to taste them. But, how in the world do I have time to bake the potatoes before I bake them a second time?"

"No worries. The recipe was accepted into the contest with an asterisk. The organizers liked the concept so much they said they would provide me with four prebaked potatoes so I would have no problem completing the recipe. And there's one extra potato, in case of emergency."

"That's a relief," Sherry said. "Now I can focus on the potato stuffing."

Before Sherry could begin reading Madeline's recipe, a cook-off runner, a most valuable assistant to the cooks, was at her side. He had bags bulging with what Sherry assumed were the recipe ingredients. The young man, dressed as a farmhand, set the bags down and said he'd be returning in a flash with her bowls, plates, and whatever else Madeline had specified was needed to complete the recipe. Sherry was instructed to choose her utensils as soon as possible.

"This event must have taken a village to mastermind," Sherry said.

"You're not kidding," the cook on the other side of Sherry said.

"What are you making?" Sherry asked. She squinted to read the name plate on her stove. "Lulu. I know a friend of your mother's. My neighbor, Eileen."

"I call her Aunt Eileen. I love her dearly," Lulu said. "You're the Sherry she's constantly talking about. She thinks you're the most wonderful neighbor and friend."

Sherry's eyes blurred for a moment. "I feel the same way about her. We should wave to her together. She'll get a kick out of that." Sherry panned the seated crowd and found Eileen dressed in a flannel shirt among a sea of flannel-adorned audience members. She was easy to pick out because her shirt was accessorized with a neon green sash. Sherry pointed Eileen out to Lulu and waved. Eileen elbowed her seatmates on either side to draw their attention to the reception she was receiving.

"Perfect," Sherry said. "She'll be elated. What was your recipe before it was swapped away?"

"Potato-stuffed chicken breast. Instead I'll be making crispy potato cake pops with apricot-mustard dipping sauce. There's stiff competition on all sides."

"Best of luck," Sherry said.

Sherry got down to work. She read the entire recipe from title to final step to get the full picture of how her next ninety minutes would work. The race to the finish line began. Twenty minutes into the recipe preparation, Sherry was having a hard time resisting the urge to intervene on some of the steps of her groundnut stew. Frequent side-eyes over to Madeline's table gave her some confidence the recipe was in good hands, but tiny details were being overlooked. The mango chutney that gave the African-inspired recipe its unique flavor profile would work better in a smooth consistency if Madeline chopped the chunks in the condiment very small, so as not to overpower any select bite of the stew. Heaven forbid a judge chomped down on a chunk of ginger. The next bite would be smothered by the lingering strong flavor. Her resistance to intervening waned and she whispered the suggestion to her teammate.

"Good idea, thanks," Madeline replied.

As soon as the first suggestion was well-received the door was open for more.

"Keep testing the sweet potato chunks," Sherry continued. "Fork tender is perfect. After that they become mushy, and the mouth feel is degraded. Whisk in the peanut butter for the smoothest consistency in the sauce. If you can't find a whisk, a fork will work but will take a lot longer. Oh, and since the potato is the star of the show, when you arrange the servings for the judges, prominently display the potato chunks across the top of the bowls."

Maybe she shared one too many tidbits because Madeline walked away without so much as a nod of the head. She returned moments later with a whisk. "How's this?"

"Perfect," Sherry said. "I'll be quiet now. If you have any advice for me, I'm all ears."

Sherry returned her attention to the twice-baked potatoes. She preheated the oven to the specified 400 degrees. Sherry was pleasantly satisfied with the quality of the supplied baked potatoes. Madeleine had written the recipes with a built-in option for various outcomes appealing to many tastes. Sherry had never attempted to write a cook-off recipe with multiple variations, but she predicted Madeline's recipe would work beautifully. The judges would have choices, all done in ninety minutes. She had a newfound respect for Madeline, despite the white lie about the Colombian chicken stew.

Sherry trimmed a slice of skin off the top of each potato and used an ice cream scoop to remove a good amount of flesh from inside. Leaving the skin intact required careful hands, one of which scooped while the other cradled the potato lovingly. She placed the flesh in a large bowl and added the specified ingredients: butter, milk, spreadable garlic and herb cheese, and chopped fresh parsley. From that point she created the topping for her ranch potato. The topping involved sour cream, mustard, chives, cumin, Monterey Jack cheese and, of course, bacon bits, which were supplied already cooked and chopped. Thankfully, Madeline had done a clear and concise job specifying many ingredients in the recipe as "prepared" or supplied a certain way. That detail saved crucial time. Madeline had done her research on what goes into a successful cook-off recipe and Sherry was more than appreciative.

After twelve minutes, one potato down, two more to go. Each large baked potato would feed the four judges. She envied their jobs because Madeline's creation smelled heavenly. The next potato variation in the recipe piqued Sherry's interest. French Bistro Twice-Baked Potato. She began with the same mash of potato pulp combined with butter, milk, and spreadable garlic and herb cheese. To amplify the French accent of the potato, Madeline's recipe called for a combination of chopped fresh herbs. Sherry finely chopped tarragon, lemon zest, basil, and oregano and stirred them into the mashed potato. The potato consistency wasn't as moist as a traditional mashed potato, nor was it as smooth. With the added pop of green herbs, the potato filling was complete. She spooned the filling back into the potato skin and prepared the French-accented topping. Prosciutto and Brie cheese would be added atop the potato after a warming in the oven. Not just prosciutto cut in julienne strips, as Sherry would have thought. The thin salty meat had to be frizzled. Another creative choice by Madeline. Sherry heated a skillet to hot and added prosciutto strips. The meat sizzled until it curled, at which point Sherry removed the frizzles to a side plate for holding. On to potato number three.

The third potato variation in Madeline's recipe was a Dahi Wale Aloo twice-baked potato. The theme was an Americanized version of a full-flavored, multi-ingredient Indian dish. Madeline had written in many shortcuts, something Sherry was appreciative of as she read the dwindling contest countdown clock behind the stage. Forty minutes remained. Once again she scooped out potato pulp. She added yogurt, chutney, cilantro, butter, tandoori masala spice blend and salt to the pulp. To finish off the potato Sherry had to prepare a raita sauce. She stirred together yogurt, a spoonful of chutney, a diced chili, diced cucumber, a shallot and salt. The smells emanating from her workstation were so enticing her stomach rumbled.

After three stuffed potatoes were swollen with revved-up fillings, Sherry laid loose foil across each and positioned them on a baking sheet. She loaded the pan into the oven. The oven's high heat would warm the potatoes, and the flavors would come together. Sherry was seeing Madeline's recipe for what it was. Genius. She hoped Madeline was having as good a time preparing the Speedy African-Style Groundnut Stew as Sherry was preparing the twice-baked potatoes.

As she always did before the final steps of any cook-off recipe, Sherry tidied up her prep area. Her organization exercise had another purpose. While collecting empty wrappers and bags, she could account for all the ingredients and double-check she hadn't left any out of the prepared recipe.

She was thankful to discover she hadn't. Her next step was to set a bowl of each of three toppings across her orderly table, and then she began the wait for the oven timer to ding.

Chapter 35

At the same time, Sherry didn't want to give the judges any reason to think she had an idle moment. She couldn't remember a cook-off where there wasn't a short lull in the action, and she had become adept at staying, at the very least, appearing to be busy. If she needed a breather during a short downtime, she created the illusion of purpose. Her go-to, non-stress exercise was rereading the recipe. It served the purpose of assuring herself she had the next steps covered. Before she began she peered out into the audience to see if there was any sign of Perry or Don. She located Wellington. Two seats away from him was Liz. There was an empty seat between them. There was no sign of Perry in the vicinity of his family. She was relieved to spot Don standing on the periphery of the audience.

"I hope Perry's okay," Sherry whispered to herself.

"Did you say something?" Madeline asked.

"I'm talking to myself, as usual. How's it going?" Sherry asked.

"So far, so good. This is a wonderful recipe," Madeline said. "I'm so glad you're my teammate and not my opposition."

"I feel the same way," Sherry said. "I'm going to grab another spoon. Need anything?"

"I don't, thanks."

Sherry left her station, noting she had a six-minute window to browse the utensils. When she reached the edge of the stage she ran straight into Ray.

"Sorry about that. I'm surprised to see you in the wings." She was drawn to the detective's wardrobe choice. "I would have never guessed you owned a plaid flannel shirt."

"That's why guessing is unscientific. You'll never see a verdict in a trial that begins with, *I guess the suspect's guilty.*"

"Duly noted," Sherry said.

"I bought this shirt especially for today. I wanted to blend in," Ray said. He puffed out his chest as he spoke.

"You do. I've never seen so much farmer dress in my whole life. Are you enjoying the event?" Sherry asked.

"I haven't gotten much time to watch, unfortunately. We have a situation."

Sherry wasn't sure she heard Ray correctly. "Did you say there's a situation? There's a security problem?"

"Nothing to panic over. Don't lose focus."

"What's the problem?" Sherry asked. Her tone was insistent.

"We're looking for Perry Colton. No one can find him. Have you seen him? I don't want to sound the alarm in the middle of the cook-off, but this is serious."

"I saw him after lunch. Maybe around one o'clock. We had a quick chat. Maybe three, four minutes. Afterward we went in different directions. I know that it's Liz Colton's duty today to keep her eye on him. She had lost him at that point. She was also looking for him. She didn't seem terribly alarmed and then I ran into him. It didn't occur to me I should be concerned. I'm sure he's around here somewhere. I didn't think he could get into much trouble. You know he's not as disabled as folks have labeled him."

"Who said he was disabled?" Ray asked.

"That's not the right word, sorry. I meant some of his immediate family say things that indicate he loses his cognitive functions every now and again. Personally, I'm not on board with that assessment. He's not a spring chicken and he has more on his mind than most people half his age. He has every right to lose track of his thoughts every now and again."

"Me, Officer Sedgeman, and his partner are keeping an eye out, as is Trooper."

"Who asked you to find him?" Sherry asked. "Liz? Wellington?"

"Now you're getting into the nitty-gritty of an ongoing search. Let's not go there. I'll tell you he needs to be found."

"You're making it sound more imperative he's found," Sherry said. "Does this have anything to do with the murder investigation?"

"Bingo. We've made some progress in the investigation. Perry is front and center," Ray said. "The time is ripe to ask him some follow-up questions. Nobody wants him fleeing."

"What progress?"

"Listen, Sherry. I hesitate to give you the facts. I'm seeing you are growing emotionally attached to Perry, as is your sister-in-law. When I talk to her she puts up a wall. I can't let how you two feel affect my duties."

Sherry sighed. "Can you at least give me one solid reason Perry has moved from mild consideration to full focus?"

"It's come to light Perry made a deal to sell the farm's cottages and the land they sit on. The conflict lies in the fact he made the deal without consulting his sons. Wellington said as much."

"I know, but I think the problem lies in the fact Jarrod wants the land for one reason and his father wanted to sell the land for another reason," Sherry said. "Perry's a nice man."

"See? There goes your wall. You're not listening to the facts. I can't ignore what's staring me straight in the face. Anyway, he needs to be found."

"I wish I could help find him. I'm kind of tied up at the moment," Sherry said.

"What are you doing away from your oven?" Ray asked.

"In every cook-off I've ever been in there's a tiny window where all the loose ends are tied up and I have a breather. That's right now. I don't want the judges to think I'm not a busy beaver so I'm searching for an illusive utensil. The moment off gives my head time to de-fuzz, for lack of a better term. A few deep breaths away from my workstation and I've got my second wind."

"You're a real pro," Ray said.

"A professional amateur, at best. I better get back. Time's ticking."

Not one for parting words, Ray patted Sherry on her shoulder. In an instant he blended into the sea of flannel and overalls. Sherry returned to her workstation. Next to her, Madeline lifted her head and gave Sherry a nod.

"Sherry, would you mind if we asked you a few questions for the media coverage of the cook-off?" Gina asked, as she and a cameraman wedged into the workspace.

"Of course not," Sherry said.

"I'll be brief. The cook-off is winding down and the last minutes are so crucial. Why is local important to you?" Gina asked.

"You could have started with a smaller topic," Sherry quipped. "Let me see. To me local means fresher, friendlier, familiar, and fantastic."

"I couldn't have said it any better. One more question. Do you have a favorite tried-and-true potato recipe? It doesn't have to be your original creation. Just one to share with our viewers."

"Off the top of my head, my go-to potato recipe is herb-roasted potato wedges, some call them steak fries, with olive oil, sea salt and Parmesan-truffle seasoning. They are to die for."

"You've inspired me to make those tonight," Gina said. "Diet be damned." She lowered the microphone. "Thanks, Sherry, and best of luck." Gina walked away as quickly as she had arrived.

"I wish I were as calm as you," Madeline said. "These last minutes are going at warp speed. I've made the mistake of checking out the other cooks. Everyone's recipe is incredible, including yours."

"Yours, too," Sherry said. "All I have left to do is top the potatoes and warm them in the oven one last time. I got lucky when they paired me with you. I'm loving creating your recipe."

Sherry pulled the pan of stuffed potatoes out of the oven. She double-checked her table to make certain she had the correct topping for each potato. Putting the frizzled prosciutto and Brie cheese on the Indian-inspired potato would not only cause global culinary conflict, but the judges would also penalize her for lack of consistency and poor adherence to the contest theme. The thought of her possible catastrophe brought a smile to her face. Cook-offs stretched her sense of adventure and her imagination, and she was having fun with herself despite the importance of the moment. A question flashed through her brain. What if this were her final cook-off? She blinked away the notion and carried on.

Moments later, the French topping sat majestically on the correct potato. She arranged the Brie and frizzled prosciutto artistically atop the next potato. In a flash of brilliance, Sherry had reserved the slice of potato skin she removed when she hollowed out the potato. Her idea was to put the oval-shaped skin askew atop the potato to serve as a beret in a nod to the country that invented the style of hat worn by artists and stylish citizens alike. She hoped Madeline appreciated her ad lib addition. She topped the ranch-inspired potato with the cheese, sour cream and herb blend. She would finish the remaining potato accordingly after the potato toppings were oven-heated. The ranch potato would get a shower of bacon. The French potato would get a fashionable beret, and the Indian-inspired potato would get a dollop of raita. After those tasks were accomplished, there was only one remaining. Plating.

Sherry assembled the potatoes on the white plates provided by the organizers. She scanned down the line of contestants. She saw everyone was on the plating phase in their preparation. No one seemed to be struggling to finish on time. Sherry recalled cook-offs involving panicked cooks who had so many steps left to achieve in the short minutes leading to the closing bell that they were paralyzed with the inability to finish. Not finishing a recipe didn't happen often, but when it did it was a heartbreaking experience for all involved. Sherry blew out a breath of satisfaction no one was experiencing the dreaded performance freeze. The closing alarm sounded. The cook-off was over.

"Cooks, what a wonderful and inspiring job you did today," Gina said as she took center stage. "Let's give these cooks a hearty round of applause."

The clapping subsided and Gina invited the cooks to have a seat with their friends and family while the judging took place. "Keep your eye on the stage. It won't be long before we ask you to return."

Sherry gave Madeline a hug before they loosened their aprons. The waiting game began. Only time would tell who the top potato team was. Sherry's first post-competition desire was to take up Gina's suggestion and have a seat while the judges completed their duties. She surveyed the audience and located her family.

"I see Isaac and Harry in their seats," Madeline said. "I'm going to say hi after I use the ladies' room and spruce up a bit. Want to come?"

"I'll meet you over there," Sherry said.

Sherry took the opportunity to scour the crowd as she made her way to her family. There was still no sign of Perry. She was excited to see Amber and Don sitting a few seats away from Erno and Ruth. After greetings all around, Sherry let out an exhausted exhale.

"Great job," Erno said. "I've never seen that format. How'd you like it?"

"I wasn't so sure I'd like it when the format was announced but I rode on my partner's coattails. We put up some pretty good food."

"Good job, Sher," Pep said.

"Thanks. Hi, sweetie." Sherry gave Don a kiss. "Amber, I've been trying to find you in the seats. Where were you sitting during the cook-off?"

"Troy and Trooper are patrolling the grounds, so I've been repositioning for the last ninety minutes to secretly keep him company. Don't tell Ray. I don't want to get Troy in trouble."

"My lips are sealed. Thanks for coming. I don't see Charlotte. Is she still here?" Sherry asked as she hugged Mimi.

"She left Mimi's diaper bag at home," Pep said. "Diaper bag is a misnomer. That bag contains snacks, beverages, bottles, a blanket, snuggly toy, diapers, wipes, a hairbrush, extra clothes, and I think some emergency cash. We could be stranded in the wilderness for days and comfortably survive off its contents. Anyway, somehow it got left behind, which leaves our survival in question."

Sherry couldn't contain an exhausted giggle. She felt a hand on her shoulder. Madeline removed a piece of potato skin from Sherry's hair, setting off a round of laughter from onlookers.

"You wear it well," Don said.

"Thanks," Sherry said.

"Madeline, great job," Pep said.

"Great job, you two," Harry said from the row of seats behind Pep's.

"Thanks," Sherry said. "Has anyone seen Perry? They're going to need him up on stage soon for the tribute to Jarrod and the farm."

"I saw him earlier, but not for a while," Isaac said. "Liz is supposed to be his companion and shadow today. I haven't seen her in a while either."

"I saw him when I first arrived. He was checking out the stage with Wellie. Not since," Harry said.

"I see you two are friends again," Madeline said. Her gaze panned from Harry to Isaac. "Glad your squabble was squashed."

"Life's too short for battles," Erno said. "Let bygones be bygones."

"Here comes Liz," Pep said as he gave a head bob in the direction Liz was approaching from.

"Great job, you gals. Has anyone seen Perry? Or Wellie?" Liz asked as she shimmied through the narrow aisle between the row of chairs.

"Thanks, Liz. You haven't connected with Perry?" Sherry asked. She considered mentioning Perry was on the police force's missing persons search list.

"I'm sure he's with Wellie," Liz said. "I can't find him either. The organizers want him to say a few words at the award ceremony. I did let a police officer know, as if Perry were a lost child."

"They're around here somewhere," Madeline said. "I got a text from Wellie while I was in the ladies' room. He's picked up a bratwurst and peppers sub."

"Hope he materializes soon," Don said. He pointed in the direction of the stage, where Gina Cousins was waving toward Sherry and Madeline. "They're signaling the cooks need to return to the stage. Good luck, ladies."

Sherry didn't wait for Madeline, who was having a word with Harry. His face expressed a dislike for whatever she was saying. Sherry wanted no part of their personal situation. She found her way through the standing audience members. She positioned herself next to the other assembling cooks on stage. Gina greeted every cook with a warm smile and a wish for a big win. When all ten cooks joined the lineup, Gina turned on the microphone to address the audience.

"Welcome back. The judges have completed their delicious task of tasting each dish and choosing the winners. Let's give all involved a grateful round of applause." Gina waited until the clapping died down before continuing. "Before we proceed to the winner's announcement, the organizing committee and sponsors wanted to take a minute to honor the

Colton family, owners of the Coastal Greater Tator Farm, and their commitment to the growing of heirloom plants. What is heirloom and why is it of importance in agriculture, especially locally, you ask?

"I'm here to educate you as well as entertain you. Heirloom plants have been grown and cultivated for many years, as many as one hundred. Each generation of the plant has the same combination of traits. If chosen correctly, heirlooms are perfectly adapted to the region in which they were developed. They contain valuable genetic resources, such as drought- or heat-tolerance. More importantly, heirloom plants often have a story—a relationship with the past—that serves as a connection to a cultural heritage. That is definitely the case with potatoes. Many Indigenous peoples, for example, have prized or even sacred heirloom crops that have been passed down for generations, sometimes surviving genocide, colonization, or other threats. Next time you eat a potato, take a moment to praise the spud that saved civilizations from starvation. Okay, cooks, I have bestowed a higher level of importance to this cook-off.

"The format of the cook-off today was unusual, and you may be asking what was up with trading recipes and teaming up. These two aspects of the contest have more in association with one another than you know. The family we are honoring right now also came up with the format."

"Interesting," Sherry said under her breath.

Chapter 36

Wellington and Perry were summoned forward by Gina. Only Wellington appeared. He took his position beside Gina. He was scouring the area until he finally asked if anyone knew where his father was. No one replied.

"I'm sure he'll be here soon," Wellington said.

"No problem. We have an extra minute to wait. He's the patriarch of the farm. I'd love for him to join us. And Liz Colton, Jarrod's wife. Would she like to join us on stage?" Gina asked.

"Yes," she called out from the audience. When she reached Gina's side she threw up her hands. "I'm no help. I haven't seen Perry. Where could he be? I turned my back for one minute and he vanished."

They waited as long as they could for Perry, but the decision was made to proceed. Wellington and Liz were thanked by Gina for the entire festival's local concept. Asked to say a few words in honor of Jarrod, Wellington conceded to Liz, whose pinched expression made it clear she wasn't thrilled to be first to speak.

"Ladies first."

Liz stepped forward cautiously.

"I didn't know I would be speaking today. I haven't prepared anything, but here I go. I miss my husband terribly. We had seven short but wonderful years married and I'm not sure what to do with myself right now. Thank goodness for the extended Colton family and the farm to keep me busy and feeling well-supported. Thank you all for coming to watch the cook-off today, and as Jarrod would say, 'stay local.'" She offered a weak smile.

The audience gave Liz a warm round of applause. She stepped aside as Wellington took over the microphone. "Yep. Thank you all for coming today and supporting the local farmers of Hillsboro County. My brother Jarrod is well-represented here today by his family. Our father is somewhere here. Jarrod and I loved the farm as kids. What a great place to grow up.

"Makes sense the cook-off is a team event. Every man for himself isn't the message of this festival. The opposite. To truly be local is to exhibit team spirit or no one wins. Cooks, you might not have been paired with the recipe of your choice, but the point is you made it work. We didn't see any bickering or ego bashing. The judges tasted the most delicious versions of potatoes I've ever eaten. Yes, I was back there trying a bite of each. Perks of the job. Kudos to all ten of you. We can't wait to shake the hands of the winners.

May the best potato win."

"Well said," Sherry muttered to Madeline, who rubbed her palms together throughout Wellie's speech. The broad grin on Madeline's face beamed in Wellie's direction.

Liz and Wellie stepped aside while Gina recovered the microphone.

"The time has come. Our exhausted judges are: Stew Bingham from the *Nutmeg News*, Francis Meltzer from the Northeast Restaurant Association, and our special guest judge, Harriet Henschell, the vice president of Connecticut Public Television. You may know her network's most popular show, *North-Eats Test Kitchen.*"

Sherry's mouth dropped open.

"The judges have performed the tastiest of tasks. Let me bring them forward to make the announcement."

The judges assembled side by side next to Gina. The ten cooks clasped their hands in front of their waists. Each held an unsteady grin. Abby Cranwell positioned herself in front of the microphone. Sherry saw Ray take a stance beside the front row of seats out of the corner of her eye. Officer Sedgeman wasn't far behind Ray with Trooper at his side.

"I regret I wasn't a judge today," Abby said. "I knew too many of the cooks personally, so I recused myself. Like Wellington, I did saunter into the judging area to taste the yummies. Gina wasn't exaggerating when she said the judges had a hard task on their hands. Ten recipes, ten cooks, ten ways to showcase the Colton farm potato. The cooks used reds, sweets, golds and baking potatoes, along with small whites, fingerlings, and purples. Are you hungry yet?"

The audience murmured while many answered "yes." When the chatter simmered down, Abby handed the microphone to Gina. At the same time, Sherry's gaze was drawn to Ray and Troy, who were involved in a loud animated conversation. When heads turned in their direction they shuffled away from the seats. Sherry glanced over to Wellie and Liz. The pair was also in a heightened state. Hands were gesticulating and heads were shaking. Wellie's phone was in his hand, and he was showing Liz his communication.

"Five teams. Ten recipes. You are all winners." Gina paused. "But hold on. There's another twist. I mean it, you are all winners. Here's the latest update. The cook-off has been generously gifted enough prize money that every team will be awarded grand prize status and three thousand dollars per person, rather than the appliance prize package that the winner would have had to pay taxes on. In case you didn't hear me correctly, let me repeat. Every team is a winner. Isn't that the most amazing symbol of teamwork and local cooperation anyone has seen in forever?"

The audience stood and applauded. Cheers resounded from the stage. The cooks hugged one another, and a simultaneous show of relieved expressions washed through the contestant line.

"What a perfect way to honor the local farmers with a collective win for everyone who used the local potatoes. That meant potatoes were the important factor in the recipes," Sherry said.

The judges shook every cook's hand while handing out a check to each. Sherry was thrilled to greet each judge. The moment was always a highlight in a cooking competition.

"Sherry Oliveri, I'm Harriet Henschel. Congratulations on your win today. I do hope we will be chatting in a different capacity in the near future. North-Eats would certainly benefit from your expertise."

"Thank you," Sherry said. As much as she intended to, she couldn't manufacture a lengthier string of words while keeping her knees from buckling. By the time she summoned the courage to elaborate, Harriet had moved on to the next cook and the moment was lost.

The ceremony wound down after the remaining judges passed through the contestant line, offering kind words of encouragement for future cooking contests. Sherry gathered her personal items, stored her check in her pocket, and found most of her family still in their seats. Don wrapped her in a big bear hug. One by one, her family and friends congratulated her on her group win.

"Charlotte didn't make it back?" Sherry asked.

"No," Pep said. "I texted her and I haven't heard back. She tends to find this and that to attend to when she goes home. She's on her way, I'm sure."

"I'm going to find Ray and have a quick word with him. After that, who wants to go see some of the trained chicken perform their tricks?" Sherry asked. "I know Mimi would love that. I would love that. If Charlotte has gone rogue I can give you two a ride home."

Chapter 37

Sherry couldn't find Ray after a brief search. The crowd was massive, and even if she made a tour of the premises the chance she'd run into him were slim. Texting him wasn't an option since she had questions rather than answers. The issue on her mind could wait. She returned to the seats her family had gathered around after the cook-off. This time she found them empty. Her energy waned at the thought of scouring the room for a familiar face.

"Sher, over here," a well-timed voice called out. Sherry turned and found her group fussing over Mimi.

"I couldn't find Ray," Sherry said as she sidled up to Don. "He's on duty, patrolling the grounds with Troy. Who knows where they are. I wanted to ask him if he'd found Perry. Strange that Perry missed the ceremony he said he would be a part of."

"Maybe we'll run into Ray if we go visit some exhibits. Mimi's itching to see the chicken talent competition. She can imitate a chicken, you know." Pep prompted his daughter to cluck like a chicken. "Talk about a child genius!"

"Good job, Mimi," Sherry said.

"Let's go see what the talented chickens are up to. Who else is in? Dad? Ruth?" Pep asked.

"Sure. Why not," Erno said.

The variety of chicken skills did not disappoint. One hen could count by tapping her chicken foot. Another hen could play a tiny piano with her beak. A rooster separated ingredients for a recipe while his hen friend placed them in a bowl. After being wowed by the chickens' performances, the group navigated their way to another attraction. Sherry wanted to see how large the winning winter squash was. Once there, Mimi painted a pumpkin along with a dozen other juveniles. After visiting all the desired activities, Mimi's yawns alerted the group the time had come to head home. Charlotte had texted she'd meet Pep at home if he was able to get a ride from Sherry. Once Mimi had started yawning, the entire group caught the bug and exhaustion set in.

The ride home was short, thankfully, as Sherry had no child's car seat in her car. Mimi had fallen asleep, so Pep cradled her in his arms with the seat belt securing them in place. When Sherry's car pulled up to Pep's cottage she was stunned to see multiple police cars parked across the intersection of the paved lane and the farm's dirt road.

"I'll take Mimi inside, Sher. Can you go see what's going on?" Pep asked. The anxiety in his voice was evident.

Sherry knew he was as worried for Charlotte's safety as she was. Mimi stirred when Pep lifted her out of the car.

"If Charlotte's home I'll send her over to join you," Pep said.

Sherry exited the car and tried to locate anyone she knew. The farmhouse seemed quiet from the outside. Her sights panned the property and picked up on a group buzzing around the storage building. She saw Wellie, Ray, Troy, and Trooper talking with Perry. Perry! Was he back home the whole time everyone was searching for him? And what were members of the police force doing at the farm rather than patrolling the festival? Was this the reason for the animated conversation Sherry witnessed near the end of the cook-off?

Sherry spotted Charlotte alongside Perry. She made her way to Charlotte's side, feeling Ray's gaze on her as she neared.

"Charlotte, we were worried about you when you didn't return to the festival," Sherry said. "And Perry. You didn't leave any word about your whereabouts." She searched the faces of those in attendance. "What am I interrupting?"

"A meeting of sorts," Ray said.

"Perry was missed at the cook-off ceremony honoring the Coltons," Sherry said.

"I had other things on my mind," Perry said.

"Who won the cook-off?" Charlotte asked. "I wanted to be there so badly." She tilted her head in Perry's direction. "There was a matter that needed me."

"Perry? Do you know who won?" Sherry asked.

"Why would I know?" Perry asked. "Charlotte brought me home halfway through the cook-off."

"We were told the concept behind the cook-off came from the Colton family," Sherry said. "The concept that the cooks work as teams and that everyone wins. I loved that surprise at the end. If you were the mastermind, kudos to you."

"You caught me. The organizers weren't supposed to credit me with the concept. I wanted local to mean teamwork. I've been pestered by so many people out for themselves that I wanted the emphasis to be on what could be achieved if everyone worked together. Potatoes saved plenty of civilizations over the centuries. It only makes sense the cook-off should be celebrated as a group effort."

"And this wonderful concept from the man people doubted was in his right mind half the time," Charlotte said.

"What's this big meeting about?" Sherry asked.

"We were all in search of Perry," Ray said. "It took a village to find him."

"Why did you leave before the honors ceremony?" Wellie said.

"Let me chime in," Charlotte said. "When I was leaving the festival for the farm to collect Mimi's diaper bag, Perry asked me for a ride home. He was tired and I was more than happy to oblige. Unbeknownst to me, he hadn't told anyone he was heading home."

"Dad, you had us all in a tizzy," Wellie said.

"I dropped Perry off at the farmhouse," Charlotte said. "I went home and found Mimi's diaper bag sitting where we left it on the kitchen table."

"You could have come back to see the talented chickens," Sherry said.

"I wish I could have but there was a glitch. I went back outside to the car, only to hear a voice calling for help. I was pretty sure it was Perry."

Sherry glanced over at Perry, who portrayed the innocence of a child.

"In the few minutes I was collecting Mimi's bag he had locked himself in the storage building," Charlotte said.

"I thought I had closed the door gently so as not to trigger the faulty handle latch," Perry said. "I was wrong. I knew when Charlotte left to return to the festival I might be stuck for hours so I started hollering for her."

"Now you know why I didn't have time to text more than a few words about why I was delayed returning," Charlotte said. "And that was only the beginning."

"Why in the world did you go in there by yourself?" a female voice asked.

Before Perry responded, Madeline joined the gathering. She took her place close to Wellie. Very close.

"This is quite a show of force," Perry said.

"Can I have a word with you and Ray?" Sherry directed her question at Charlotte.

Sherry met Charlotte and Ray a few feet from the others.

"How long have Madeline and Wellie been seeing each other?" Sherry whispered.

"I first noticed they were getting close at the end of the summer. Not long after she gave up on her unrequited love for Harry," Charlotte said. "I think they make a cute couple. She melded into the family so nicely. She's a calming influence despite being chatty to a fault sometimes."

"That's not what I witnessed the first time I met them here," Sherry said. "Patti and I were both taken aback by some combative behavior between family members."

"I was about to say, that was until Wellington became increasingly agitated with Jarrod's attention to outside interests rather than focusing on the farm," Charlotte said. "Then the gloves came off. I could hear it all from my kitchen window."

"Do either of you have any reason to suspect Madeline having some involvement in Jarrod's murder?" Ray asked.

"I admit I had reservations about her being innocent. Until today," Sherry said.

"Today?" Ray asked.

"Today at the cook-off I saw a new side to Madeline. She was patient, a great recipe writer, and a wonderful cook. I admit I pushed her a bit by questioning how she was preparing my recipe. She handled the pressure gracefully. I wanted my recipe to be made to the best of her ability and she did that. That's not all."

"Go on," Ray said as Sherry collected her thoughts.

"Madeline wrote the notes that Perry's been finding around the farm."

"She confessed to that?" Ray asked.

"She didn't exactly confess," Sherry said. "But I have proof."

"If she did write the notes why would you think she's innocent?"

Chapter 38

"Why would she threaten Perry with the notes?" Charlotte asked. "He's been incredibly generous to her. I don't understand."

Sherry reached in her coat pocket and removed a folded piece of paper. "Today at the cook-off we were given another recipe, instead of our own, to read, digest, and prepare to the best of our ability. To prove we were versatile cooks. I was given Madeline's recipe and she had notes jotted down the margin all over the sheet. The red-inked notes match the red print on the notes found around the farm. Ray, if you agree, I'll ask her, right now, in front of you."

Ray leaned over Sherry's hand and eyed the recipe. "It does look like a match, but she's not the only one in the world with a red-ink, thin-tip pen."

"Another point. Madeline lied to me about something, and when I called her out on it she said she wouldn't lie again. With your approval I'd like to prove her correct."

"Be my guest," Ray said.

The huddle dispersed and regrouped around Madeline.

"What's this about?" Madeline asked.

"Madeline, did you write the notes Perry's been collecting around the farm, mostly on his front door?" Sherry asked. "Remember, you owe me a straight answer."

Madeline sighed. "I'm sick and tired of people thinking they can meander on to Coastal farms property and go prospecting for land sales. That means you, Harry Chan, wherever you are. No one should tell my boyfriend's father when it's time to sell his farm. Not even his sons. Only he gets to decide. I thought once the word of the notes got out people would not be interested in living on the farm." Madeline's voice quivered as she emphasized her final word.

"Madeline, your notes could be construed as threats," Charlotte said. "I'm not sure Perry thinks the note writer was trying to help him."

"Perry knew all about the notes," Madeline said. "I told him I had a way to scare any would-be developers off his tail. I didn't exactly tell him what the plan was, but you understand, don't you?" She directed her question at Perry, whose relaxed expression spoke volumes.

"I think I get it now," Perry said. "You were only trying to help. Did you know about this, son?"

"Madeline is a determined woman," Wellington said. "I knew she was up to something. I couldn't figure out what. My biggest hope was that she had nothing to do with Jarrod's death. She's a passionate woman. All I can say is I've never been so relieved in my life that she only had your best intentions in mind."

"See?" Madeline asked. "I didn't kill anyone. Jarrod got himself killed without my help. And, if we're being completely honest here—" She paused and shifted her sights to Ray.

"That's what we're aiming for," Ray said.

"To be completely honest," Madeline continued, "I wanted to prove Wellie had nothing to do with the murder. Just in case someone thought he did."

"Was that someone you? You thought I might have killed my own brother?" Wellie said.

Madeline scoffed. "You thought I might have had a hand in the murder, why can't I have a wild thought, too?"

"Can we please return to Madeline's question about why you, Perry, went into the potato storage building by yourself today?" Ray asked.

"Farm management procedure. I go in the building every single day. Many times a day during harvest season. I know where every bin is stored, with what variety of produce, and the amount each bin contains. I check the top layer of every bin for freshness. If the potatoes need rotating I do that. If the bins need an update on their labeling I do that. Tending the crop is my pride and joy. Charlotte knows all this. She's documenting the process. I've gone over my care procedures with her multiple times. That's another reason I want a farm manual published. People think it's plant, pick, profit. Easy-peasy. Think again."

"The process has been documented," Charlotte said. "It's far from unusual Perry should go in the building by himself. As he said, he does it every day."

"Yup," Perry said. "Today, I had a bad gut feeling. Something wasn't right. I've had a nagging feeling since early this morning. I couldn't stay at the festival any longer. I had to come home and look for myself."

"Look for what, sir?" Ray asked.

"I know the building's been searched as part of the murder investigation, but I know every inch in there. If anything was disturbed I'd find evidence of it. I don't like the idea of an uninvited trespasser lurking around the farm."

"And did you find anything?" Wellie asked his father.

"I did," Perry said. "I was about to tell Detective Bease. I've got it with me."

"Wait, you skipped a few details. How did you get out of the locked building? Did Charlotte use Bernie again?" Sherry asked.

"Bernie?" Ray asked.

"Bernie is the iron skillet I gave to Charlotte," Sherry said. "She used it once before to open the lock on the door. Bernie makes a great battering ram."

"I can attest to that," Wellie said. "Bernie sprung me free."

Ray pinched his lips shut and widened his eyes. Sherry smiled at his understandable skepticism.

"I didn't use Bernie this time. I need her in tip-top shape for a Dutch pancake I'm teaching myself how to make. Without her I had to implement a different plan. There's a pitchfork by the door. Through the other side of the locked door, Perry instructed me on how to get the job done without harming myself," Charlotte said. "We're a good team, right, Perry?"

"That's right," Perry said.

"Why were the police called?" Sherry asked. "This all sounds like a mishap, not a crime."

"Just a precaution," Charlotte said. "What if Perry was hurt or I couldn't get the door open with that giant dinner fork?" She pointed to the pitchfork. "Or, heaven forbid, there was an intruder hiding in there. If someone's being held against their will, more than likely they've been commanded to sound calm under the menacing eye of the captor. Funny, I had a bad gut feeling too. I called the police right before I went in for the rescue."

"We arrived in the nick of time. No one was injured except the battered lock mechanism," Troy said with a wry smile. "Trooper and I combed the area for intruders. We didn't find anyone. Meanwhile, Ray and Charlotte unhooked the pitchfork prongs embedded in the door. Charlotte's got some left hook."

"What did you find while you were locked inside?" Ray asked.

Perry reached into the pocket of his well-worn barn coat. "A business card was wedged under the corner of the small reds' bin. Those are the ruby jewels of the potato family that people cook then top with sour cream, dill, and smoked salmon. Or pesto, fig jam, and goat cheese. I was inspecting them. They need special attention due to their tiny size. They were taking on a touch of moisture underneath. I need to adjust down the humidity level in this cold weather. Anyway, the card fluttered when I rotated the top layer of reds." He handed the card to Ray. Sherry inched closer to get a look.

"Harry Chan," Ray read aloud. "With a notation. '3.5 M.'"

"I'm not happy about the card being in with the harvest," Perry said. "I pride myself on the hygiene of the space. I'm going to update my visitor policy. Harry Chan is not welcome to help himself to any potatoes. And he knows it. He's not a renter and half the time I get the feeling he's waiting for me to keel over so he can have a go at a farm takeover," Perry said with no uncertainty. "I'm giving him the benefit of the doubt he wasn't in there against my word." He peered over Ray's shoulder. "If I didn't know any better I'd say the writing was Jarrod's handwriting. Wellie, take a look."

Wellie received the card from Ray and nodded. "Yup. Jarrod makes the most elaborate letter *M*. His middle name is Mount and he used to practice his signature all the time when we were young. He proclaimed he'd be famous one day and needed to practice his signature for his future fans. What a guy."

"Is everything all right?" Isaac walked up behind Perry and put his hands on his shoulders.

"Isaac Rowe," Madeline said. "Just the person we want to speak to."

"He's not the one we want to speak to," Ray said.

"He should be the one you talk to," Madeline said. "Isaac is Harry Chan's on-again, off-again best friend. There's a good chance Isaac was the one who dropped Harry's business card in the storage building."

"What's going on?" Isaac asked.

"Perry was locked in the potato hotel." Madeline pointed to the building. "He attracted a lot of rescuers."

"Glad you're okay," Isaac said.

"Have you been helping yourself to some potatoes recently?" Ray asked.

"Not me. I've had my fill of potatoes for a while," Isaac said. "Why are you asking?"

"We were talking about Jarrod's murder," Madeline said. "Have you told the investigators about your deal with Perry? For the cottages? Some people weren't too keen on that tidbit leaking out, especially Jarrod and Harry."

Ray made a noise that Sherry couldn't interpret. "Maybe he *is* the one we want to talk to."

"If he asked me about it I told him," Isaac said. "Why are you bringing that up, Madeline? I keep telling you the deal's set in stone. You can't change our minds. Neither can Harry."

"I don't recall you telling me this. Refresh my memory," Ray said. "You bought the farm's cottages?"

Perry cleared his throat. "Years ago, Isaac and I shook on a real estate deal. He was helping the Colton family out. Helping us keep the farm a farm. We were making some sacrifices, so the big picture didn't change. The deal was based on Jarrod's plan of succession. I liked Isaac's interpretation of the plan. Jarrod's motivations weren't as honorable at the time. Jarrod had begun to see me as a frail old man in the last ten years and he presented a plan to me that I refused to understand, much less agree with."

"So, no deal," Ray said.

"Yes, I made a deal. Isaac and I made the deal without my sons' knowledge, on my terms. Sorry, Wellie, I'm trying to protect your inheritance as best I can. Sorry you're just learning about this now," Perry said.

Wellington threw up his hands. "I don't seem to know much about anything that's going on around here."

"It's for your own good. Especially with what's going on these days," Perry said. "That's why Charlotte and I have left you boys out of the farm manual we're scripting."

"Why's that?" Wellie asked.

"Look at where I am right now. I'm running a fifty-plus-acre farm. Pretty well, I might add. I want to ensure whoever takes on this career after me knows exactly what they're getting into. From the perspective of the boss."

"I get it," Wellie said. "Don't gloss over the fact you admitted you sold off the cottages. If it weren't for Madeline's pursuit of buying a cottage I may never have found out until the real estate changed hands. How dumb would I have looked? I already look idiotic to Madeline for not knowing what my father's doing with the farm. Dad, when was I going to learn about the whole matter? After you die?" There was a tinge of bitterness in his tone.

"That was the timetable, yes. Unfortunately, some people got so nosy they uncovered the deal in progress. You should be thanking me."

"For what?" Wellie asked.

"If you'd known about the pending transaction for too long, you might have been the one murdered," Perry said.

Sherry's mouth dropped open. "What do you mean?"

"My deal with Isaac is about ten years old. We shook on a deal to have him buy the cottages and acreage, all about five acres. He was a man I trusted. He presented himself as an honest man who would always have the future of the farm aligned with my vision. We set up a dollar amount and filed for the appropriate permits to have some farmland rezoned to residential. Did I mention that was ten years ago? Isaac's been living on the farm for the last couple of years as a renter in good faith that one day the deal would be legitimate. Whenever the freeze on farm rezoning is voted on and lifted the deal would go forward. Augustin moves at a snail's pace when change is happening." Perry laughed with an edge. "I'm the same way."

"While all of this was unfolding, was Jarrod aware of the fact he had no chance to sell the cottages?" Sherry asked. "Did he know about your handshake deal?"

"He was becoming increasingly aware he was being tested for his loyalty to the Colton family and our farm," Perry said. "The more he pulled away from the day-to-day operations the more I felt he couldn't be trusted with the farm's best interests in mind."

"And the more you exhibited forgetful symptoms?" Wellie said. "This is all beginning to make sense in a strange way."

"Stress can take its toll, yes," Perry said.

"Perry, is there an update about your health you'd like to share with this group?" Sherry asked. "In the long run opening up would benefit the situation." Sherry stepped closer to Charlotte and lowered her voice until it was barely audible. "Did you know about this? About Perry being a whole lot healthier than he's let on?"

Charlotte pinched her lips tight before relaxing her expression. "Maybe. How about you?"

Sherry lowered her head and examined the ground. "Not for very long."

"Would anyone like to fill the investigator in?" Ray asked. "This is like watching a couple of mimes perform a three-act play. I'm lost."

"Okay, okay," Perry said. "I've been putting on an act. But for good reason. When I got wind of Jarrod and Harry researching how to sell the farm out from underneath me, I could have gone one of two ways. I could have thrown in the towel and given them what they wanted, or I could have fought for what I wanted. I decided on the second plan, but with a twist. Yes, I did have a case of vertigo months ago and I made lemonade out of lemons. People around me couldn't wait to label me incapacitated. Why not test their loyalty by giving them what they wanted. Sometimes I was fully there, a minute later I wasn't. People began to speak freely around me as if not only was my mental state failing, but my hearing must be as well. The things I learned are amazing!"

"Dad," Wellington said as he shook his head slowly. "What you did isn't right."

"For an old man I still have a few tricks up my sleeve," Perry said. "Unfortunately, the plan began to backfire as I inched closer and closer to giving my sons the right to sign for me. That was not a smart decision."

"Did your plan collapse when you gave Jarrod, and then me, power of attorney?" Wellie asked.

"You had to have known that would open the door for one or both to explore selling the land," Isaac said. "How far was Jarrod from getting a sale completed would you say, Perry? That might be the catalyst for someone to commit murder. There's a lot of money at stake."

"A lot of money you stand to lose," Wellie said. "Dad, you may have painted yourself into a guilty corner in the eyes of the investigators."

"Right now, if I were any one of you, I'd think I was the murderer," Perry said.

"Dad, don't joke about this," Wellie said.

"I'll speak on everyone's behalf. I'm so worried it's you, Perry. I wrote the notes to try and help you. I can't help you if you truly are guilty. If you confess to feeling threatened and that's why you did it, you could plead self-defense," Madeline said.

"How many folks are on your suspect list, Madeline?" Wellie said. "I really need to watch my step around you."

"I keep my eyes open," Madeline said. "Another reason for my notes. To get the murderer to confess. Perry? Are you the murderer? Now's your chance to confess."

"Perry didn't murder Jarrod, Madeline," Charlotte said.

"You guys can argue about this all day, or you can accept the truth. Jarrod couldn't sell the land, even if he had power of attorney," Isaac said.

"Here's the truth. Nothing's for sale. Because the three cottages are mine," Wellington said.

"What?" Madeline asked. "Wellie, listen to what you're saying."

"No, the cottages are mine, or at least will be one day," Isaac said. "Perry and I shook on a deal. My lawyer said that was all it took. And we set the price, which is now a fantastic price considering how many folks want to live on the shore. Ten years ago, you could hardly give the land away. Perry didn't think he needed a lawyer to document the deal because the land was so affordable. Thank goodness for the price we settled on because in today's market a handshake wouldn't hold water. Over a certain selling price, a handshake between parties isn't valid."

"Sorry to burst your bubble, Isaac. Dad? Do you want to be the one to tell Isaac about the trust you put the cottages in when you hit your mid-seventies?" Wellie asked.

"How do you know about the trust?" Perry asked.

"Jarrod and I've been bickering since you had your first bout of vertigo. I needed help on the farm. He wasn't offering any. I needed support to try to convince you hiring some outside help doesn't equal losing control of the business. Push came to shove and Jarrod and I had a knock-down, drag-out altercation one day. He was strutting off to Long Island with Harry Chan to further his real estate career at the total expense of the Colton name. He was meeting with a high-powered lawyer who was going to prove in court your uncovered deal with Isaac was invalid." Wellie glanced in Sherry's direction. "He took your boat."

Sherry winced at Wellie's thinly veiled accusation she may have been in cahoots with Jarrod by providing the trip to Long Island. "Not my boat. My fiancé's boat. That's his livelihood and he doesn't question passengers' motives for riding the boat."

"He didn't exactly welcome me with open arms when I tried to board," Wellie said.

"Of course not. Why would he? He described an enraged man running down the dock screaming something he couldn't make out. Your own brother told Don to hurry and back the boat out. He pointed out a madman hauling it toward the boat. At the time Don thanked Jarrod for keeping the rest of the passengers safe. Don was doing his job." Sherry knew she was coming off defensive, but Wellie had challenged Don's actions and that touched a nerve.

"Anyway," Wellie continued, "later that day I spoke to Jarrod on the phone when Liz finally insisted he pick up my call. He told me that he and Harry were in Long Island meeting with a top real estate attorney who spent lots of research time discovering the cottages were tied up in a trust. Imagine Jarrod's surprise at that revelation. Harry must have been completely deflated. Turns out Dad went behind our backs and we had gone behind his."

"What do you expect? The way you boys were acting I wasn't sure either of you wouldn't do something drastic to claim a piece of the pie," Perry said. "Besides, my deal with Isaac was based on a promise he gave me along with the handshake. I was beginning to come to the realization he might not keep that promise."

"Dad, did you think one of us would murder you to inherit land we can't even afford the inheritance tax on?" Wellie asked.

"You two didn't pass the test when I feigned dementia. But in the end the farm belonged in the family. I wanted to set up a trust that gave you boys the land in due time, keeping the farm a farm, and ensuring no one went bankrupt in the transfer."

"I have something to say. The only thing Wellie is guilty of is trying to help you run the farm minus your uninterested son, Jarrod," Madeline said. "His suggestion to hire outside help isn't the same as signing way the farm. It's the opposite. Don't be so paranoid. And, may I add, you've hired outside assistance, so who are you to criticize your son?" She pointed at Charlotte.

Sherry was astonished to see Perry's mouth turn up into a smile after being tongue-lashed by Madeline.

"All very admirable, Madeline," Isaac said. "Sadly, the trust means nothing. I could prove that in court. We shook on my right of first refusal for the entire fifty-five acres. That means if someone offered you a better deal, including Harry Chan, I can offer one dollar more and it's mine. And the deal includes any land transactions within the Colton family. If you need convincing, my lawyer will be on your doorstep in half an hour to explain how you've reneged on a contract. The law doesn't look kindly on double-crossers."

"I knew I shouldn't pay a lawyer to do the work a free handshake could accomplish," Perry said. "Lawyers have no idea what they're doing."

"Dad, you said your deal with Isaac was based on a promise, too." Wellie said.

"That's right. Your fancy lawyer will need to convince me and everyone else that your intentions were to save the farm from being anything other than a farm. We made a deal based on that premise. Your right of first refusal must be based on the premise you're purchasing the farm to save it from developers. You agreed to that. You might have kept the cottages as is, but when you move onto purchasing the farm, I have no doubt you'd be on the phone in minutes to none other than Harry Chan, developer to the stars."

"I knew their frenemy act was a façade. They're in it together and Jarrod was the mastermind," Madeline said.

"I don't need the cottages. The trust can govern those," Isaac said.

"Dad, you're giving the farm away. If we sell the cottages to pay the taxes on the rest of the fifty acres when Augustin decides our nearly free ride is up, you can't sell to Isaac based on a price that's a decade old. From the other perspective, you're a hustler, Isaac, and you know it."

"At the time my intentions were to save the farm and keep it as is," Isaac said. "Just as Perry wished for. Let's face it. Ten years have passed since we shook. You can't expect me to not see the wonderful opportunity presenting itself now."

"See? You and Jarrod and Harry Chan were all after me. Is it any wonder I've had to fake dementia to get to the truth?" Perry said. "Detective Bease, arrest these men."

Ray couldn't contain a smirk followed by a smile. "Sir, they've done nothing illegal. Yes, it certainly does appear everyone's after your valuable land parcel. Now can we get back to the matter of Jarrod's murder?"

"You have a way of simplifying matters," Sherry said to Ray.

"Sir, after your lengthy explanation of family issues, I'm interested to learn, in your opinion, if you can boil down the facts to the one reason you think Jarrod was murdered?" Ray asked.

"Jarrod was murdered because someone didn't appreciate he had changed his mind," Perry said.

Chapter 39

"Changed his mind?" Ray asked. "About what?"

"About most everything," Perry said. "The folks who may have been depending on him to cash in were about to receive the letdown of their life. Jarrod was about to make public he was coming back to the farm and there was nothing that would sway him in another direction even after he had spent months, maybe years, renouncing the farming business. That was going to rub a lot of people the wrong way."

The prolonged silence was broken by a car struggling to get traction on the loose driveway stone. After the car was parked Harry stepped out.

"Well, this is a fine welcome," he said with a broad smile.

"You may be face-to-face with the murderer," Isaac whispered loud enough for Sherry to hear. "This guy's been rubbed the wrong way."

"I wanted to make sure Perry was accounted for," Harry said. "What a relief he's here."

"I can count on you, Harry, to keep your eye on the prize," Isaac said.

"I could say the same about you," Harry said. "At least we're now on the same wavelength. Watching out for Perry is the number-one priority."

"I'm impressed you took our warning to steer clear of the cook-off," Isaac said to Perry.

"You and Harry told Perry he ought to go home before the cook-off was over?" Sherry asked.

"He can thank us any time," Harry said.

"I'm fully capable of making my own decision whether to come home early or not," Perry said. "You two are trying to continue to make me look flaky but that cat's out of the bag."

Harry ignored Perry's comment. "What's going on here?"

"We were discussing Jarrod's murder with Detective Bease, in particular what the motive may be," Charlotte said. "It seems you've known Jarrod came very close to selling the cottages out from under Perry."

Harry kicked a stone with his sneaker. "It's all for the best. It's a complicated issue that dates back many years. I know Isaac and Perry made an agreement that had multiple layers. Isaac swooped in at a time when Perry needed a trustworthy investor, for lack of a better term, to purchase a small portion of the farm to save the productive portion. Isaac made the deal of his lifetime. The deal began to sour for Perry when year after year went by with no movement on rezoning the land. The land value is going up and up but the price they shook on stayed bargain-basement low."

"Scene two, enter the developer with the big cash reserve," Isaac said. "Harry Chan. The twist is Harry doesn't approach Perry with a new and improved offer, he approaches Jarrod, who is at a point in his life where he's newly married and maybe seeking a more attractive lifestyle. The farmland at today's price would certainly buy a wonderful lifestyle for Jarrod. But, how to get Perry to sell? The kicker is Harry gets so chummy with Jarrod he finds out Jarrod has a newly acquired power of attorney from Perry. With that power comes the ability to sell the land on behalf of Perry. Harry, am I getting the story straight?"

"One detail is missing," Harry said. "You didn't seem to have any qualms about cozying up to Jarrod in hopes you could rekindle the original deal, but this time with a new cosigner. Jarrod was jumping on board to take advantage of his own father. How could you have lived with yourself taking such advantage of an elderly man as well?"

"You realize I'm right here?" Perry said. "And since you were late to this shindig you've missed one detail about me that was revealed."

"I hope it wasn't bad news," Harry said. He winced as he prepared to hear what Perry was about to say.

"I have bad news for everyone. I am as fit as a fiddle," Perry said with a glint in his eye.

"That's not bad news, sir," Harry said. "And I wasn't cozying up to Jarrod so much as offering the Colton family options for the future, or the present."

"Can you tell me who owns the cottages?" Madeline asked. "I'd like to stay in mine as long as possible."

"Of course you would," Isaac said. "Who wouldn't with the deal Perry gives you. I should have claimed poverty a few times to see my rent reduced."

"Oh, come on, Isaac," Harry said. "You're the last person who should issue a complaint about any favoritism from Perry. If the many Augustin boards overseeing the farmland transaction had accepted your request to purchase the cottages years ago, you'd be rolling in dough. We wouldn't be here trying to figure out who killed Jarrod."

"Do you know who killed Jarrod?" Madeline asked with prying eyes aimed in Harry's direction. "Maybe you couldn't broker a deal with Jarrod that satisfied your need to develop all the available farmland into mega-mansions?"

"Don't think I didn't try," Harry said. "That's not illegal, you know. And attempted business deals don't automatically become murderous in the process. You're being dramatic."

"You went so far as to hire a lawyer to circumnavigate Perry and Isaac's handshake deal as soon as you found out Jarrod had power of attorney. That's kind of suspicious," Charlotte said.

"No offense, Charlotte, being the scientist you are, you should know. Doing research is the best way to avoid making serious misjudgments. Jarrod and I had little information to go on until we made a trip down to Augustin's tax office. Miss Cammie is a tough nut to crack, but we were persistent. She responded when we used more honey than vinegar. When Miss Cammie hinted tax records showed a pending decision on the cottage land that could change tax payments on the farm on many levels, we knew the time was right to start a bid for the land."

"Unless Isaac's first right of refusal is enforced. In that scenario, if you make a bid, he has every right to bid one dollar more and he wins," Wellington said.

"Or he loses because he can't afford what we can," Harry said.

"Or Perry defers to the court system to get his original deal enforced," Sherry said.

"That would take a team of high-priced lawyers on behalf of Perry," Harry said.

Perry groaned.

"Dad's indigestion says it all. He's not willing to go that extra mile." Wellie shook his head.

"Something is bothering me about the night Jarrod was murdered," Perry said.

"What's that, sir?" Ray asked.

"We were having a family dinner. We haven't had a family dinner in years. When my wife died I lost my interest in family gatherings. What was there to celebrate?" Perry's mouth drooped to a frown.

"We asked Dad if we could all have dinner together to get him excited about the cook-off featuring his potatoes," Wellie said. "I invited Madeline."

"Did the dinner serve its purpose?" Sherry asked.

"I thought Dad was excited by the end of dinner. Apparently I was wrong. Today he didn't stay through the entire cook-off. He didn't stay for the honors given to Coastal farm. His baby. Dad, what was that about?" Wellie said.

"I wasn't feeling festive. I had a nagging feeling something wasn't right on the farm. Plus, these two told me how pale I looked. That got into my brain." He tipped his head in Harry and Isaac's direction. "I saw Charlotte heading toward the parking lot, and I asked her for a ride home if that was where she was headed."

"You seem okay now," Wellie said.

"I made a full recovery," Perry said. His reply was clipped.

"I was looking out for your well-being. That's all," Harry said.

Perry grumbled an inaudible reply.

"What bothered you about that night, besides the fact Jarrod passed away?" Sherry asked.

"I had spent the afternoon teaching Jarrod and Liz how to get Ruby to behave dragging the harvester rake," Perry said. "Both had expressed an interest in pitching in for the portion of the harvest where the soil has been turned and combed, and a rain comes through and resettles the earth. A remarkably high number of concealed spuds rise to the surface and the rake finds them easily. It's a very satisfying process. The kids wanted me to get excited about the cook-off and I wanted them to get excited about their renewed interest in farming the land."

"Their renewed interest comes at an opportune time considering the rumors of the farm selling peaked over these last weeks," Charlotte said. "Why would Jarrod suddenly have a change of heart? Is that the change of mind you were referring to?"

"Yes, he had a change of heart and mind," Perry said. "He asked me to bring them up to speed on a way to help around the farm. I got every indication Jarrod was giving up the real estate salesman dream and returning to his roots."

"They didn't seem very happy at dinner," Wellie said. "Are you sure they'd made up their minds?"

"They were probably tired. You can't jump back into manual labor without feeling the burn," Perry said. "They were both in need of a shower when the lesson was over. They went home and returned in time for dinner. All spruced up."

"And what bothered you about that night?" Ray asked.

"Jarrod was wearing the same getup that he wore to dinner when he was found behind the tractor. Didn't he go home after dinner?" Perry asked. "That bothers me."

"You didn't tell me that," Sherry said to Ray. "That's strange. If Jarrod's time of death wasn't until the early morning, where was he all night? He obviously never made it home to sleep and change out of his dinner clothes." She glanced in the direction of the potato storage building. "Think about finding Harry's business card with a notation in Jarrod's handwriting. Was Jarrod locked in the building all night? Is that when he dropped the card? Does any of that make sense?"

Chapter 40

"What would he be doing in there in the dead of night?" Wellie said.

"Beats me," Perry said.

"Here comes the person you need to ask," Charlotte said.

A gold sedan pulled into a parking spot next to Sherry's car. Liz opened the car door before leaning across to the passenger seat. After a few minutes she exited the car toting whatever she gathered off the seat beside her. "Perry, for goodness sake. Here you are. You've given me all sorts of fright."

"I don't need a babysitter, Liz, but thanks for your concern," Perry said.

She continued lecturing Perry as she neared. "Obviously you do if you can disappear without letting anyone know. I've already lost someone I loved; I couldn't bear to lose another." She scanned the group. "Hello, everyone. Detective Bease, you were at the festival, now you're here. You're working overtime. What's everyone else doing here? Are we celebrating Sherry and Madeline's cook-off?"

"In a way," Madeline said. "And tending to other business."

Liz lifted a tote bag. "I brought back the containers for the leftovers you gave me from Jarrod's memorial service. I think I've consumed enough potatoes in the last week to outlast any cravings for a long time."

"Be careful what you say, Liz," Harry said. "Perry doesn't want to hear you're sick of potatoes. I know from experience."

"Oh, so sorry," Liz said. "Jarrod would have been so happy with all the potato celebrating Augustin's been up to."

"We were just talking about you and Jarrod and the night he was murdered," Ray said. "I'm still putting the pieces together of the scene that night through the early-morning hours up to his death. As we were reconstructing that night we've come up with questions. One of which you have the answer to, if you wouldn't mind."

"Anything I can do to help," Liz offered.

"The night of the murder you and Jarrod had dinner here with the other Coltons and Madeline, correct?" Ray asked.

"That's right," Liz said. "We had beef soup with potatoes and crusty garlic bread and a wonderful salad that Madeline made. She's a great cook. I was starving and so was my husband."

"Because you had a session with Perry on using the tractor and harvester attachment?" Ray asked.

"That's right. I learned more about running that machine that day than in the hours Jarrod's tried to explain it to me on paper. There was a lot to learn. I was thankful for the break in the middle." She directed her gaze toward Isaac.

"Is that what you were doing when I called about another plumbing emergency?" Isaac asked. "You didn't mention you were in the middle of something important."

"Our customers always come first," Liz said. "I appreciated a moment away from the dos and don'ts of running heavy machinery."

"You were called away to help Isaac out?" Ray asked.

"Yes. I didn't want to make him wait. He's had a devil of a time with his plumbing and we're trying to cut response time down to the bare minimum until we can figure out a long-term solution. Unfortunately, that's looking like a full replacement of his water intake system. Jarrod was dragging his feet on that ultimate step, but the time has come."

"And how long were you away from Perry's lesson?" Sherry asked.

"Longer than I'd hoped. Maybe forty minutes, give or take a few minutes," Liz said.

"Perry, what did Liz miss while she was working with Isaac?" Sherry said.

Perry shook his head. Sadness swept across his face.

"Perry?" Charlotte urged.

"Charlotte, I can't," Perry said.

"Perry, what did Liz miss in your tractor lesson when she left to help Isaac?" Charlotte asked. "It's important."

"Charlotte, why are you pressing Dad?" Wellie asked. "He's clearly uncomfortable."

"She's trying to get me to say something I don't want to say," Perry said.

"Then don't," Wellie said. "You're not obligated to say a word."

Perry sucked in a deep breath. Charlotte took a step closer to him, as if he may lose his balance at any moment and she would provide aid.

"Perry, are you feeling ill?" Liz asked. "You're pale. He may be having an episode."

"I wish I were," Perry said. "Then I wouldn't have to do this to you. Detective, the night Jarrod was killed, he and Liz were going through something. Yes, she was resigned to learning to farm, but she didn't know until the dinner that Jarrod had quit his job at Down Home Realty."

Liz gasped. "Don't worry, Perry. Jarrod didn't mean what he said. That was a mistake on his part. We were moving to a beautiful home near the shore. Jarrod would never quit his new job. He was just about to hit it big. He promised. We'd be done with this farming lifestyle." The shrill desperation in her voice pierced the air. "Perry, your memory is fuzzy. I don't think you're remembering that night correctly."

"Liz, you missed the update on Perry's condition," Sherry said.

"Oh, no. It's worse than everyone knows? I thought so," Liz said.

"The opposite," Madeline said.

"What Liz never learned from me while she was tending to Isaac's plumbing problems was the portion of the lesson where I turn Ruby's engine off," Perry said. "It's a whole process in itself. It's not as easy as turning the key. Not even close. Ruby's a feisty old gal and likes to be coaxed to power down. I think she knows there's a chance she may never come back on again. A jiggle here and wiggle of the gear shift and a waggle of the sticky key. In a certain pattern. Maybe multiple times."

"I'm still willing to learn. Why in the world would that have anything to do with Jarrod's murder?" Liz asked.

"Ruby was running the morning I was called to the farm," Officer Sedgeman said. "If someone didn't know how to power her down she might be left on in hopes the gas would run out."

"Is this what's been bothering you, Perry?" Charlotte asked. "Is this why you left the cook-off early?"

Ray reached in his coat pocket. He showed Liz the card.

"My business card," Harry said. He reached in a pocket and produced a matching card. "I have an extra right here. Would anyone else like one?"

"This was found in the potato storage building." Ray pointed to the building a few yards away. "Were you in there recently?"

"I've never been in there in my life. Potatoes and I aren't compatible. They give me terrible gas. I don't see what everyone sees in them. When I mentioned that fact to Perry in passing one day, he banned me from ever going in the building. He took my digestive issue as a personal assault on his livelihood. From that point on, I did all I could to rebuild what I thought was a friendship, to no avail. That's why I warned Liz not to mention being tired of potatoes if she ever wants another."

"We have reason to believe the notation on the card is in Jarrod's handwriting," Ray said.

Liz studied the card for a moment. "Nope. He doesn't make his *M*'s with the curly tails anymore. He changed his signature when he passed his real estate license test. He insisted he was going to be signing so many contracts he needed to simplify his autograph so his name would be easily recognizable. You know, a lead to the next sale. Harry hands out his card like candy. The card could be anyone's."

"Harry, what do you think the notation on the card, 3.5 M, refers to?" Ray asked. "And did you write it?"

Harry closed his eyes as he appeared to give the question careful consideration. "I wrote that." He produced a red pen from his pocket. "That's the price I gave Liz when she asked how much the cottages would sell for on today's open market. She asked that I write the amount down because she didn't think her husband would believe her. She was trying to convince him to make an offer to his father at the price he and Isaac shook on. I mean, if she can't get a family discount, why was Madeline getting such special treatment?"

"I'll tell you why. I saw young love blossoming. I'm not a monster. I want the best for my sons, and Madeline treats Wellie like a king," Perry said. "I wanted to keep her close, so he'd stay interested."

"Thanks, Perry," Madeline said.

"How does this always get back to Madeline's love life," Ray whispered to Sherry.

Chapter 41

"If we're done here," Liz said, "I'd like to follow up with Isaac about his plumbing issue. I think Perry needs a rest, too. When he's tired I take anything he says with a grain of salt."

"I have one more question for you, Madeline," Sherry said.

"Me?" Madeline said. She sought a glance from Wellie, who nodded his head. "Okay."

"Did you free Liz from the storage building the night of Jarrod's murder, after the dinner at Perry's farmhouse?" Sherry asked.

"Let me think," Madeline said. "You know I free someone from in there on average of once a week, I'm guessing. My cottage is the closest and I can hear the old door latch click pretty clearly, followed by a call for help. Liz and Jarrod were the first to leave dinner. I helped Perry do the final cleanup, then Wellie wanted to walk me home. He's so sweet." She smiled at Wellie.

"And?" Ray urged. The tightness of his jaw was evident as his patience seemed to be wearing thin.

"And we didn't get too far before I realized I had forgotten my new gloves. He jogged back to the farmhouse to collect them. That's when I heard a call for help. Liz had locked herself in the storage building. Sherry, how did you know that? Are you psychic?"

"I'm definitely not psychic," Sherry said with a dry laugh. "If I was I'd have a lot more cook-off wins under my belt. Imagine me knowing what the judges were thinking and being able to cook their preferences."

"Could we stay on track?" Ray asked. "Madeline, how did you get the door open?"

"I have a bunch of tricks to get the latch to behave. That night I used a hairpin. Sadly, I snapped it in the process and it's ruined. That was my last one. I need to buy some more if that latch isn't replaced soon."

"Did you go inside the building that night?" Ray asked.

Madeline shook her head. "Nope. Liz said she was fine and didn't need any more help. I propped the door open and told her to hurry out before Perry sees the door open. That building environment is as finicky as Ruby and Perry monitors it like it's a newborn baby."

"I don't know what this is about, but if you think I was in possession of Harry's business card the night of Jarrod's murder, I wasn't," Liz said. Her gaze was directed at Sherry. "I showed it to Jarrod and we had a chuckle over what could have been and, yes, well maybe, I put the card in my coat pocket. And, yes, Madeline's right, I went into the potato storage building after we left dinner."

"That's an unusual time to go in there," Wellie said. "There's barely any light in there."

"That building has more people coming and going than Grand Central Station," Perry said. "You know, I'm trying to keep the temperature consistent in there, folks. I have a business to run and frozen potatoes aren't on my list of sale items."

"And why did you go in?" Ray asked Liz.

"The reason was nothing sinister. On the contrary. I wanted to make Madeline's wonderful twice-baked potato recipe she shared with me before the cook-off. I helped myself to some russet potatoes. With Perry's blessing, of course. He may have forgotten I asked him as I left dinner."

"Thanks, Liz. That's a fine endorsement," Madeleine said.

"She didn't ask me," Perry said.

"Does your hairpin look something like this?" Sherry asked. She fished in her coat pocket and produced the hairpin Erno gave her at the Ruggery.

"Exactly, but that's not mine," Madeline said. "I was down to one and broke my last one helping Liz out."

Sherry sent an encouraging glance in Ray's direction. He had to have something he could add to her developing theory. He opened his mouth. Before he could speak, Charlotte began.

"Liz, if Madeline freed you the first time, why did you knock on our door asking for help?" Charlotte said.

"Interesting, yes. Liz, you had been locked in the building after dinner, freed by Madeline, and you wanted to get back inside the building hours later in the pitch dark?" Ray said. "Why is that? Why were you still on the farm? And where was your husband?"

"To answer Charlotte's question, I borrowed Bernie from Charlotte the night of Jarrod's murder to whack the sticky door handle on my second trip to the storage building. I had two hairpins in my hair that might have worked after seeing Madeline's trick, but both had fallen out of my hair at some point," Liz said. "I saw Charlotte's house light on and asked for help. Isn't that right, Charlotte?"

"I got up to sooth a very fussy Mimi at around two. Wasn't long after I heard a faint tap on the front door. I opened the door and there was Liz. She said she'd dropped something inside the storage building. One of her potatoes. She chose four from the bins and by the time she left the building she only had three. We all agree, Perry would be upset if a stray potato was loose on the floor. She said she'd been fretting about the mishap since earlier in the evening. She'd also had a fight with Jarrod, she said, and fell asleep in their car waiting for him to return from an after-dinner walk."

"You believed her story?" Ray asked.

"Why wouldn't I?" Charlotte asked. "These things happen. Add to that, I was bleary-eyed from waking from a deep sleep. My brain wasn't registering the full picture of what was going on. I didn't give the matter much thought while Mimi was crying. I couldn't go with her and leave Mimi, so I lent her the next best thing to open the door. Bernie."

"All true," Liz said.

"Why hadn't you asked for help finding Jarrod?" Sherry asked.

"We were in a timeout," Liz said. "He grumbled to me all through dinner. Wellie was right. We'd had words and he was off on a walk to clear his head. It's happened before. Better to take a timeout than to say something regretful in the heat of the moment. Unfortunately, I think that's where he ran into the murderer. Somehow he was carried back to the tractor, where he was found. That block of time between seeing Madeline and waking from an uncomfortable nap doesn't exist for me. As I said, I'd fallen asleep in the car. I was horrified when I woke up and it was after midnight. Then I remembered about the potato I'd dropped. I thought the day couldn't get any worse. I was wrong."

"Did you get Bernie back?" Sherry asked Charlotte.

"I did. Liz must have left the skillet on my front porch when she was done," Charlotte said. Her tone was questioning.

"Have you used Bernie since?" Sherry asked.

Charlotte didn't answer until Ray prompted her with the same question.

"I attempted to. I was all set to teach myself how to make a Dutch pancake. I had all the ingredients ready and waiting and I pulled out Bernie to preheat her. That's when I noticed she'd been injured. There's a new scratch across the surface that I'm sure will cause any food to stick. I didn't know how to tell you, Sher."

"I'm so sorry," Liz said. "I apologize for the scratch. I'll replace the skillet. I feel awful. In the dark I didn't see the damage. There was a huge spider on the double doors. Instead of crushing it I tried to steer it away by banging the skillet beside it. It worked. Maybe I was too aggressive and nicked the skillet."

"Ray, did you say Jarrod was killed by a blow from a pitchfork?" Sherry asked. "Maybe Bernie was used as a shield to fend off the pitchfork blow, resulting in a scratch."

"A job for forensics," Ray said. "Forensics has definitely confirmed that Jarrod had wounds consistent with a pitchfork assault."

"Jarrod disappeared after dinner," Sherry said. "Perry and Wellie went to bed?"

"I did," Perry said.

"I went over to Madeline's for a nightcap," Wellie said.

"And a snuggle," Madeline said.

"While all that was going on, who powered up Ruby?" Perry asked.

All heads turned in Liz's direction.

"If Wellie and Perry didn't, did you, Liz?" Sherry asked.

"The key was in the ignition. Call me silly, but I moved the machine because I wanted Jarrod to believe I was sorry we fought. I wanted to show him I could be helpful on the farm, and he could continue his real estate career. All was well." Liz's voice trailed off as her gaze lifted skyward.

"Dad, you left the key in the tractor?" Wellie asked.

"I'm old and forgetful," Perry said with a glint in this eye. "So, sue me."

"Detective Bease, if you had Liz on your suspect list, I think you owe her an apology," Madeline said. "No hard feelings?"

Sherry's mouth dropped open. Ray's stayed clenched shut.

"Everyone's stressed," Liz said. "No harm, no foul."

"Madeline, do you have other suspects on your list?" Wellie asked. "Or have we run the gamut?"

"Funny you should ask that, Wellie," Harry said.

"Why's that?" Wellie said.

"You know my lawyer says the trust is broken with the passing of Jarrod. You have every right to take over ownership of the farm," Harry said. "You are sitting in the driver's seat."

"What are you talking about?" Liz asked. "Jarrod said he and I were both on the trust agreement. Isn't that right, Perry? Wellie and I are the remaining owners now that Jarrod has passed in such an untimely way. I will honor him by accepting our share of the farm. We were preparing to rejoin the daily functions, at least until the market is right to sell."

"Were you hoping that was soon?" Wellie asked.

"Jarrod had a time frame in mind, yes," Liz said. "Harry can attest to that. I'll honor Jarrod's wishes."

"You weren't in the trust agreement, Liz," Perry said.

"Well, I just assumed," Liz said. She waved her hand through the air as if to bat away the injustice of it all. "But I'm the recipient of Jarrod's assets, so that's as good as being in the trust."

"Don't expect much," Isaac said.

"He's right," Harry said.

Liz's mouth dropped open.

Silence swept over the gathering until Liz exhaled. "Perry, how could you do this to me? I gave up everything that was important for a good future to save the Coltons. We could all be living in the lap of luxury if you'd only give up the notion farming is somehow romantic. It's not. It's a nightmare." Her voice grew shrill. "Jarrod is such a fool. I'm such a fool."

"Jarrod told you about leaving his job and returning to the farm," Ray said.

"Of course he did. I may not have welcomed the idea with open arms, but he sweetened the deal. He told me about the trust and in time the farm would be ours. Why would I think I wouldn't be included on the trust document? Perry is the world's most generous man. Just ask Madeline and Isaac. Of course, my father-in-law saw me as a devoted family member, because I am. As his son's wife I am his daughter by marriage. Nothing can change that. Jarrod's passing only solidifies my place in the family."

"Not sure how that's true," Harry said.

"Anyway, I own my portion of the farm now and I will treasure that role for as long as need be," Liz said.

"If that's the case, let me continue with your farming education," Perry said. "Learning to operate the tractor was lesson number one. Lesson number two: Keep your eyes on the humidity levels in the storage space. I had to lower the humidity in the storage building the morning Jarrod's body was found," Perry said in a casual tone. "The air quality had spiked to a stage I hadn't seen before. Made me wonder who had been in there for a long time."

"You think Liz was trapped in there longer than she thinks?" Madeline asked.

"Or was someone else trapped in there for longer, much longer, than she was? Someone who may not have been alive," Sherry said. She knew Ray might not appreciate her speculations, but his silence relayed the fact he was intently listening.

"And did Liz return to the building not only to pick up her potato, but to move Jarrod's body?" Sherry asked. "If she saw Charlotte's house light on she may have a witness, so she made up a good reason to return to the building. One that Charlotte would second as the truth."

"I'm glad Liz had the presence of mind to go clean up her mess. You know I don't like the storage area out of order," Perry said. "Ruins the contents. Potatoes seem hardy but they are as fragile as bananas if not treated right. The wrong air quality can spoil the entire harvest."

"Thank you, Perry," Liz said. "You know, it was only three or four hours."

"What was?" Ray asked.

Liz had no reply.

Sherry and Charlotte exchanged glances.

"Liz?" Perry said. "Do you have something you want to tell us? Were you and Jarrod in the storage building hashing out your argument? Is that how Harry's card got in there? Jarrod showed you the cottage price and you went ballistic because he had proclaimed you two were now full-time farmers, not real estate moguls?"

"And did you use Ruby to pull Jarrod out of the building so the humidity levels didn't fluctuate enough to alarm Perry?" Sherry asked.

"If you did you were too late," Perry said. "I have a new humidity monitor that signals my new phone something's up. I have a full report on that night's mishaps."

"Dad, are you kidding? A monitor? A new phone?" Wellie asked. "Go ahead. Knock me over with a feather."

"Thanks to Charlotte," Perry said.

"You all are so paranoid. Stop listening to Perry," Liz said with a snicker. "Fine. I was hoping Jarrod and I would move far away from the farm and live happily ever after in the lifestyle I knew complemented our aspirations. He changed his mind, I may have overreacted, we argued as couples do, but after that I have no idea who murdered him."

"I do. Your fingerprints were all over the pitchfork, Ruby, and the tractor wheel. Wellington found your lost hairpins in a layer of mud under the tractor. Right, Officer Sedgeman?" Ray asked. "Did you use the pitchfork to render Jarrod unconscious then finish him off with Ruby?"

"Or did you use Bernie while Jarrod tried to fend off your attack with the pitchfork before you turned it on him?" Charlotte asked.

"Jarrod promised me so much," Liz said. "I gave him plenty of time to deliver. You can't dangle a pot of gold in front of someone and expect them to say, 'no, thanks.'"

"I saw the same gold and I said, 'no, thanks, I'll take the potatoes,'" Madeline said. She smiled in Wellington's direction.

Officer Sedgeman and Trooper stepped forward. "Elizabeth Colton, you are under arrest for the murder of Jarrod Colton." He clicked the handcuffs on her wrists and led her to the police car.

Chapter 42

"Hi, Patti, it's Sherry."

"Hi," Patti said.

Sherry was emotionally exhausted. Her droopy tone relayed as much. Reclining on her bed was the perfect setting for the phone call she'd been procrastinating making for the past hour.

"So, what's new?" Patti said with a suggestive lilt in her voice. "Anything you want to tell me about your future?"

Sherry gave procrastination another minute to hang around.

Patti continued. "Before we get down to the nitty-gritty, I heard Liz Colton was arrested this afternoon. It's already all over the newsroom here at MediaPie."

"That's right. In a nutshell, Liz wanted more out of life than Jarrod was willing and able to give her."

"And how are Perry and Wellington handling the arrest?" Patti asked.

"Perry had a gut feeling Liz may have been guilty. I think that prepared him for the outcome. In a surprise turn of events, the men Perry thought was trying to take down the farm, Harry Chan and Isaac Rowe, turned out to be the people who exposed Liz's dark side."

"How did they do that?" Patti asked.

"Harry and Isaac put their heads together and gave up the idea of pressing for the farm's development. They pushed Mayor Drew to hold the honors ceremony for the Coltons. They saw the honors ceremony at the cook-off as an opportunity to provoke the murderer, if he or she was in attendance. It was a gamble. They convinced Perry not to stick around for the ceremony. They didn't want Perry getting hurt. They also gambled on the fact the murderer might realize if Perry wasn't at the cook-off he very well might be home alone. That's when Ray, Officer Sedgeman and Trooper raced to the farm."

"And Wellington?" Patti asked.

"Wellie lost his brother," Sherry said. "Sadly, Jarrod had turned the corner on his decision to return to the farm life. His relationship with Wellie was in the repair stage. In the end, both brothers are farmers at heart. Overalls and flannel suit them both best. For Wellie it'll take time for the wounds to heal. Despite the loss of Jarrod, I predict he and Madeline will have a peaceful life together."

"Considering everything that's happened, do you think the writings on the wall for the Coastal Greater Tator Farm?" Patti asked.

"Yes, I do. In a good way. Off the record, Charlotte pulled me aside after Liz's arrest and said her collaboration with Perry has been so successful he offered her a position implementing a business plan to get the farm into the modern age of farming. She'd be the farm manager," Sherry said. "That's a much better solution to the farm's uncertain future. Having a committed, non-family member in an oversight position can only be a good decision, especially if it's Charlotte."

"Perry's okay with that move?" Patti asked.

"Perry trusts her implicitly," Sherry said. "Charlotte said Madeline and Wellie have made plans to join forces and work full-time on the farm."

"It's going to cost plenty to move the farm into the modern age," Patti said. "I saw a lot of rust on the machinery."

"Charlotte finally got a look at the financials. Turns out cash flow is looser than Perry's let on. His mattress savings account has bloomed into six figures over the decades. Must be a pretty firm mattress."

"My mother has a mattress account," Patti said.

"I wonder if Erno does?" Sherry asked.

The women shared a laugh.

"Charlotte has a better business plan for Perry's stash. Growth, investment and reinvesting in the farm," Sherry said.

"That's amazing," Pattis said. "Something good has come out of this mess."

"Charlotte will make sure the farm preservation grant Augustin is promising for the next five years comes to pass, and quickly. I'm sure Miss Cammie will have a hand in overseeing that outcome. She's already called me with that good news. She has no problem challenging the bureaucrats who are holding up the process for no good reason. The trust that protected the cottages from being sold is now broken after Jarrod's death. The family will most likely sell what they need to sell and scale down the farm while ramping up an heirloom harvest that will command a hefty price and a cult following. They'll be looking for committed investors for small shares of ownership," Charlotte said.

"Charlotte will be working for the farm full-time. What about her science work?" Patti asked.

"Charlotte's science background will lend the perfect hand to the farm. Her documentation skills are a perfect match for her journal work with Perry.

He has ambitions to sell their farm journal commercially."

"Also amazing," Patti said.

"Charlotte will also make sure Pep puts a potato toast on Toasts of the Town's menu. Perry said he was thrilled with the prospect of a Greater Tator Bacon–Hash Brown Toast with many optional add-ons, like sun-dried tomatoes or olive tapenade. I guess he's come to terms with how well bacon and potato go with each other. To top off everything, Perry offered Pep and his family a chance to purchase their cottage, at a family discount."

"Kudos to your whole family for putting the farm first," Patti said.

"And Ray is planning on asking Madeline's sister, Lulu, out to dinner," Sherry added.

"All good news," Patti said.

Patti paused. Sherry remained silent. Had she really made up her mind? Any last-second doubt she harbored disappeared when Patti continued.

"I need an answer, Sher. I know this is a difficult decision, but nothing is irreversible."

Sherry pictured Harriet Henschell's encouraging smile at the cook-off. "I'm moving forward with the interview," Sherry said with conviction. "Don's all for it. My family's all for it, and most importantly, I'm all for it. Sign me up and let's see where this takes me."

"Excellent," Patti said. "I'll call them and text you what the next step is. I'm proud of you."

Recipes From Sherry's Kitchen

Snickerdoodle Sandwich Cookies

Servings: 12

1 cup butter, softened
2½ cups granulated sugar, divided
2 eggs
1 teaspoon vanilla extract
3 cups flour
½ teaspoon cream of tartar
½ teaspoon baking soda
½ teaspoon cinnamon

Cream-Cheese Filling

8 ounces cream cheese, softened
¼ cup butter, softened
4 cups powdered sugar
1 teaspoon vanilla extract
1–3 tablespoons milk

Preheat oven to 375 degrees.

Spray baking sheet with cooking spray.

In a mixing bowl, beat butter on medium speed for 2 minutes. Add 2 cups sugar and continue to beat for 2 more minutes. Add eggs and vanilla extract and cream until combined and mixture is light and fluffy.

In a separate bowl, combine dry ingredients: flour, cream of tartar and baking soda.

Add half of the flour mixture to butter mixture and combine. Add remaining flour mixture. Shape dough into balls.

In a small bowl, combine cinnamon and ½ cup sugar. Roll cookie dough balls into mixture and fully coat.

Place cookie dough balls on baking sheet, allowing 2 inches between cookies for baking.

Bake at 375 degrees for 9–11 minutes.

Cool.

For the cream-cheese filling:

In a large bowl, combine cream cheese, butter and powdered sugar. Scrape sides of bowl as needed.

Add vanilla extract and combine. Add milk, a little at a time, to reach cheesecake-like consistency.

Spread filling onto half the cookies. Top with a second cookie.

Store cookies in refrigerator until ready to serve.

Speedy African-Style Groundnut Stew

6 boneless chicken thighs
$\frac{1}{2}$ pound sweet potato fries, thawed, cut in 1-inch pieces
$\frac{1}{4}$ cup mango chutney
2 tablespoons smooth peanut butter
1 cup canned diced tomatoes with green chilies
salt and pepper to taste

Preheat oven to 350 degrees.

Place chicken and fries in a large baking pan, season with salt and pepper, and bake in the preheated oven for 20 minutes.

Meanwhile, in a medium saucepan, combine the chutney, peanut butter and tomatoes with chilies and cook over low heat until it just begins to simmer.

After the chicken has baked 20 minutes, spoon the chutney sauce over the chicken and continue to bake for 15 more minutes until bubbly and browned.

Serve chicken and sauce over fries.

About the Author

Devon Delaney is lifelong resident of the Northeast and currently resides in coastal Connecticut. She is a wife, mother of three, grandmother of two, accomplished cooking contestant and a recent empty nester. She taught computer education and Lego Robotics for over ten years prior to pursuing writing.

Devon has been handsomely rewarded for her recipe innovation over the last twenty-plus years. Among the many prizes she has won are a full kitchen of major appliances, five-figure top cash prizes, and four trips to Disney World. She won the grand prize in a national writing contest for her foodie poem "Ode to Pork Passion." Combining her beloved hobby of cooking contests with her enthusiasm for writing was inevitable.

When she's is not preparing for her next cook-off, Devon may be found pursuing her other hobbies, including playing competitive USTA league tennis, gardening, needlepointing, painting, jarring her produce and hooking rugs. Her standard poodle, Rocket, is her pride and joy and keeps her on the path of sanity.

You can learn more about Devon at www.devonpdelaney.com.